LANDFILL LIZARDS

BY EDWARD J. MCFADDEN III

SEVEREDPRESS

LANDFILL LIZARDS

ISBN: 978-1-923165-16-8

"The killers are the people who are ruining the world to line their pockets, poisoning us, burying us under garbage!" — John Brunner, *The Sheep Look Up*

1

Patriot Landfill & Recycling Center, Scorched Mesa, Arizona, *10:19 MST, present day*

Garbage is life.

And death.

It was also a way to make a living.

Oscar Rayos understood this even as a boy. In his youth, the dump was a magical place where society's castaways became treasures. The landfill was a far-off lifeless trash planet where he played war amidst an endless supply of broken toys, bicycles, and an assortment of fixable household items that provided much-needed income for a little kid who had expensive tastes in BMX racing equipment.

As an adult the Fill served a more practical purpose; it paid the bills, filled his days, and helped Oscar forget why he was stranded in the wastelands of Scorched Mesa.

Everyone else had lit out for Friday night fun, and it was Oscar's responsibility to close the dump for the night. He enjoyed closing the Fill, walking the perimeter, and feeding and watering Tank, the landfill's security system. Some despised the rank stench of garbage baking in the sun, but Oscar didn't mind it. The dump without patrons and trash-rats, the constant growl of equipment, and the crinkle, snap, and pop of man's forgotten things being broken down always served to ease his eager nerves.

He locked the office door and headed out into the dump, his rubber boots kicking up dust and grit.

Failing sunlight angled through a stack of automobiles like a dying flame, daggers of light bouncing off bent chrome and broken glass. The entrance gates stood open, and Oscar pulled them closed, and wrapped the chain through the fence, but didn't lock the padlock.

A line of wrecked cars ran along the western edge of the landfill, the access road beyond, and Tank stood in the tunnel-like gap between the pile of crushed autos and the fence. The rottweiler and black labrador mix sat, his keen eyes focused on Oscar as he approached.

"Hey, buddy," Oscar said as he knelt and handed over a dog bone. He wasn't supposed to be sociable with the dog. Trash-master had bitched at him about it many times, but Oscar didn't care. When he'd first arrived at the Fill, a broken and disgraced ex-Army sergeant, Tank had been his only friend. Sitting at the top of the refuse pile in the dark, drinking beer and howling at the moon with the huge black and brown beast had gotten Oscar through some cold nights.

The line of crushed cars ended and gave way to the scales area in front of the separating warehouse, where vehicles were weighed prior to and after drop-off to determine how much recyclable waste had been discarded. The facility's large bay door stood open, and Oscar and Tank went inside.

Oscar pressed the close button as he stood aside. The door rumbled down and stopped with a thud and a rattle of metal.

Tall concrete partitions that tapered down to three feet jutted from the walls creating stalls that were filled with recycled and processed trash, some of which had value. There were stacks of cardboard, various types of metal, like aluminum and steel, and several of the bins held mounds of plastic and one paper. Oscar worked recycling sometimes, but he preferred working the main refuse line. There was something about the unprocessed garbage heap that said possibilities to Oscar, and he knew one day he'd find his diamond in the refuse.

Oscar set the alarm, killed the lights, and slipped out a side door with Tank in tow.

A cloud of vultures filled the sky, and they squawked and cried, dive-bombing the main garbage pile like pelicans nabbing fish from the sea. The area Oscar liked to call the Grassy Knoll towered over the fresh trash pile. The man-made hill was compacted layers of trash covered in soil that over time had formed a mound. This was done to minimize odors and environmental impact, though on hot days the stench of the Fill could be smelled for miles around. Large stacks that released gases like methane produced by the microbial activity that broke down organic matter stuck from the top of the devil grass-covered knoll, and buried within the mound there were liners and monitoring systems to prevent environmental contamination.

This made Oscar smile. Who the hell cared about contamination out in the desert where only the toughest creatures dared to call home? He did, and he often wondered why, only to be reminded of the answer; he had nowhere else to go.

To the right of the Grassy Knoll was a graveyard of large, hulking pieces of old equipment and piles of refuse waiting to be stripped and crushed by eager Fill employees, of which there were none.

A line of fresh garbage two hundred yards long and fifty yards deep separated the dumping area from a finely manicured dirt field. Waves of heat rolled over the decomposition zone, a complex mix of woods, metals, glass, cardboard, unclassifiables, and other biodegradable items forming a stratified landscape, each layer preserving a snapshot of the discarded artifacts of daily life. The pile sat on a clay base to limit ground seepage, and the trash was a chaotic blend of colors, textures, and shapes. Plastic bags fluttered in the dirty breeze like flags, and broken toys and discarded furniture painted a peculiar picture of how people lived. Oscar wondered what the distant inhabitants of Earth would think when they excavated the archaeological melting pot.

Two yellow bulldozers with cheetah-like rust spots sat atop the trash pile, and behind them a backhoe sat idle, an American flag hanging from its lifted basket. Eventually, there would be a second Grassy Knoll and an area to the south had already been cleared for the next dumping field.

The walk around the trash field and the Grassy Knoll took ten minutes, Tank padding along behind him, and the partners found nothing out of place. Dusk pressed on the desert and Oscar paused along the southern fence and gazed across the stretch of desert that separated Twilight Dunes from the dump. Few lights sparkled in the trailer park, and Oscar figured most folks—like him—weren't home from work yet or had decided to make a stop at their local watering hole to blow some of their meager paychecks.

A cloud of white light filled the eastern horizon. Oscar rolled his shoulders and cracked his neck. He'd served at the Cactus Ridge Proving Ground, though he couldn't say he missed the place. Being stationed at the base had been a prominent step on the path that led to his ruined life.

The Army's private entrance to the dump was locked, the security booth dark, but still Tank spent extra time sniffing around the booth and along the fence. When the big mutt was satisfied, the duo moved on, Tank's black fur blending into the growing darkness.

A low growl carried over the garbage.

Tank stopped walking, his gaze straying toward the section of the Fill where lost things went to die eternal deaths. Objects too big and bulky, or items that required additional environmental protections before they could be buried, sat in piles and stacks. Air conditioners waiting to have their gasses properly drained and disposed of, rusted metal and machines, stacks of steel drums and cylinders of various sizes, a pile of tires, and an uncountable number of other trash items that would most likely sit in what Oscar called the Wasteland long after he'd shuffled off this mortal coil.

"What is it, bo—" Oscar's words caught in his throat.

The dark form of a person moved in and out of the shadows that danced among the trash.

3

Oscar reached for his sidearm, but he wasn't carrying his revolver on this day. Coyotes sometimes found their way into the Fill, but he hadn't seen one in a long time.

Tank's growl grew in strength as it carried over the dump. The beast pressed to the hardpan and crawled forward on his belly, the bronze-like hair around his neck glowing in the darkness. Thin clouds fleeted across the star-dappled sky, and shards of metal and broken glass sparkled like diamonds in the pale moonlight.

The Army maintained a restricted dumping area within the Fill because the powers that be didn't want trash-rats like Oscar looking through the base's garbage. Some of the base's refuse went to the regular landfill pile, but there were other things—blue unlabeled barrels, crates, and huge steel components to machines that Oscar could only visualize using the strongest of his imaginative muscles. There were Army jeeps, old weaponry, their barrels filled with concrete, rusty supply chests, furniture, and piles of brass from discharged shells waiting to be recycled. Oscar had never seen anything put in the restricted zone leave the area, and like the dump employees, dealing with garbage that was out of sight was perpetually out of mind.

Surrounded by chain-link fence topped with concertina wire, the Army's area dominated the eastern section of the dump. Tank pressed to his feet and trotted to the edge of the restricted area, the canine following the dark shadow that darted in and out of the garbage piles as if unaware of Oscar and Tank's presence.

Medical waste containers waiting to be burned were stacked before the incinerator, but that wasn't what drew Oscar's attention.

The southern edge of the Army's restricted zone butted against the incinerator area. This was by design. The Army produced a fair amount of medical-like waste, and their refuse accounted for a good portion of what the Fill burned. There was a hole cut in the fence, and a boy stood before the breach peering into the restricted area.

Tank barked twice, the echo of his aggression fading into a throaty growl.

The kid froze.

Oscar pulled his Maglite from his hip and turned it on. "Tommy?" Oscar yelled. He couldn't see the kid's face, but Oscar had caught the boy in the dump so many times he couldn't think of who else the intruder might be.

The kid darted into the shadows and was gone.

Tank surged forward and gave chase, but the beast came to a screeching halt when Oscar whistled.

"Tommy?" Oscar called as he worked his way around a pile of mixed refuse and a stack of broken wooden pallets.

The slit in the fence hadn't been made with metal snips or a saw. The fence all around the four-foot hole was stretched and twisted as if something heavy had barreled into it. Links were torn, their metal curled, and the uneven broken edges looked as if they'd been pulled apart using great force.

Oscar shined his light into the gap, and only the beady glowing eyes of desert rats stared back at him. He ducked through the hole, the scent of chemicals and rot filling his nostrils. There were unlabeled fifty-gallon drums, sealed wooden crates, and a series of pallets holding metal parts of machines that were long lost to the sands of time. He chuckled. Most folks on base would call the trash surplus, and half of it was probably still on an Army inventory log somewhere.

He saw a sparkle in his peripheral vision, and he spun around. "Tommy? You're not in trouble if you come out now. But if I find you in here…" Oscar delved deeper. There were several miniature versions of the Grassy Knoll at the center of the restricted zone, their single stacks pumping rank gas into the night.

Oscar panned his light around.

One of the burial mound-like hills had been disturbed.

Tank growled and let loose with a sharp bark.

"What is it, boy? Show me."

The dog trotted to the mound as Oscar tracked the canine with his light.

"Dang," Oscar muttered. The mound had been dug up, like a dog had been searching for a bone, and there was a pile of dirt and debris.

Tank inched forward, sniffing at the excavated area.

LED light drove away the darkness revealing a dark hole. The layers of soil covering the garbage had been stripped away and an odd assortment of bones sat at the bottom of the shallow pit. The bones appeared to have succumbed to intense heat, transforming them into a grotesque melted fossil. All form and definition had been contorted and liquefied, creating an unsettling mass that evoked a series of unsettling memories for Oscar. Though the bones were destroyed, it was clear the creature had been big. Twice the size of a crocodile and similarly sculpted.

He looked over his shoulder and scanned the dump. If it had been Tommy who had dug up the remains, he was gone now and all that was left for Oscar to do was decide if he was going to call Trash-master. He chuckled. No way that was happening on a Friday night. No way that was happening any night.

5

Things in the dump were usually meant to be there, so Oscar knew what to do. He collected a shovel and spent fifteen minutes covering the exposed carcass with dirt and trash, Tank watching him the entire time like Oscar might do a less than thorough job.

When he was done, he slipped out of the restricted area and repaired the fence. Oscar always carried snips and fence ties on his person while at work. Fence repair was one of his duties, and like a ranch hand trying to protect cattle from wolves, Oscar's job was to make sure if someone... or something... broke into the dump, it wouldn't be easy. In addition to Tank and the building alarms, there were motion lights and four cameras, though only the one at the gate worked.

"Night, buddy," Oscar said after Tank was fed and watered.

The beast watched Oscar like he was never going to see him again.

As Oscar slipped through the gate and locked the padlock the canine whimpered ever so slightly, and a wave of hot guilt broke over Oscar's heart.

West End Avenue was free of vehicles, and Oscar walked south down the center of the road, both sides of the sand-encrusted street a barren nothingness save for a few scraggly wind-sculpted trees and clumps of devil grass fighting their way up through the parched earth. Music carried on the trash-laden breeze, the lights of Twilight Dunes coming alive one by one in the distance.

2

Moonlight painted the desert in stark black and white. A gentle breeze stirred sand and grit, and the garbage gods had been kind on this night. The southerly wind pushed the stink of the dump away from Twilight Dunes, not that Oscar noticed the dumpster perfume anymore. A coyote howled in the distance and its mournful cry was answered by two others.

Oscar cut through the thick hedgerow of Arizona rosewood that surrounded the narrow arroyo which sheltered forty-eight mobile homes of varying degrees of economic prowess from the scouring desert winds. He passed under a crude portcullis made of old wood and discarded metal that was covered in kudzu vine, its peak adorned with a peeling painted sign showing a setting sun, the words Twilight Dunes across its bottom.

The trailer park was coming to life and lights sparkled along rooflines and snaked down lampposts. Christmas lights shined 365 days a year in Twilight Dunes, and this gave the community a perpetually festive feel. Music and the murmur of voices and TVs leaked from trailers, and somewhere a ball bounced rhythmically against the side of a trailer, the hollow rap carrying over the trailer park like distant gunshots.

Thinking of Tommy, Oscar veered left and tracked the sound.

"Hey, Oscar," came a smoke-ravaged voice from the darkness. The trailer on the corner of Cross Street and Number One Street was dark, but Oscar saw a faint shadow sitting within the screened front porch. He knew Stacey was sitting there in the darkness, her young son most likely watching T.V. or playing video games alone in the trailer. Stacey was one of many hard-luck cases in the Dunes. Her husband was killed on base in an "accident"—a fancy word for "you'll never know what happened to your loved one." With no other realistic options, Stacey had decided to keep Joey in school, which meant staying in Scorched Mesa. The woman had done her best, but she found too much solace in the bottle and the smoke.

"Hi, Stacey," Oscar said.

"Hey, Oscar," she said, her speech slurred. "Why you always in a hurry?"

Oscar said nothing as he picked up his pace.

"Why don't you sit down and have a drink," she cajoled. "I've got some good whiskey I've been saving for something... special."

"Keep saving it," he said, but felt bad so he added, "Maybe another time." There would never be another time. At least not with Stacey.

The trailers on Number One Street, which ran along the southern edge of the Dunes, were quiet and Oscar found the source of the bouncing ball.

"Jesse, have you seen Tommy?" he said.

The teenager stopped throwing the tennis ball against the trailer and looked around as if Tommy might appear out of thin air. Then he hiked his shoulders and said, "Like today?"

"Like in the last hour or so?"

"Naw, man, I ain't seen him," the kid said, and went back to throwing and catching his ball.

Oscar wanted to correct the kid's English but knew it was a waste of time. In many ways, the lost souls of Twilight Dunes weren't what troubled Oscar most. It was the children staring at a future for which they were ill-prepared and poorly supported. He said, "If you see him, tell Tommy I'm looking for him. In fact, tell him to come see me."

Jesse nodded but he was no longer paying attention.

The older he got the more Oscar felt his opinions tilting toward curmudgeon, and he knew if it was left up to the younger generation to take care of him in his old age, he'd be struggling to change his own diapers. He supposed he deserved it.

As he made his way to Middle Street Oscar was greeted by a field of glowing eyes. The Pride blocked his way.

Ms. Perriweather was the resident cat lady, and she ensured that the eight strays that roamed the trailer park were fed and watered, though the costs of the animals were shared by the community. Perri made cat food from donated leftovers, and some families made their contribution via money to Perri, or in the form of monthly food deliveries.

Newbies often balked at contributing—especially the self-proclaimed dog people of which there were several in residence, but it only took one desert rat crawling through their cornflakes to bring newcomers around.

As if to maintain the essential pecking order of the animal kingdom, a dog barked, and the cats scattered like teenagers at a house party when the cops arrived.

Oscar's camper was the third up on the left side of Middle Street, the road that ran down the center of the park. His standard camper wasn't old, or new, but lived in. He'd purchased an abandoned trailer, had it removed from the site, and paid to have his house pulled from the CRPG base and parked on the spot. Oscar's front yard consisted of a horseshoe court and a screen porch attached to the camper.

He unzipped the screen door and stepped inside.

An odd cackle-like bark that sounded like a chicken yodeling carried over the Dunes.

Oscar paused for a heartbeat, but when there was no return cry, he continued into the camper.

Friday night beckoned like a Siren's song, but he wasn't sure what he wanted to do. It had been a long day, and he was tired, but he needed something to eat, and a few drinks weren't the last things on his wish list. Oscar resolved to get changed and head over to Toby's, the park's sub rosa devil juice joint, which was run out of Toby and Paula Jentry's home.

Oscar pulled off his work shirt, grabbed a beer, and headed for his tiny bathroom.

As he stood over the sink Oscar's dirty face glared back at him from the mirror, and he licked his lips as he considered how much he'd aged in the last ten years. When he left Boston, his face had been free of wrinkles, his eyes aglow with possibilities. Now canyons cut across his sun-bleached cheeks, his eye sockets dark hollows that made him look like a heroin addict.

Oscar took a long pull of beer. His shoulder-length hair was pulled back in a tight ponytail and his oversized ears, which had earned him the nickname Dumbo in grade school, were sunburned, skin perpetually flaking from the scarred skin.

But it was the overall posture of his face that had changed the most. Old pictures revealed perpetual smiles, his lips slightly curved no matter the situation or pose. Now as he looked into the mirror, though he had plenty to be thankful for, he had little to be happy about and it showed on his face like a roadmap of failure paved with bad luck, poor decisions, and an unquenchable anger.

The bedroom was still a museum dedicated to Monica, and as he searched his small closet for a clean shirt, he saw her clothes exactly where she'd left them. Her dresses, the items on her nightstand, and her slippers which still sat on the floor by the bed were covered in three and a half years of dust. Oscar still had trouble believing she was gone, and suddenly he didn't feel like going out or doing anything other than crawling into bed with a bottle.

"But you promised me you wouldn't do that anymore," came the voice of his dead wife. They talked often, and it was she who was pushing him to get on with his life, maybe even find someone new, but Oscar just didn't have it in him. He wasn't sure what was in him anymore.

He finished his beer, said farewell to the empty, and tossed it in the recycle bin. As Oscar pushed out the trailer door into the thickening night a voice leaked from the shadows.

"Yo."

Oscar reached back into the camper and turned on the porchlight. "Hey, Roscoe," he said.

Roscoe Bendly was a friend and the wife of a close friend who was still in the service. She'd been stationed at the CRPG, but was recently discharged and was waiting for her husband to find his way home. Dark-skinned, petite, muscular, and tough as nails, Roscoe was more of a badass than her husband. If she didn't beat you down using one of the several martial arts she'd mastered, she'd shoot you. Twice. She tipped a beer to her lips, her eyes sparkling in the harsh porchlight.

"Where you heading?" she asked. "I was thinking maybe we coul—"

Another primal coughing bark echoed over Twilight Dunes.

"What the hell is that?" Oscar said.

A sizzle, like a giant rat getting fried as it bit into one of the many power lines strung about the Dunes, rose above the wind and the scrape of sand pushing over sand.

All the lights in Twilight Dunes blinked out, the hum of ACs died, and TVs and music fell silent.

Power outages in the desert were common, and soon the rumble of generators would fill the night.

"What the hell now," Roscoe said as she pushed to her feet, downed the rest of her beer, and abandoned the bottle on the arm of her chair. "I'd say you can have the five cent return, but we here in Arizona don't give a pig's fart about the fu—"

For the second time in as many minutes Roscoe was interrupted by an unusual sound, but this time it wasn't the strange cry of an unknown animal.

The shriek of a woman broke the stillness, followed by the sound of squawking chickens, a barking dog, and people yelling and screaming.

Roscoe headed for the screenhouse's door and Oscar said, "Hold up a minute."

He darted back into the trailer and retrieved his pistol. He'd turned in his service weapon when he'd left the Army, but he'd won a Smith & Wesson .38 revolver in a card game, and though the weapon was worn, it worked perfectly. Oscar loaded the gun and spun the cylinder as he glanced toward his closet where his real weapon was stowed. A Benelli M2 semiautomatic, but he didn't think he needed that level of firepower.

Pistol in hand, Oscar rejoined Roscoe.

Finding the source of the commotion wasn't hard.

The partners followed the frenzied sounds of disturbed chickens and chattering humanity and found Mr. Erickson holding court outside his doublewide. If there was a mansion in Twilight Dunes, it was Mr. E's place. The trailer was a modular home, though it did have an axel that allowed for wheels that were long gone which qualified it as a mobile home. The old man was surrounded as he gave an account of what had occurred to the onlookers.

When Oscar arrived on scene he asked, "What's happened?"

Mr. E didn't pause in his pity party, but he pointed toward the rear of his trailer. His place was one of the few that had a fenced backyard because of his poodle, Henry. The gate was open, and Oscar and Roscoe threaded through the crowd into the man's backyard.

A patio with new furniture, an elaborate chimenea, and a basic outdoor kitchen gave way to a patch of weed-ridden turf, and beyond that, there was a doghouse and a chicken coop.

The coop had been busted open, the chicken wire containing the exterior portion of the enclosure torn away. A chunk of the roof was missing, and if Oscar didn't know better, he'd swear he saw teeth or claw marks in the wood. Coyotes would chew through metal to get food, but Oscar had never seen anything like this.

"Coyotes?" Roscoe asked.

Oscar didn't see any of the telltale signs of coyotes; clumps of hair stuck to the splintered wood, paw prints, urine… but there was blood, plenty of it.

A crimson puddle marred the sand just beyond the coop, and a pile of feathers held together by a chunk of flesh sat at its center. The side of the chicken coop was splattered with blood, and a trail of red five-toed footprints trailed away from the carnage. There were two-inch slices at the tip of each digit delineating claws, and the prints didn't resemble the padded paw prints of coyotes at all, though it was clear whatever had made the tracks walked on all fours.

The blood trail led to a hole in Mr. E's fence, the stark desert landscape silhouetted in the jagged opening like a rip in time leading to another world.

3

Saturdays at the Fill were always chaotic. It was an 'all hands on deck' situation and the only day of the week Trash-master pretended to do his job. The cycle was always the same. Early dump-offs from weekenders who didn't want to get caught in the crunch and had spent their week loading up gave way to the lunch lull. Then came the afternoon rush comprised of tired, frustrated, and time stretched patrons who couldn't appreciate the dump for what it truly was, an oasis of renewal. Oscar hated the intrusion, and it irked him to know that Joe Public had no idea what life would be like if their detritus wasn't disposed of. Civilizations had fallen because of insufficient trash sanitation.

"The customer is always right," said the Landfill Manager, Trent "Trash-master" Masterson. The pencil of a man wore jeans, a blue shirt, and a tie. A tie at the dump!

Oscar mock-saluted as he pulled on his gloves and went to tell old man Karver that TM said he could leave as many AC units as he wanted, and that Oscar would assist him. Total bullshit for a half-an-hour before closing time on a Saturday night, but on Saturdays Trash-master only cared about public perception, and Oscar and the rest of the crew could spend the other five workdays making things right. As angry as it made him sometimes, Oscar had to admit the strategy wasn't totally without merit. Not that he had a say, and since the result was Trash-master mostly leaving him alone the rest of the week, it was a small price to pay.

Oscar directed Karver to back up to the Wasteland.

Both bulldozers growled, Wasten and Curby at the controls as they crushed, moved, and buried the day's garbage that hadn't survived the sifting of the recycling operation. Moxie worked the backhoe, a cloud of buzzards and small birds a dark reflection in her sunglasses. Pickups, cars, trucks towing trailers, and rental vehicles lined the refuse pile like puppies suckling on their mother. Truck beds were swept out, children rummaged for toys, and Trash-master looked out upon his domain like the King of Junkland.

Oscar and old man Karver unloaded his environmental timebombs, Oscar doing most of the work. When they were done, there were twelve window AC units stacked like children's building blocks amidst the other lost garbage. Karver got preferential treatment because he was

Trash-master's buddy, but when the old guy slipped Oscar a twenty all admonishments and jealousy faded like bitterness for one's parents.

"Where did they come from?" Oscar asked.

"People have these things lying all over the place. Garages, porches, backyards, and basements," Karver said. "They know they can't put them to the curb because of the freon, and they're too busy and too lazy and too preoccupied to bring the units to the recycling center, so…"

"How much each?"

"Twenty-five to fifty."

Oscar glanced at the stack of AC units. They were all basically the same size. "Why different prices?"

"Different people," Karver said as he got in his truck, closed the door, and drove off.

Oscar stood in the pickup's dust cloud, the old man's final words echoing inside his skull like a rifle blast. That was it, wasn't it? For all the talk about all people being equal, money and status would always be humanity's kryptonite, regardless of color, race, or creed.

"Let's go, Oscar. I want to get out of here tonight," jabbed Wasten. Wade "Wasten" Crosten was the Fill's most experienced and longest-tenured operator, and thus he spent all day every day sitting on his ass in a fan-cooled cab, and he never let Oscar forget it.

Oscar waved and smiled.

Over the next half-hour, the stream of Joe Publics diminished, and Trash-master even closed the gates five minutes early. In a transparent call for a volunteer, he said, "Who wants to make a little extra cash? Who's staying?"

Everyone looked at Oscar like he had the last slice of bread on Earth, but then Wasten surprised him. "I'll hang around for a bit."

Oscar chuckled. Not a commitment to close, and Oscar figured Wasten had another reason for staying.

Before someone grabbed his coveted spot, Oscar said, "I'll close."

"Thanks, Oscar," said Moxie as she pulled her hair tie and her raven locks spilled around her shoulders.

"Yeah," mumbled Curby and the others, and Oscar soon found himself standing alone before the refuse pile watching Trash-master lock and alarm the office. One less thing Oscar needed to do—but why had the boss done it? He never locked the office.

Oscar opened the gate and waved as the boss left.

A gunshot pierced the stillness, followed by cackling laughter.

He chained the gate and went in search of the marksman.

Wasten was shooting cans behind the recycling building.

"That's why you wanted to stay," Oscar stated.

The operator pulled a beer from a Styrofoam cooler and tossed it to Oscar. "Had to test this baby and the wife and neighbors get prickly." Wasten held out a silver Colt .357 Magnum with a wooden grip. "Wife don't even know I have it."

"She doesn't like guns?"

"Not ones that cost almost two thousand bucks," Wasten said.

Oscar whistled, opened his brew, and took a long pull, the bittersweet scent of the hops blending into the rancid aroma of the garbage breeze.

"Want to fire it?"

Oscar did.

As Oscar blasted trash, he told Wasten what had occurred at Twilight Dunes the prior night. "Whatever it was ripped through the fence and tore up the chicken coop real good," he said. "Mr. E says he lost three chickens and there wasn't any sign of them. Except blood, a few feathers, and a lump of flesh."

"Did you track it into the desert?" Wasten asked.

Oscar lowered the gun. "No. Who gives a turd about what's out on the desert?"

Wasten gazed west in the direction of his house. "Thing is... I had Deputy Sheriff Iquiro out at my place last week."

Oscar lifted an eyebrow as he fired off two more shots. The gun clicked empty, and he opened the cylinder and shook out the brass. He knew Kendra. She was a straight shooter who always went the extra mile to help the citizens, and that often put her at odds with her superiors. She drank in Toby's sometimes, and he liked her and had even tried to work up the courage to ask her out, but he'd never managed it. It wasn't that he was shy, but he was a bit insecure. Kendra was attractive, smart, had a great job, owned a house in the nicest section of Scorched Mesa, and what did he have to offer? A weak military pension, a rusted trailer, and a broken psyche?

"I don't abide the law, but..." Wasten struggled to find the words. "You know how we can't smell nice things, right?"

Oscar nodded. The crew at the Fill had discussed many times how it was impossible to get the stench of the dump out of one's nostrils, and how the rank scent tainted every other smell. Roses became air freshener covering the scent of human waste, chicken smelled like animal rot, and perfume morphed into burnt plastic and charred wiring.

"Well, I'm out back grilling—you know what a nice view I've got, and I caught a whiff of something that turned my stomach." Wasten accepted the revolver from Oscar and began stuffing bullets into the cylinder. "Outside of the flu or getting bit by a snake, you know that doesn't happen often. Wife calls my stomach Old Ironsides." Wasten snapped the gun's cylinder closed and stared at Oscar for any sign of recognition. "You know what that is, right?"

Oscar shook his head no, but he knew. He'd learned that it was always best to let your elders feel like they had the upper hand and knew more. Then they let their guard down. But at forty-eight Wasten was only nine years older than him, and when Oscar looked at the man, he saw himself in ten years—if he was lucky.

"Didn't they teach you anything in the Army?"

"Not much that's useful."

Wasten sighed. "The USS Constitution? The iconic wooden-hulled frigate that's been in the fleet since the War of 1812?"

Oscar knew all about it, but he said nothing and shrugged.

"Anyway, this smell really starts to eat at me. Like I'm not hungry anymore for the steak I'd been waiting on all day. So I put the heat on low, close up the BBQ, and go play bloodhound. It was dark, and you know how it is. Something can be ten feet away or a thousand feet, and you don't know until you're lost in the devil grass, am I right?"

Oscar nodded as he and Wasten switched positions.

Wasten aimed and blew three cans off their perches atop a washing machine waiting to enter the recycling building. "I didn't have to go far before I found it." He paused to build suspense. "A black-tailed jackrabbit—at least that's what I think it was before something got hold of it, which…" He shrugged. "Those SOBs are fast."

Oscar knew there were bobcats out in the desolation that were fast. "A cat?"

Wasten shook his head. "The thing was torn up like I ain't never seen. Clumps of matted fur clung to exposed sinew and bone, and its vacant eyes…" Wasten waved a hand. "One of its big ears was torn off, the other twisted and bent, and its entrails spilled from a hole in its torso that looked like…"

"What?" Oscar pushed.

"Like it had been chomped on by a shark, or something else with powerful jaws and plenty of teeth. The thing's limbs were broken, but that ain't why I called the cops." Wasten emptied the gun and dumped the brass. "It was the smell. As I stood there looking down at the mess, I realized it wasn't the cause of the stench."

"What was?" Now Wasten had Oscar's full attention.

As he reloaded, Wasten said, "I trek out into the nothingness, right? No flashlight, and I'm wearing sandals—sandals for shit's sake, but I'm three scotches deep and what do I care, right? A few days in the hospital away from this place and the nag would be a vacation, right?"

Oscar said nothing. The man was almost there.

"Anyway, I wasn't thinking straight," he said. "I hear this strange clucking noise, then I came upon…" He fired the gun six times, put it down atop an empty fifty-gallon drum, and said, "A huge pile of shit. At least, that's the only way I can describe it."

"You mean like animal waste?"

"Yeah," Wasten said. "Nasty stuff that looked like the biggest serving of soft chocolate ice cream I'd ever seen, and it wasn't just the smell. It looked like a whale had crapped. There were bones, sticks, rocks, and stuff sticking from it and there were streaks of blood like strawberry preserves through yogurt."

The analogy made Oscar's stomach grumble. "What did Kendra say?"

"What the hell was she supposed to say? She took pictures, put some of the shit in a water bottle, and told me to stay away from it like I was going to bring some home to the wife as a prize."

And with that, the wind filling the sails of the conversation fell dead.

When the twelve-pack Pabst Blue Ribbon was gone, the boxes of ammo empty, and the ground covered in brass, Wasten said, "I best be getting home."

Oscar held the gate open as Wasten drove his new Chevy through the gap. He didn't wave or look back as Oscar closed the gate.

The sun sat on the western horizon as Oscar started his rounds. Tank, who had hidden from the Saturday crush of patrons and who was deathly afraid of gunshots—thankfully this fact was little known—appeared at Oscar's side as he walked the perimeter.

He was passing the military entrance when the ring of metal hitting metal carried over the dump. It sounded to Oscar as though something had fallen… or been knocked over… in the Wasteland.

Tank growled and chirped.

Memories of the melted fossil stirred, and curiosity drew Oscar onward.

The hole in the fence was still patched, and he found no other breaches. The incinerator was dark, and shadows danced within the waste waiting to get transformed to ash.

Tank pressed to the ground and barked repeatedly until Oscar put his hand on the beast's head and told him to calm down.

A dark shape rose from the garbage, an absence of light that stood out against the dusk seeping over the land.

Tank whimpered.

The blackness formed into the visage of a massive lizard. Tall spikes of shadow protruded from a ten-foot tail, and four thick limbs held a narrow midsection aloft. The angle of the falling sun elongated the Gila monster's flat head, but it was the eyes that cemented Oscar's feet to the hardpan.

Two dark orbs glowed in the grayness as the creature's nictitating membranes retracted. Unlike a Gila monster, the beast's pupils were vertical slits reminiscent of a predatory reptile, and they emitted a faint light that pierced the encroaching darkness.

As the form came closer Oscar saw green bioluminescent patterns traced along the creature's body like a child had smeared the darkness with a highlighting marker.

Oscar looked over his shoulder, searching for help despite knowing there was none. He glanced down at Tank and sorrow washed through him.

The huge dog was shaking, his muscles flexing, teeth bared as he growled. Tank wanted to investigate, but Oscar held the canine back.

A deep sense of terror leaked through Oscar, the stench of his own fear so strong he knew the monster in the darkness could sense it.

The massive shadow pulled back, a narrow head pointing upward, a dark snake-like whip Oscar assumed was a tongue lashing the growing darkness. A wail, not unlike the odd calls he'd heard the prior night, thundered over the dump, and that was enough for Oscar. He knew a battle cry when he heard one.

"Attack!" yelled Oscar.

Tank bolted forward, barking, the dog and the shadow on a collision course.

Then the shadow dissipated like smoke on a strong breeze and the radiant stripes disappeared.

The dog didn't trust his eyes, but Tank didn't go far before he gave up the ghost and skidded to a halt, his head alternating between jerking around in confusion and bowing to sniff the ground.

Oscar shook his head to clear the cobwebs. Had that just happened? He looked around again willing there to be another witness, but only junk stared back at him through the deepening night.

4

Moonlight angled into the camper painting half the small space in harsh black and white. Oscar couldn't sleep, the day's events spinning out of control through his mind, rationality fighting with his senses that insisted he'd seen something... abnormal crawling through the trash. It was the size that kept sleep at bay. If a coyote, bobcat, or other beast had broken into the dump, Oscar wouldn't care. But this...

He tossed and turned, struggling with the question of whether he should tell someone what he'd seen. But what had he seen, really? And what credibility did he have? Add to that his past... Oscar had no choice but to wipe the prior night from his mental slate. That was the only option. He knew from experience there was no limit to how far he could fall. There was no bottom and he was clinging to the walls as it was, and Oscar certainly didn't need more trouble at work.

The distant cry of a coyote filtered into the trailer, and the curtains fluttered in the gentle breeze streaming into the camper. He was sure the air was tainted with the scent of garbage, but he didn't smell it anymore. Shadows flitted around the room as the curtains wavered, and a beam of moonlight fell on Monica's ring holder, which still sat atop the dresser. The black ceramic hand sculpture held several rings on its outstretched fingers, the most prominent of which were her engagement and wedding rings. He couldn't see them in the half-light that filled the camper, but Oscar knew the black ceramic fingers and palm was marred by thin white crack lines.

Monica had hurled the piece at him, rings and all, and he could still see her in his mind's eye sitting at the dining table gluing it back together just as she'd tried to glue their lives back together when he had been assigned to the Cactus Ridge Proving Ground.

The light wavered and the diamonds that made up the engagement ring sparkled. Then he was there again, reliving all the heartbreak, anger, and betrayal.

Rain lashed the large window that looked out on the Mississippi River. Oscar had chosen the place special, and he'd paid extra to have a first-floor room with a balcony that stretched to the river's edge. The rumble of water rolling over stones eased his mind and helped him build his courage. He lifted a finger of scotch and downed it when he heard the shower turn off. His anniversary wasn't the only reason he'd left base for the weekend. Oscar had a shit-sandwich to deliver, and he was running out of time.

Monica pushed through the bathroom door, a towel wrapped around her thin frame as she worked her long black hair with a second towel. "That felt good," she said. "The water at the base is never hot enough for me."

"Water that could cook an egg isn't hot enough for you," he said. They had dinner reservations and he wanted to get the argument over with before they headed out into the wild. Monica had no problem arguing in public—she was Italian, and it was in her DNA, but him…

Monica saw the two empty mini-bottles of Glenlivet on the nightstand and said, "You started without me?"

A frown crept over his face. He couldn't help it. "Can I get you something?"

She licked her lips, a cloud passing across her face as her gaze strayed to the carpet. She said, "No, I shouldn't."

That odd comment threw him off, but he had a job to do, and he had best get to it. Still, he hesitated, the fear that his wife might leave him this time heating him with worry.

Sensing the guilt rolling off him in waves, she asked, "What is it?"

He yanked off the Band-Aid with one sharp pull. "I've been transferred."

She froze, arms in the air, the white towel on her head, her mouth hanging open.

"Cactus Ridge Proving Ground at Scorched Mesa."

"The desert!" she shrieked. "What the hell did you do this time?"

That comment led to a hostile exchange about Oscar's past failings and his inability to gain the promotions that Monica expected and felt he deserved.

When they'd battled to a stalemate, tears leaking from her eyes, Monica began her secondary assault.

"Well, I don't know if that's going to work," she said.

"What are you saying?" He'd known it might come to this and he was prepared to leave the service to keep his wife.

She said nothing as she shook her head.

"I'll quit. Do something else. I can—"

"What? What are you going to do that gets me medical coverage?" Monica shrieked. "There aren't many jobs for people that blow shit up!"

That wasn't exactly true, but… Medical coverage? Oscar's brain went to work calculating, his mind spinning up a series of scenarios, none of which were good. "Why do you care about medical coverage all of a sudden? Are you alri—"

"I'm pregnant."

Oscar jerked back like he'd been stabbed. Talk about pulling off the Band-Aid. He didn't know what to say at first, then he shotgunned questions. "How? How far along are you? How long have you known?"

Throughout the barrage, Monica stared at him with pity carved into her beautiful features, and when he was done, she latched onto the last question on his list. "I found out last week after I went to the gynecologist."

Heat spread through Oscar like a toxic cloud as he calculated dates, his memory recalling the box of unopened tampons that had been sitting on the back of the toilet for weeks. And she'd just had her annual checkup a couple of months prior. "Gynecologist?" His voice cracked as the pieces of the puzzle came together.

Three days slipped away, and Oscar was raking the trash line as Moxie worked one of the dozers when a black army pool car tooled through the dump's gates and parked in front of the admin building. The bulldozer still rumbled, but Moxie stared at the car as well, the machine's plow lifted, garbage falling from its tooth-like spikes.

The car door opened and Civil Affairs Officer, Second Lieutenant, Carol Devito folded herself out of the car as she protected her eyes from the bright sunlight with the back of her hand.

Oscar knew Carol, but not well. She'd served at Cactus Ridge during his time there, and though she looked at him like a bug she wanted to squash, when it came time for Oscar to call it quits, she was a big help.

The second lieutenant looked around like she was searching for something to shoot, her short blonde hair slicked back, her green dress uniform tiptop.

Oscar felt her eyes on him, and then she was gone into the cool environment of the administration building.

An hour before quitting time Alice Noxbury wandered out into the dump to find Oscar. Alice was Trash-master's assistant, and the de facto manager of the landfill most of the time. Invisible spiders crawled over his body as he followed Alice to the office.

Oscar thought he knew what the boss might want. Surely the Army guys had seen the repair in the restricted area's fence and had come to ask if anyone at the dump had seen anything unusual. Perhaps there'd been a problem at the base? And now Trash-master was tasked with asking all his people?

As it turned out that wasn't what the boss wanted at all.

Trash-master looked Oscar up and down and said, "As we were talking Carol asked to take a walk so she can count her visit as an inspection, and what do we find? The ground behind the recycle building littered with brass. You know anything about that?" His boss's voice boomed through the small office.

Oscar was elated. No need to lie about what he'd seen, but the relief didn't last long. He couldn't throw Wasten under the bus and he was responsible for closing so he said nothing.

"Looked like magnums," said Trash-master.

Oscar considered his lie. It was more complicated than it appeared on the surface. If he said he didn't know, then Trash-master would assume someone had breached the security of the dump, and that would cause all kinds of bad things. If he owned up to it in any way, he was going to get his ass reamed, but that would most likely be the end of it, so he decided to apologize and hope he didn't get in trouble.

"Damn," Oscar said. "That's so my bad."

Trash-master eyeballed him as if he wasn't completely sure what Oscar had admitted, which of course was the point.

"Are you saying you left those casings there?"

"Yes, sir. I was checking out a buddy's weapon, Tank barked and… well, I forgot to clean up my mess." Of course, target shooting wasn't permitted on landfill property, but even Trash-master's hypocrisy had its limits. "It won't happen again. You have my word." Whatever the hell that meant.

Trash-master nodded.

The nastiness out of the way, Oscar figured maybe he could sneak in a question. He asked, "What did the Army want?"

The king of Junkland gave him the stink-eye as Oscar and his boss stared at each other, locked in a game of visual chicken.

Oscar looked away.

"It's on a need-to-know basis, and you don't need to know," said Trash-master. "Now get back to it."

"Thank you, sir," Oscar said. "I appreciate the leniency, sir." It never hurt to kiss ass, especially when you were knee-deep in a lie.

Oscar was out back of the recycling building picking up the brass when Trash-master lit out, peeling through the gate, leaving only a trail of dust behind. Oscar could only imagine why he was in such a rush.

He finished his task, but before joining Wasten out in the Fill, he headed for the office. With the boss gone, it was the perfect time to go fishing for information.

Alice sat at the reception desk like a magistrate waiting to pass judgment on a miscreant who's taken a crap on her lawn. Oscar thought she could be a good-looking woman if she cared, but as it was her bird's nest hairdo, makeup-free face, and clothes that said "I just rolled out of bed" more than they said "sexy" made her look frumpy and old. Her glasses were perched on the tip of her nose and when she saw Oscar, she smiled.

"Hey, Alice. All good?" Oscar said. He hated chitchat, probably because he sucked at it.

"Surviving. You?"

He shrugged. "What did the greenies want?"

She harrumphed. "You didn't come to see me?"

"Of course, I did."

She sighed. "Are you trying to get me fired?"

"Come on, Alice," Oscar said. "You know those green bastards never tell the truth. Yes, they're here to protect you and your freedom... blah blah blah, but if it came down to them or you, they'll lock the base's gates and leave you to die so fast your head would spin off into space."

She looked at her desk, then back up at him, pity in her eyes. She knew his story, how he'd ended up at the dump, and Oscar was constantly getting romantic vibes from the woman, but he felt nothing. He waited her out.

Alice sighed long and hard, and Oscar thought she might blow the papers off her desk. Even though the boss wasn't there, and Oscar and Alice were the only ones in the building, she looked around, lowered her voice conspiratorially, and said, "They were in Trash-ma... Trent's office and I only heard a few words that he repeated. He can be a loud cuss."

Oscar drew her in with his eyes and licked his lips, doing his best flirt move.

She demurred. Alice was a married woman, and ten years his senior, and Oscar was damaged goods. She shook her head. "I heard the words bioluminescent, mutant, and..." Alice's gaze strayed to the floor.

"What?"

"Deadly," she said.

That made Oscar's hands tingle. "Any paperwork?"

She chuckled. "But I'll keep an eye out," she said. "For you, Oscar."

Oscar nodded his thanks and left.

The wind gusted and dirt devils spiraled across the landfill.

Oscar knew from experience that if the Army was poking around it had to be bad and he didn't know what he could do about it. He was the smallest fish in the smallest pond, and that meant he had the smallest teeth, if he had any teeth at all.

5

For the next two days Oscar put his head in the sand. He went to work, came home, ate, and went to bed. It was the Friday night card game at Toby's that drew Oscar out of his shell. He still didn't feel like company, but he'd had enough self-flagellation and he was tired of staring at the four walls of the camper that seemed to be closing in on him with each passing second. Plus, Earl would be at the game and if anyone knew why the military was poking around the Fill it would be him.

Moonlight painted Twilight Dunes in silvery shadows, the murmur of his neighbors and the scent of their BBQs bringing a smile to Oscar's face. For a community of lost souls living on their last dollar, Oscar felt there were few places that suited his current life better.

A huge shadow with a narrow reptilian head fell across the street, its jaws hanging open, spiked teeth elongated by the moonlight.

Oscar stopped walking, felt for his sidearm, which wasn't there, and let a thin stream of air escape his lips. He pulled his flashlight and turned it on.

A Gila monster sat perched on a rock by the roadside, its oversized silhouette cast by the moon suspended in the southern sky. The beast's head was angled upward, its long tail flat against the stone.

The creature boasted a stocky build and was at least two feet in length. Its short, stout limbs ended in powerful claws, which Oscar knew the beast used to dig and burrow into the sandy desert soil. A bold mosaic of black and orange arranged in a captivating pattern of irregularly shaped bands along its body gave the appearance of movement and its skin was heavily textured and featured small, granular scales. The beast's thick tail, which the bigheads said served as a reservoir for fat storage, allowed it to endure long periods without food. Its eyes were small and bead-like, better for seeing in the dark which served its nocturnal lifestyle.

He wasn't afraid of the beast, yet he felt uneasy. Oscar gave the creature a wide berth. Even though the beasts never attacked humans, they'd been known to bite when scared and the lizard's venom glands in its lower jaw dispensed a powerful poison via its sharp teeth. The venom wasn't lethal to humans, but its effects were far from pleasant. The Gila monster was a slow-moving and solitary creature that spent most of its time burrowing underground or hiding in rocky crevices, but he'd seen them move faster than he'd believed possible.

Oscar sucked in a breath.

Was his mind playing tricks on him? Under the hard light of his LED torch, he thought he saw the faint tracings of green bioluminescence leaking from the creature.

He rubbed his eyes, and when he looked back in the Gila monster's direction, it was gone.

Toby's was crowded as it always was on Friday nights, but there was a table in the corner of the patio reserved for the game with a sweating pitcher of beer and a team of mugs waiting at its center. Two of the players were already seated at the table and he said hello to Roscoe and Earl as he took a seat.

"Who else is playing?" Oscar asked as he poured himself a beer.

"Toby's in tonight along with Mr. E," Roscoe said as she lifted her beer and took a long pull.

"Toby?" Oscar said with his mug halfway to his mouth. "Paula can handle T's Friday night rush on her own?"

Roscoe said, "Toby agreed to make a substantial donation to the Pride's food fund so Ms. Perriweather is filling in for him."

Toby's was a fenced-in area behind Toby and Paula's doublewide covered by an elaborate tarp system that had multiple layers. A basement-style bar picked from the Fill sat three, and there were tables of various states of functionality and appearance packed beneath the canopy. Toby was behind the bar, the man's balding head shining under the floodlights mounted beneath the canopy.

Mr. E arrived. A big man with a walrus mustache, very little was known of his history. When anyone delved into his past he clammed up like a criminal, and for all Oscar knew, that's exactly what the man had been in his past life. It didn't matter to Oscar what the man had been, all he cared about was what he was now, and Mr. E afforded him the same courtesy.

The group played by old school rules and the dealer rotated and picked the game that was played. So it was that the game became a carousel of Omaha, seven-card stud, five-card draw, and Caribbean stud poker. The friends played, drank, and as lips loosened Oscar turned the discussion toward the base.

"Did you hear the Army community relations bigwig paid a visit to the dump?" Oscar said.

Everyone focused on their cards except Earl, who looked up and said, "Who?"

"Carol Devito."

Earl whistled. "What did she want?"

"I thought you might know. Any weird rumors out at the base?"

Earl took a sip of his beer, discarded two cards, and accepted their replacements. "You know how it is out there, Oscar. Information is more valuable than discharge papers."

What Oscar knew was he'd been a midlevel policy puppet, security, hired help who did what he was told when he was told to do it, and in the end, he hadn't even managed to do that. Earl. He was a black Jack Reacher. "Yeah, I hear you. I didn't see very much of the high-security areas," Oscar said.

"Except that one night," his dead wife Monica reminded him.

He let the conversation take a backseat as they played, Earl sucking down half a beer for each hand. When Earl was five beers deep, Oscar re-engaged.

"You hearing any chatter about anything odd out on the desert?" Oscar floated.

"Like?" Earl asked.

"Strange killings? Mutilated animal corpses, odd waste piles, mutants, that sort of thing?" Oscar expected his friend to laugh, but his face grew grave.

Earl took a long pull of beer and eyed Oscar like a desert rat he was preparing to kill. "Where did you hear that nonsense?"

Oscar had hit a nerve, so he hiked his shoulders and let the guy go.

"Ahhh," Earl said as he looked around the table. Nobody met his eye except Oscar. "You know as well as I that the government tests all kinds of biological and chemical weapons out there, and not only in the desert. I've seen some of the labs, the cage facilities, and…" He waved a hand.

Oscar knew the man was straying onto confidential land, but everyone around the table could be trusted, and what the hell could they do with the information anyway?

Earl straightened, a sign that he'd made a decision. He said, "Did you guys hear about the closing a few months back?"

That got everyone's attention, and Roscoe stared openly, Toby froze with his beer an inch off the table, and Mr. E licked his lips, which Oscar knew he only did when he was nervous or worried.

"Cactus Ridge was put on lockdown," Earl said. "Carol, Ms. PR, barely acknowledged the situation. Employees were not allowed to leave, and those coming to work were not allowed in. The Army claimed there were no injuries, no damage, and that no threats were reported at the proving ground."

Oscar's heart pounded in his ears.

"What I heard was the lockdown was in response to the temporary loss of a vial containing a VX nerve agent or biological specimen. Ms.

PR said the material was recovered and the entire incident was the result of a mislabeling problem."

"Do you believe that?" Roscoe asked.

Earl made a sound like a broken trumpet and didn't speak again.

Oscar didn't believe the Army's story for a minute. But what of it? The trusted souls sitting around the table hardly had enough energy left at the end of the day to get to the supermarket, let alone use inside information to challenge the United States government.

Roscoe nodded and stuck out her chin in the direction of the road.

Through the sparse vegetation drooping from lack of water, Oscar saw Tommy standing beneath a floodlight mounted to a dead tree that served as one of the street's two light poles.

Oscar said, "Deal me out of the next hand." He got to his feet and threaded through the crowded tables, cut through the hedge, and approached Tommy.

"Where the hell have you been?" Oscar said, his tone rough, though he wasn't really angry. Oscar and the other adults in Twilight Dunes all helped raise the few youngsters that called the park home, and that meant Oscar's primary task wasn't to be the boy's friend, but one of his surrogate fathers. The kid's mother did her best, but teenage boys were a challenge even under the best of circumstances.

The kid looked at the ground, studying his shoes. He was an average-looking kid of typical size, his clothes a bit threadbare, his face tainted with dirt.

"What were you doing in the dump the other night?" Oscar pushed.

The kid didn't look up.

"Tommy, I'm talking to you. What were you doing in the dump?" Oscar said a little too loudly. He looked over his shoulder. All chatter at T's had paused and all eyes were on them. Oscar lowered his voice. "I've told you not to go in there. Did you make that hole in the fence?"

"No, no," Tommy said. "It was there when I—" The kid bit his lip as he realized he'd just admitted to the crime. His shoulders sagged and he said, "Yeah, it was me. Sorry. But I didn't do nothing. Swear. I was just scavenging."

"Did you go into the restricted area when you found the hole in the fence?"

Tommy shook his head emphatically. "No way, you know the shi— stuff that's in there."

Oscar sighed. He hated pushing the kid. He didn't have much and his outlook wasn't good, so it was Oscar's job to not only discipline the kid but build him up. "I'm proud of you for coming to me and taking your medicine."

Tommy looked up sheepishly, then his gaze fell back to his feet. "That's not why—not the only reason I came."

"Why then?"

"You need to see something," Tommy said.

The card game was put on pause. Toby worked the bar and Mr. E headed home as Oscar, Roscoe, and Earl followed Tommy. Pairs of eyes glowed from the vegetation before Perri's place, the Pride laying low for the night. Cats were creatures of the night, but out on the desert, they didn't have the size and strength to dominate the darkness. The trio strolled down the street and into a copse of mesquite trees that ran along the edge of the narrow arroyo that sheltered Twilight Dunes.

Tommy led as the party threaded through the trees, their gnarled branches adorned with small, feathery leaves. The bark on the tree trunks was dark and weathered, which contrasted sharply with the tree's delicate foliage. Fragrant cream-colored flowers protruded from the ends of branches, and some of the flowers had wilted and fallen apart revealing twisted seed pods.

The party's flashlights bloomed in the darkness, pale light leaking over the desert as the group emerged from the trees.

Dark splatters marred the sand, the LED lights turning crimson to black. Bloody prints that looked like human hands trailed away into darkness.

"I heard about Mr. E's coop. Has there been other reports of attacks in the area?" Earl asked.

Oscar was tempted to tell the man what he'd seen, but he kept his lips pressed shut.

"You had a lot of questions earlier." Earl rolled his shoulders and cracked his neck. "It's time to settle this once and for all," he said.

"I'll go get the guns," Roscoe said.

"Um, no you won't," Oscar said. It had to be said, but he was sorry it was him that had to say it. Roscoe was tougher than he was, and nobody liked being told what to do.

"I'm sorry," she said, her tone ice. "But our friendship doesn't give you the right to tell me what to do."

"Still, you're not coming."

"Try and stop me." She turned to leave.

Oscar grabbed her elbow, and she shook him off, so he appealed to her sense of friendship. "Think of it from my perspective, Roscoe. You come with us, do something heroic, and get killed or hurt. I promised Rick I'd look out for you."

"Well, Rick isn't here."

"No, he's not," Oscar said. "Please. Indulge me this one time."

"Fine." Her face twisted like she'd drunk spoiled milk.

With that settled, Oscar sent Tommy home, and eight minutes later, Earl and Oscar stood at the edge of the desert, flashlights in hand and weapons at the ready.

Oscar hadn't changed his clothes, and he carried his loaded Benelli, and his revolver was stuck in his waistband, extra ammo in his jacket pockets.

Earl. That was a different situation. The man had donned a black knit cap and an all-black outfit. His Glock was on his hip, and he carried his military-issued weapon that he'd purchased upon discharge, a fully loaded M4. He looked as serious as a heart attack and that eased Oscar's caterwauling nerves. He'd been in the military, but he wasn't on Earl's level. He didn't even know where Earl's level was.

Shadows danced across the desert, the wind whispered and sighed, and the endless tinkle of sand being pulled over sand carried over the desert. The partners wound around thickets of devil grass and scrub pine, the moonlight angling through the vegetation patterning the ground in a mosaic of odd shapes.

Flashlights pushed away the darkness, but beyond their glow, the blackness was an impenetrable wall. Coyotes howled, lizards bleated, and the chorus of insects and nightbirds filled the stillness.

After a couple of hundred yards, the bloody footprints disappeared, and the duo followed black drips over the hard white terrain.

When they'd gone half a mile Earl dropped to a knee and examined the ground.

The trail was gone, but the bright security lights of the dump glowed like a nuclear cloud on the horizon.

6

Severe LED light pushed away the blackness as Oscar and Earl inched their way across the barren wasteland that surrounded the landfill. The air carried the sharp scent of mesquite with an undertone of smoke, and it brought back memories of the campfires he used to build with his dad during their hunting trips in his youth. Dad was gone twenty years now, and Oscar had trouble picturing his face in his mind's eye and knew that soon his father's image would be lost except for the pictures that proved he existed. Oscar wouldn't even have that. The night symphony squeaked, rattled, and bleated, and coyote howls and the growling and shrieks of bobcats carried over the desolation.

The blood trail was completely spent, and the duo had seen nothing else unusual. Oscar's nerves still danced as he held the Benelli, finger on the trigger, safety off and ready to fill anything he didn't recognize with #4 turkey shot.

Earl's Glock was holstered, and his rifle hung over his shoulder as he led the way around tall patches of devil grass, pricker bushes with stiletto-length spikes, and through a copse of twisted mesquite trees with small olive leaves.

"Do you have any theories about what we're following?" Earl asked.

Oscar had only known the man a couple of years, but he understood the subtext. Earl had already asked if there had been any other reported incidents. Oscar hadn't related what he'd seen in the landfill, and Earl was asking again, politely.

When he didn't respond Earl made a sound that could only be interpreted as a display of irritation.

Guilt leaked through Oscar like sewage clouding clear water. This man was helping him. Hiking out into the bleak desert in the dark and for what? Because a coyote stole a chicken? But to that the rational side of Oscar's brain reminded him that coyotes didn't leave five-fingered footprints.

"Whatever," Earl said. "I get hurt out here and you're the one with blood on your—"

"You wouldn't believe me if I told you," Oscar pushed out.

Earl stopped between two huge clumps of devil grass and turned to face Oscar. "Try me," he said.

Oscar spilled it as the pair continued walking, the whole thing, from the first encounter to the last, filling in pieces that his partner already knew.

Earl said nothing when Oscar was done, his gaze straying to the dump and locking on its cloud of light that hovered over the desert like a UFO. A long minute passed before Earl lurched back into motion and said, "For what it's worth, I believe you. I've seen enough crazy shit in my day to never discount any possibility especially when the government is involved. I should've asked this before, but you've got your keys, right?"

"I do," Oscar said. "But we can't use them to get in." He left that hanging out there like a fart in Sunday school.

Earl didn't stop walking or look back.

Oscar said, "The camera at the gate works. The others don't. I'm assuming we don't want to announce our presence. Regardless of the situation. Right? So no front gate and I don't have keys to the Army's areas. Oddly, the Army's entrance and their restricted area don't have a single camera."

"Fancy that," Earl said.

As the duo approached the landfill, they killed their flashlights as they dropped to the hardpan and waited in the darkness at the edge of the dump's light cloud. Security lights were always aglow to keep scavengers of the human and bestial variety out of the landfill.

A chicken-bark shriek echoed over the desert, followed by a long hiss that emanated from inside the dump.

The sounds of barking and whimpering set Oscar's chest aflame.

Tank.

Oscar surged to his feet, and Earl pulled him back to the ground.

"No emotions from here on out, kid," Earl said.

The pair was on the southern side of the dump. No dust hung in the air and not even shadows moved within the Fill. The recycling building could be seen to the left of a field of crushed cars and steel drums that separated the building from the boundary fence. The open dirt field that would become Grassy Knoll Three covered a large expanse along the fence before giving way to the main refuse pile, the Wasteland, the incinerator, and the military's restricted area.

"So how are we doing this?" Earl asked.

"There are a couple of spots where I always have to repair the fence… don't ask," Oscar said. "There are more twist-fixes than there is chain-link. We open a slit and use that, assuming we don't find where our friend entered."

"I doubt very much the beast we're tracking is the cause of your fence breaches," Earl said. "This animal, whatever it is, has been coming and going for a while. It's been taking chickens, pets, and desert creatures for weeks, maybe months, and there could be more than one of the things. Add to that the central location of all the activity is the landfill. No, it's more likely they have a tunnel or some other way into the dump."

That thought made Oscar's bowels loosen and a nasty heat spread through him like sickness.

"No sense waiting," said Earl as he pushed to his feet and strode into the gray zone that separated the cloud of light from darkness. When he started to jog, Oscar got to his feet and followed.

When the partners reached the chain-link fence that surrounded the landfill, they got low, weapons up and ready, heads on swivels. Nothing moved beyond the fence, and Oscar gave the 'follow me' sign as he inched his way east.

A sharp yelp, then barking and whimpering.

"Tank needs our help," Oscar whispered, and he doubled his pace as he scanned the fence for patches. "This doesn't seem very smart," came the voice of his wife Monica. His mouth fell open to respond to her, but then he remembered Earl was with him and he pasted his lips shut.

Oscar found a patched section of fence, dropped to a knee, and began undoing repair ties. "We shouldn't be doing this," Oscar said to make himself feel better and share the mistake with Earl.

"No shit," said his partner.

Oscar smiled. Earl was committed and he'd expected nothing else.

The dump at night was a surreal mix of possibilities and dangers that made the senses tingle and the internal alarms blare. Under the shroud of grayness, the landfill transformed into a surreal and eerie landscape, where the discarded remnants of human existence took on a different character. The once vibrant colors faded into shadowy silhouettes as the landfill settled beneath an otherworldly calm and floodlights illuminated the sprawling expanse of forgotten lives.

Earl cleared his throat. The night air was heavy with an amalgamation of odors—decaying organic matter mingled with the acrid scent of plastics and chemicals. The distant buzz of the transformer that supplied power to the dump disturbed the stillness as the scavengers of the night hid within the trash, their eyes glowing in the gloom.

The wind whispered through the mounds of garbage, ghostly voices sharing tales of the objects' former lives. Broken toys, worn-out furniture, and obsolete electronics stood as silent witnesses to the transient nature of the human experience.

Earl and Oscar navigated this nocturnal realm, winding through the labyrinth of waste, their movements stealthy.

A sharp bark that ended in a yelp and cry brought Earl and Oscar to a standstill.

"He's over by the incinerator," Oscar said as he burst back into motion.

Earl fell in behind him.

A calamity of ringing metal and the metallic screech of a monkey hooting pierced the night.

Oscar spun and fired, the boom of the shotgun thundering through the trash.

Red spinning glowing eyes stared at Oscar and Earl from the shadows.

Earl turned on his flashlight and laughed.

A toy monkey wearing a dirty yellow shirt and torn white and red striped pants slammed two small cymbals together as it shrieked, its head jerking around.

"You missed it," said Earl.

Oscar leveled the gun, fully intending to blow the toy away, but thought better of it. It was bad enough he'd already given away their position, but the toy chose that moment to give up its ghost again and fall still. He lowered his weapon.

The wind gusted and despite the heat, a chill tweaked the tips of Oscar's fingers and toes. He stared at the mechanical monkey, memories of the incident stirring. Oscar was paralyzed by the memory. His mistake. The mistake.

"Are you O.K.?" Earl put a hand on Oscar's shoulder.

"Yeah, I'm fine." But he was anything but fine. Oscar's mind spun backward, the images rolling over the backs of his eyeballs so fast his head spun from the memory.

The sterile white corridors of the research facility echoed with the low hum of machinery, the only constant in that cold place. Oscar was on patrol, and he navigated the warren of steel doors and cold linoleum floors with a sense of unease settling in his stomach like a lava rock. He hated this place and it only served to stoke the fire in his gut that never ceased, an unquenchable anger he was having trouble controlling. The world had taken his wife, and everyone needed to pay.

The muffled sounds of a monkey yelling and hooting leaked into the passageway. Oscar approached one of the animal testing rooms and pressed his ear to the door. More yelling and painful animal cries.

He hesitated as he glanced furtively down the corridor. This was none of his business, but something compelled him to investigate, his ego and anger-driven sense of justice clashing with the clinical indifference of his station in life.

And he was looking for a fight, whether he knew it or not.

Oscar eased the lab door open, and he was met with a scene that scarred his memory.

A cage housed a trembling, wide-eyed lab monkey, its fur matted, its eyes filled with terror.

The researcher, a sergeant Major Oscar knew as Dr. Detrich, loomed over the trapped creature, wielding a syringe with a callousness that made Oscar's hackles rise.

"Stop!" His voice cracked as Oscar burst into the room, his hands shaking with a mixture of fear and anger, a wave of consequences breaking over him.

Dr. Detrich turned, his expression a blend of bemusement, annoyance, and surprise. "What's your problem, Oscar? This is none of your business."

But it was Oscar's business, at least that's what his righteous mind believed at the time. The lines between professional detachment and humanity blurred as he saw the fear in the monkey's eyes. The beast whimpered, pleading. Oscar's vision went red, anger burning his stomach as rage took control. He lunged for the syringe, his fingers closing around it and tearing it from the doctor's hand.

"There are protocols," Oscar said. "And from what I can see, you're not following them."

The sergeant major smirked, his arrogance undeterred. "This is science, Oscar. We're pushing boundaries here. You wouldn't understand."

Oscar's eyes flashed with defiance. "I understand perfectly." He locked eyes with the scientist in a silent standoff, the tension in the room escalating.

The monkey huddled in the corner of its cage, eyes darting between the two humans.

Oscar brandished the syringe, its needle glinting in the harsh overhead light. "I wonder what this will do to you?"

Dr. Detrich scoffed, "Put that down, Oscar. You're acting the fool."

The blinding heat of rage filled Oscar with anger. He was beyond reason. He'd lost Monica, the only thing in the world he cared for, and he'd be damned if he was going to stand by and watch an innocent animal get tortured.

Monica spoke in his head for the first time then. "Calm down, baby. Calm down."

But he was gone, lost under the weight of injustice, a surge of adrenaline lighting him up like a Christmas tree.

Dr. Detrich's eyes widened, a moment of uncertainty flickering across his face. The room fell silent, broken only by the labored breathing of the monkey. Dr. Detrich stepped back, his features contorting with fear.

Oscar lashed out and rabbit punched the guy in the chops.

The researcher dropped like a sack of potatoes.

Oscar panted harder than the monkey, his breaths coming in ragged bursts, the fog of anger subsiding as he stared at the fallen scientist. What had he done?

The monkey, though still caged, seemed to regard Oscar with a curious, almost grateful, gaze.

As he stood amidst the repercussions of his anger, the sterile walls of the research facility closing in around him, the weight of his choices crushing him, Oscar tried to help the scientist up, but the man was having none of it. He fled the lab screaming like Oscar was a murderer, yelling for help, and Oscar saw what remained of his life swirl down the drain. Funny thing was, he recalled not giving a shit.

The wailing of Tank snapped him from his reverie, and he looked up to find Earl staring at him.

"Are you alright?" Earl asked. "You... weren't here for a minute."

Oscar nodded in the affirmative that he was O.K. and said, "Understatement of the year. Now let's go help Tank." He gathered his courage, lifted his shotgun, and darted into waste wonderland in search of his friend.

7

Tank's whimpering drove out the echo of crashing cymbals as Oscar peeked around the corner of the incinerator building, gun up, nerves dancing just beneath his skin. Each sound the canine made caused his blood to boil harder, but Oscar lowered the heat of his emotions. He couldn't help Tank if he wasn't dialed in and focused, not to mention that a lapse in judgment could get him killed.

Moonlight angled over the trash heap, and shadows frolicked and fought within the refuse, the shrieks of the mechanical monkey fading from his mind. Light from the perimeter lamps diminished as Earl inched forward into the darkness, panning his rifle around as he swept across the collection area before the incinerator. The dark maw of the metal beast stood closed, but a flash of silver caught Oscar's eye as he pushed off the recycling building and trailed after Earl.

When Oscar arrived at Earl's side, he found his partner examining an army of shiny metal tanks, their neck rings capped off, their valve mechanisms, and safety caps gone. The cylinders were sealed with welded caps.

"Doesn't look like any of these are meant to be opened... ever," Earl said.

"I'd like to meet the guy who welded those caps. What ar—"

Tank's barks and wails reached a crescendo, and the commotion was answered by a series of primeval chirp-barks.

"They're not labeled," Earl said.

"None of this was here when I closed," Oscar said. Or were they? He'd come this way, hadn't he?

"The greenies come in the place when it's closed?" Earl chuckled. "Of course, they do, what was I thinking?"

"Thing is... this stuff can't be burned, so why didn't they put it in the restricted area with the other lost items?" Oscar said. He was having trouble thinking straight with Tank's cries of pain bouncing around inside his head.

Oscar went around the cylinders and worked his way along the edge of the restricted area, the Wasteland, and the fresh garbage field to his left.

Earl hissed for him to stop. "The sound is coming from over there," he said as he pointed to the Wasteland.

Oscar nodded and changed course.

The partners cut between the Wasteland and a pile of fresh refuse waiting to be churned under earth. A diverse collection of discarded items formed the bulk of the heap, each piece bearing the scars of abandonment. Tattered fabric waved in the breeze, entwined with broken lumber and weathered containers, their labels faded. The trash pile's vibrant colors were muted by dirt, decay, and darkness, and broken shards of glass glinted. The trash pile emitted such an unpleasant aroma it even registered on Oscar's trash-dampened palate, the mix of decay, mildew, and the lingering traces of discarded consumables like raw sewage crawling up his nose. Insects scuttled about, and flies filled the air, reclaiming the refuse as their domain.

Oscar batted flies away from his face as he pressed his back to a stack of forgotten crates containing old computer monitors—more work that had been sitting around the Fill since before Oscar's arrival.

Earl fell in beside him, and with their backs covered, the partners stared into the gloom of the Wasteland.

"Time for some light?" asked Oscar.

"Wait one second," Earl said.

Shadows writhed within the darkness, a large shape moving about. Metal crashed as something was knocked over and a loud hiss carried over the dump.

The squeaks and titters of the desert rats ceased, and their glowing eyes disappeared.

Tank shrieked, gurgled like a drainpipe, and fell still.

Oscar screamed, crashing cymbals ringing in his head, the scared glowing eyes of a monkey staring at him from within the blackness. Oscar didn't feel so brave anymore, and the moisture migrated from his mouth to his armpits and suddenly the Benelli felt very heavy.

Adrenaline urged Oscar forward, gun out before him. His legs were on fire, and his back screamed, blood pounding in his head. "Light it up!" he yelled, and the world blossomed with angry LED light.

A ribbon of glowing nuclear green swung from the blackness into the cloud of light as something huge and brown and covered with an intricate mosaic of hardened plates slammed into Oscar.

Earl also got hit and he screamed, the flashlight flying from his hand. The torch hit the ground with a *pop* and sent waves of strobing light over the scene before winking out.

The blow knocked Oscar from his feet and pushed the air from his lungs. He hit the hardpan in a tangle and lost the shotgun.

A chicken-bark followed by an elongated hiss rose above the sound of Oscar's heart trying to break through his chest. He rolled onto his side. Something huge moved about within the dust cloud stirred up by the commotion, and the ground trembled like it did sometimes when Moxie dropped something really big off her hook.

Earl managed to stay on his feet, and he fired into the darkness, but Oscar couldn't see what the man was aiming at.

With an effort that almost took him down, Oscar struggled to his feet and retrieved his weapon.

Whatever had knocked the sense out of Oscar was nowhere to be seen.

Another chicken-bark roar, but this time Oscar wouldn't be denied. He sprinted into the darkness, cutting around a pile of tires and slipping into the Wasteland.

Earl took cover behind a pile of wood that had been stripped and neatly stacked—someone at the dump had gone through a lot of extra trouble, but wood was expensive these days, so he understood.

Gunshots rang out as Earl laid cover fire.

Worry ate at Oscar's stomach. What if a stray bullet hit Tank? A ricochet? Sweat dripped down his back as he pushed the thought away. If he didn't get to Tank soon it wouldn't matter.

Gunsmoke hung in the air as the partners inched forward through the darkness. When Earl came to his flashlight, he picked it up and tapped it against his leg, but the torch didn't come back on.

It was then Oscar remembered he had his Maglite on his belt. He pulled it free and lit the night.

Earl gasped, and that simple sound made Oscar's stomach fall out his ass. Nothing shook Earl. Nothing.

Tank lay on his side, the rottweiler and labrador mix's dark fur covered in blood. The beast's eyes found Oscar, and he started whimpering again and the cries cut through Oscar more than any sharp blade ever could. The bronzish hair around the dog's neck was dark, and a large open wound ran down the canine's side. Rib bones, sinew, fat, and muscle could be seen in the gaping wound, and blood spilled out onto the hardpan. The beast's ribs had done their job. None of the dog's organs were exposed, and though the beast was panting hard, Oscar thought it was fear eating his friend.

Oscar dropped to a knee and stroked the dog's head, which was wet with sweat and splattered crimson. White foam, tinged red, oozed from Tank's clenched jaws, and with a twist of satisfaction that brought neither happiness nor relief, Oscar saw flesh caught between the canine's bloody teeth.

"At least you got a piece of..." Oscar didn't know what to say because he had no clue what Tank had gotten a piece of. Maybe not no clue, but he knew nothing, and the feeling was starting to irritate him.

Earl took off his tactical vest, stripped off his shirt, and pressed it to the wound on Tank's side to staunch the bleeding. The beast whimpered and cried, but his dark eyes no longer darted about, and he'd stopped panting.

Tank's right front leg was twisted at an odd angle and one of his ears was missing a chunk of flesh. Oscar saw no claw marks, but the wound itself was red and already looked to be infected, though Oscar knew that wasn't possible.

Oscar and Earl worked hand in hand, and after several minutes they'd managed to put temporary bandages on all the beast's major wounds, and they'd stopped the outflow of blood. Despite this, Tank seemed to be getting worse.

The dog no longer made a sound, his eyes occasionally rolling back in his head as he drifted in and out of consciousness. Oscar nudged the beast every few minutes as Earl tried to get a signal on his cellphone to call for help, but he had no luck.

Tank's eyes closed, and when Oscar tried to rouse the dog, Tank didn't respond.

"We're losing him," shrieked Oscar. "But why? We stopped the bleeding. There doesn't appear to be any internal injuries."

Earl stared at him with pity.

"What the hell is it?" Oscar was on the edge and in danger of careening off the road. Tank was a friend. Maybe his best friend and he couldn't just stand by and watch him die.

"Maybe..." Earl looked away.

"What?" Oscar yelled so loudly his throat hurt.

"Whatever got him might..." Earl shook his head. "Could be some type of poison."

Oscar jerked back like he'd been slapped. Questions, and none of them good, filled him with concern and horror.

"You need to get him help. Fast!" came Monica's voice from Oscar's subconscious.

"We need to get him out of here," Oscar said.

Earl whistled and got to his feet. "The animal hospital..."

Oscar glanced at his watch. It felt like days had passed since he was sitting peacefully with his friends playing cards and drinking beer, but it had only been an hour and a half. It was a weekend night, and even if it wasn't, the vet would be long closed.

"We'll take him to the twenty-four-hour walk-in clinic just outside the base. They're always open." Alliance Medical Services was nicknamed Aunt Sue's MS because that was where the Army folks went when they didn't want Uncle Sam to know the intimate details of certain medical procedures and ailments.

"Will they help him?" Earl said. "Doctors can be prickly cusses."

Oscar pointed at the gun on Earl's hip and said, "If need be, we can make them."

"I ain't going to jail for a dog," Earl said. "No matter how cool said canine might be." Then to Tank, "Sorry buddy."

"Come on!" Oscar pleaded. "Shelly is probably on duty. She'll do it if you ask nicely."

"If you're so damn sure, why don't you take him?"

The boom of something huge falling to the ground thundered through the Fill.

"We're not done here," Oscar said. "I'm gonna find what did this." His gaze shifted to where the noise had come from. "And I'm allowed to be in here after closing, you aren't. I can say I heard crying, investigated…"

"How are we going to get him to the MS?"

"I've got my keys," Oscar said. "You can take a Fill work truck."

"Me? Shouldn't you drive the work truck?" Earl asked.

Earl had a point, so Oscar said nothing.

"We should both go. We can come back with reinforcements. Maybe do recon in daylight first. These things aren't going anywhere. It's stupid for us to be wandering around here in the dark now that we know how dangerous these things are."

"All good points," Oscar said. "But I'm staying. Come on. You're wasting time. Time Tank doesn't have."

"I want to stay," Earl said.

Oscar sighed. "Let's flip for it."

Earl said nothing.

Oscar tossed a coin in the air and said, "Call it."

"Tails."

The coin glinted as it bounced off the hardpan.

Oscar trained the Maglite on the quarter.

It was heads.

Oscar went to the service panel on the back of the admin building and disabled the alarm and the gate camera while Earl retrieved a Fill vehicle, an old pickup that was used around the yard and didn't have plates and wasn't registered. The duo carefully lifted Tank and placed him in the truck bed, the beast unmoving, unconscious, and unresponsive.

"Thank you, Earl," Oscar said. "If need be, tell the cops when they catch up with you at the clinic that I made you do it. Say I put a gun on you. Threatened you."

"Don't you worry on me."

"Save him," Oscar said. "Please."

Though he did his best, pity slackened Earl's expression.

Oscar didn't hold it against the man. Earl knew his story and had even met Monica, though she'd been nothing but a skeleton, skin, and half a brain by then.

Coyotes argued and the night symphony blared as Oscar opened the Fill's gates so Earl could pass through.

Earl didn't wave or look back as the truck bumped up onto the road.

Oscar watched the pickup's taillights until they dissolved into the darkness. Then he relocked the gate and checked his weapons.

As if in challenge a low cackle-bark that rose in volume and pitch pierced the night.

Light green glowing streaks moved within the trash piles, the breeze whispering and bringing the scent of oil mixed with trash.

A clicking sound, like a chain being drawn over metal, carried over the dump.

Terror and anger rooted Oscar to the hardpan, the rational side of his brain telling him he should be in the pickup's cab with Earl doing everything he could to save Tank.

But he'd already done all he could, and now he was going to find the beast that had diced his friend.

And when he did, he was going to kill it.

8

Silence settled over the Fill, the only sounds were Oscar's harsh breathing and the tap of metal on metal as something wavered in the gentle breeze. The tips of Oscar's fingers and toes stung with apprehension. His tough words to Earl only moments before had fled like so many good ideas after midnight. That unchecked bravado and righteousness had cost him so much, but still... Who would he be without it?

The wind whispered and he heard Monica's voice soothing the tumult of emotions raging inside him. "You don't need to do this alone," she said.

"But I want to," he answered. Oscar checked the Benelli for the tenth time, and eased his hand over the revolver's handle, reassuring himself that the weapon was there and ready.

He walked along the fence surrounding the restricted area, and nothing but shadows and desert rats moved within.

A clang of metal to his right, and Oscar spun, settled on his feet like he was preparing to catch a ball, and aimed the shotgun into the blackness. A flash of radiant green and then a massive, elongated shadow fell across the incinerator's loading area.

Floodlights were mounted on each corner of the incinerator building, and nothing moved within their puddles of light. Oscar didn't see the creature, but he felt... something. A presence. A malevolence that meant him harm.

A low hiss carried over the dump, and Oscar was moving again, the rational side of his mind screaming warnings, but that part of Oscar's team never held much sway. Anger. Revenge. Emotions the primal side of his brain used as weapons that wouldn't be deterred. The lizard of his brain wasn't that much different than the brains of the wild creatures that called the desert home, and that was a stark reminder of Oscar's position in life. Yet none of that changed the situation or his goal.

Clicking, a hiss, and a series of low chicken-barks that sounded too much like laughing for Oscar's tastes.

He was almost past the incinerator building when two eyes appeared in the stygian darkness to the south. Oscar jerked to a stop, terror cementing his feet to the hardpan.

Nictitating membranes retracted revealing eyes that radiated brightness, a haunting radioactive brilliance. The creature's pupils were vertical, mirroring those of a predatory reptile. That told Oscar the beast wasn't an overgrown Gila monster. Their pupils were horizontal and didn't glow like their diet was tainted with nuclear waste.

Waste…

Oscar didn't finish his thought because his breath caught, and his head filled with the static of disbelief and fear.

Under the cloak of darkness, within the trash heap where light surrendered to an all-encompassing void, an absence of light darker than night began to sculpt itself into an entity. It was as if the void yearned for form, for substance.

A subtle manifestation emerged, and a huge silhouette tinged in glowing green formed in the darkness. The absence of light coalesced into an undefined shape that danced on the periphery of Oscar's perception, teasing the boundaries between existence and emptiness. Spectral tendrils of shadow reached out like fog probing the air.

Cold sweat rolled down Oscar's back.

As the seconds slid by, Oscar unable to think, act, or move, the formless shape sought definition, and the silhouette morphed into a discernible shadow. The contours sharpened, defined by glowing green streaks, and the image cast an eerie semblance of a giant lizard on the canvas of darkness.

A huge creature materialized out of the darkness into a cloud of light.

The creature bore a striking resemblance to an enormous Gila monster that had undergone a profound and horrific metamorphosis. Its limbs were muscular trunks, and additional spines and bony protrusions stuck from its legs, tail, and back, creating a dinosaur-like appearance. The creature's long, razor-sharp claws gleamed in the unforgiving light, its eyes dulled by its closed nictitating membranes that shielded the creature's eyes from the severe LED light.

Normal Gila monsters had sagging skin, but this beast's torso was muscular and thick, and its armored skin which was usually covered in pearl-shaped thin bones had transformed into a complex mosaic of hardened plates, resembling a fusion of organic armor and crystalline structures.

Bioluminescent patterns adorned the mutant's entire body, producing an unsettling spectacle of shifting colors and patterns reminiscent of a healing burn victim.

The creature's head, flat and triangular, resembled that of a snake, with a flat snout and jaws lined with teeth. Oscar saw that it had been the beast's tail that had knocked him on his ass. Having evolved into a potent weapon, the beast's tail displayed increased muscularity and a prehensile quality, and to Oscar's amazement, the creature used the python tail to wield a bat-like piece of wood.

Pain jarred Oscar's side where he'd been whacked, and his gaze locked on the creature's teeth. He knew from experience out in the desert that Gila monsters produced venom in their salivary glands at the end of their lower jaws, unlike snakes, whose venom is produced in glands behind the eyes. He'd been bitten a couple of times, though he was no expert, but he knew a Gila monster's venom was propelled from a gland via tubing at the base of its lower teeth and then by capillaries into grooves in the teeth. From there the venom was chewed into the victim.

He recalled Tank's condition and Earl's speculation about the canine being poisoned.

The massive beast threw back its head and shrieked as it sprang forward.

Stung from his wonderment, Oscar fired. He pulled the trigger until the Benelli clicked empty and then he pulled the revolver.

But the lizard was faster, and apparently more intuitive, because it had slipped behind a pile of refuse as #4 turkey shot peppered the garbage.

Oscar darted into the shadows and took cover behind locked crates of documents waiting to be burned. He swung the shotgun over his shoulder and looked back the way he'd come.

Green bioluminescent streaks cut through the trash, the sounds of clanging metal and the booms of falling items echoing over the dump. Desert lizards are usually stealthy beasts, but the creature's size was making it difficult for the monster to navigate the maze of detritus without disturbing any of the many tottering piles throughout the Fill.

He aimed the pistol and fired, six even shots spread out over a twenty-foot span of trash. Bullets pinged and thumped, the echo of the gunpowder expanding making Oscar's ears ring. Frustration burned his stomach as he stuffed the revolver in his waistband and fished in his pockets for shotgun shells. As he pumped bullets into the Benelli's magazine, he felt the creature getting closer, his skin crawling with a sixth sense that had saved his bacon more than once.

A cackle-bark shriek emanated from behind the incinerator building. The beast was trying to come around and get him from behind. There was no cover from that direction unless he sprinted across the unloading area before the massive firebox to the trash heap, during which he'd be fully exposed.

But mini-Godzilla didn't have a gun, and how fast could the thing be? Faster than him came the answer, and the decision of flight or fight was made for him.

Oscar put his back to the crates and stared into the gloom. He still had his Maglite, and he considered lighting the beast up. Sweat dripped down his forehead into his eyes, the stink of his fear worse than the reek of trash.

He went for his light but as his fingers grasped the smooth metal the monster surged from the darkness, eyes aglow, teeth glinting.

The shotgun thundered, six booming shots that tore away the darkness. At last loading Oscar had stuffed an extra shell in the firing chamber, and as it turned out the extra shot might have saved his life.

With the fluidity of water, the beast surged at Oscar, shifting, twisting, and weaving like a crocodile as it came on. The first five shots grazed the creature with scattered shot, but the sixth shell hit the beast and it squealed as it changed direction.

The shriek of pain brought a smile to Oscar's face. Despite its hardened and shielded skin, the beast was vulnerable. He dropped into a crouch, reached for the revolver, remembered the gun was empty and that he didn't have any ammo for the .38 on him, and instead went about reloading the Benelli. He only had five shells left, and after he'd stuffed them into the magazine, he chambered a round.

Here he was again, alone, with no witnesses to the fact the mutant existed. He felt for his phone. Pictures were worth a thousand words, but in the darkness, with the beast camouflaged and moving fast through the trash, there was no way he'd get a picture that would prove anything.

But a corpse would prove plenty.

The lizard's tail whipped and knocked over a rusted metal cabinet that fell to the ground with a hollow gong.

Oscar only saw the green streaks of the creature as it moved, and his nerves danced as he recalled how the animal had tried to circle around him. He shifted on his feet, swinging the Benelli.

With a crash of metal, the mutant launched over a stack of broken furniture and old mattresses, jaws flexed open, sharp teeth bared. The creature's eyes were aflame, and if Oscar didn't know any better, he might have thought the beast was a dragon about to incinerate him with its fire breath.

A rank wind pushed into Oscar as he dropped and rolled, the lizard's claws sailing inches above him, the air in between sizzling with motion.

Oscar angled the shotgun up and fired, but the creature was like smoke, and the shot missed as the giant lizard landed atop a forlorn amalgamation of trash.

The lizard skidded to a stop and turned to face Oscar.

With a battle cry Oscar hadn't commanded his vocal cords to utter, he opened up with the shotgun, its barrel spitting white-orange rage as the round metal pellets streaked from the barrel and whistled through the air. The snap of the empty shells being ejected and the gentle thump as they hit the ground was unusually loud amidst the chaos as Oscar's world shrank to a five-foot circle around him.

A wail of hideous pain cut through the night.

Oscar pulled his flashlight, turned it on, and pressed it to the Benelli's magazine like a sight as he panned the gun around, the light driving away the darkness.

The lizard stood watching him from forty yards away, its eyes locked on him.

Oscar felt the anger behind those eyes. The desperation. The hunger. He aimed the Benelli at the creature but didn't fire. He had one shell left, and it was in the firing chamber. No way he was walking around the dump unarmed with a giant mutant Gila monster running around.

The beast's eyes swung like searchlights, then blinked out as the creature scurried over a pile of trash into a field of rusted equipment and bald tires.

Oscar gave chase, then slowed when he saw the slick crimson trail leading into a field of discarded things.

Squeaking rats pushed to the edge of Oscar's bubble of light, their beady eyes suddenly defiant. Godzilla was gone and the vermin once again ruled the trash-roost. The creatures came forward in a wave, and Oscar stomped his feet and charged the creatures, his victory with the lizard urging him onward.

There were so many rats, some of which were the size of dirty poodles, that the beasts could have easily overtaken Oscar. As it was, and evolution being what it was, the creature's tiny brains couldn't fathom a coordinated attack with a creature one hundred times its size, and the rats scattered like birds after a gunshot. He realized fast he was probably giving himself too much credit and that the rats probably weren't that hungry.

The battalion of rodents scuttled into the pasture of forgotten items, the entire crowd heading in the direction of the restricted area.

Oscar followed. He'd been going nonstop for over two hours. His beer buzz had worn off, and his knees pulsed with pain. He'd hit the beast—he was sure of that, but he hadn't managed to kill the creature, so he didn't have a corpse... or his proof.

Time to remedy that.

He followed the lizard's trail of blood, the crimson splatters and five-fingered footprints stark black under the stare of the Maglite.

9

Oscar heard rats scurrying through the garbage just beyond his cloud of light. The footprints trailed into a canyon of threadbare tires, hills of rubber that would pollute the Earth long after the Fill was buried by time boxing in the path. Blood drips decorated the trail, but the black dots were getting smaller, and the tracks were fading as Oscar went on.

He could tell by the trail that the creature's front right appendage was damaged. The forward right print was nonexistent in spots or nothing more than a dark slash on the hardpan, which told him the claw was being pampered.

There was movement ahead like a gathering storm, but it wasn't a rainstorm pushing through the narrow canyon of tires.

The Maglite's glare rendered the world in a harsh black and white that had a three-dimensional quality because the black tires and light-brown hardpan were a stark backdrop even under the softest light.

Tiny glowing eyes surged into the whiteness like a crashing wave, a horde of rats climbing over each other only to be held back by the alphas of their kind that led the charge. The advance group sat on the path, several of them sitting upright on their back legs, ears twitching, sharp bucktooth-like teeth gnashing. In his mind's eye, Oscar pictured the rat leaders with their front legs crossed, looking all pissed off. The field of smaller beasts crowded in behind the leaders, and for the briefest of instants Oscar asked himself if he'd been outsmarted.

But he be man.

Screeching and whining carried through the rubber valley as three of the larger rats came forward.

Oscar leveled the shotgun. He couldn't fire because he only had one shell left, so he searched around for weapons and found none.

The entire horde burst into motion, a flowing mass of gray flesh, the smaller rats almost overtaking the alphas.

Oscar had decided to turn tail and run when he discovered a mound of weapons.

The lead rats had slowed, and the beasts were crawling on all fours and licking the blood.

He secured the Benelli on his back via its strap. Then he shifted his attention to the heap of tires on his right and selected the largest one. He pulled the tire down off the pile, set it upright on its nonexistent treads, and took a deep breath. To say he was unhappy about the situation wouldn't be totally true. He cracked his neck, gripped the tire, and rolled it as hard as he could toward the rats.

Oscar didn't wait to see if his rubber weapon struck home. He started pulling tires and hurling them. One after the other, like a machine, using the last of his energy, burning everything he had left.

Soon eight tires were barreling down the narrow alley and Oscar ran behind them like an admiral commanding his ground troops.

The beasts scattered, and Oscar kicked rats as he ran, punting the beasts that were too fat and too slow to get out of his way.

Ahead the trail turned sharply right. It was the end of the tire valley and a chain-link fence topped with razor wire blocked the way forward.

The fence was broken open and the wounded beast had fled into the restricted zone. Oscar thought of the breach he'd discovered several days back on the southern side of the Army's area. This hole was bigger and there was much more damage, and it was going to take Oscar at least half a day to repair.

Like the first breach, the chain-links all around the hole had been stretched and twisted until they gave way. The trail of blood was almost gone, but many of the broken links were black with drying blood, and a piece of brown and black skin with a bright green stripe was caught on a broken link and rippled in the breeze.

Behind him, in the darkness, the rats chortled and sang, and when Oscar looked back, he saw the vermin were already feasting on what remained of the lizard's blood, their eyes glowing in the LED light. The Maglite hardly deterred the beasts, and he hadn't killed a single one. That brought neither pleasure nor pain. He was no killer, that was for sure. And he didn't terminate life for no reason. Even when there was an excellent reason, taking the life of another living thing is a crime against nature, unless it's to preserve one's existence, and even then, there were those who said that was God's decision and not his, not that he ever considered the opinions of said people.

Oscar had known he was no killer as a boy just like he'd known the landfill was his comfort zone. It had been the death of a frog, a small amphibian, no more than an inch long, that had shaped this ethical mountain and guided him through the years of his young life.

It was a hot summer day, not as hot as the desert, but hot. The memory of that day was so strong, he had viewed it and refined it so many times, that it was like watching a rerun of one's favorite T.V. program. It replayed as Oscar gripped the Benelli and stared into the restricted area.

Fishing for carp and goldfish with tiny balls of bread was one of Oscar's primary summer activities as a youth. Young Oscar and his friend Rob often trekked through the woods behind Rob's home to a small lake where they would waste the days sitting around catching fish and throwing them back into the pond.

On this day as he and his buddy trekked through the woods with their poles and an empty white bucket, they came across a frog struggling to find its way back to the water.

Rob easily captured the amphibian and imprisoned it in the pail.

Young Oscar had little issue with this. He'd detained turtles, frogs, fish, and sometimes large spiders and crickets, but he always fed them and let them go after a couple of days. Except for the turtles which he let loose in his backyard. Some of the boxers made a home there, while others disappeared despite young Oscar's best attempts at fortifying the old stockade fence that surrounded the yard.

It was the fireworks that set young Oscar's stomach ablaze.

Rob always had a banger or a bottle rocket, and on this day, he produced a cracker that had been broken off the end of a bottle rocket.

"What are you—" was all Oscar got out.

Rob lit the firework and dropped it in the bucket.

So many ideas flew through his head that Oscar was frozen, paralyzed by indecision. He wanted to reach into the pail and jerk the cracker out. He wanted to save the frog.

The firework exploded, the sound magnified by the hollow bucket, which held together.

Unfortunately for the frog, it wasn't as lucky. What remained of the beast was splattered on the side of the bucket; blood, entrails, fat, sinew, and bone leaking down the melted and white-charred plastic. Within the morass of flesh, a blackened eyeball had stared at Oscar.

He felt the rage that would settle just beneath his control for the rest of his life, and he punched Rob with everything he had.

That was the last time they'd gone fishing, and the once inseparable friends only spoke when required to. The incident left Oscar a changed person, but not Rob. Oscar heard years later that the boy who had grown up to be a man had killed and tortured two women. It had made Oscar feel like crap because he'd seen the killer inside his friend, even as a young kid.

All that considered, Oscar was also a hunter, but rats weren't frogs that were trying to sink tiny teeth into his hide. Oscar knew that when you were hunting and you hit a deer, sometimes they sprang away in search of a quiet place to die. He'd tracked wounded bucks for miles, and if it took walking miles to find mini-Godzilla, and put an end to the mystery and fear, he would do it if he—

A loud chicken-bark-cackle that Oscar had come to associate with the mutant lizard carried over the landfill and tossed him from his reverie.

Oscar inched through the hole in the chain-link fence, gun up, finger on the trigger, the rats squealing behind him. Shadows writhed and faded within the mounds of discarded items, the stench of oil and chemicals driving out the rot-dominated scent of garbage.

He didn't enter the restricted area often, but Oscar knew the western side where he'd entered was considered long-term trash. The greenies used the term to describe equipment and consumables that no longer had any value or use but couldn't be destroyed for various shady budgetary reasons that amounted to kicking the can on huge losses.

Stacks of crates containing outdated food rations, hulking pieces of peculiarly shaped metal that had once been parts of unknown machines, and a variety of drums and cylinders, each unlabeled and stacked neatly, filled the yard. There were old vehicles, loads of dented and rusted helmets, forlorn boots, and weapons, the gun barrels of the old guns filled with concrete.

A sour-sweet wind pushed over the dump. The blood trail diminished to an occasional black drip or a partial hand-like footprint. What hadn't diminished was Oscar's ability to track the creature. The beast was big, which meant many of the escape routes through the trash were far too small for the creature to traverse without causing a calamity, so there were few paths the mutant could tread.

The highlight of the restricted area was what Oscar called the technology graveyard. This pile of electronic remnants served as a monument to the transient nature of technology, a necropolis where once cutting-edge components now rested, replaced by sleeker, more efficient successors that would soon join them.

Amidst the debris there was a disorganized heap of computer garbage and a boneyard of obsolete electronics. Towers of antiquated monitors, their screens now dark or shattered, stood like silent relics of a bygone era. Circuit boards, once the nerve centers of innovation, were cracked and broken, their transformers crushed, their wires stripped of their former glory and precious copper. Mainframes, once mighty engines of computation, slumbered in their obsolescence, their colossal frames rendered obsolete by the relentless march to get smaller faster. An array of abandoned switches and routers sprawled chaotically, their interconnected pathways severed and forgotten. Metal veins, once pulsating with data, hung lifeless like hair, waiting to be recycled.

The remains of the blood trail led through hanging strands of copper, and Oscar used the tip of the Benelli to move them aside.

Nothing moved within the maze of computer monitors and old brown metal boxes that had once adorned every desk.

Oscar eased through the salvaged wires, dust lifting from the hardpan. The wind shrieked and whistled as it fought to get into the confined area, and it was easy to see nobody had been this way for some time. Dark dust speckled with black grit covered every vertical surface, and there were no footprints except those of the beast backtracking over each other. The creature had come this way many times, yet the garbage appeared undisturbed. Rust stains dripped onto orange-brown spots on the path, but they were unmarred. Birds' nests filled many of the sheltered areas, and white droppings littered the ground.

The blood trail was gone, and of the mutant, there was no sign other than its wake of prints.

After several minutes of following the footprints that delved deeper into uncharted territory, Oscar came upon a pile of green telephones, the old-school kind with a keypad, a curly wire, and a handset. Most of the pile was stacked neatly—for a dump—, but a large section along the bottom of the stack had been torn away and a dark maw opened on blackness.

Here the ground had been recently torn up, and five-fingered prints trampled each other and led into the hole.

Oscar plunged his head into the opening and sniffed, then jerked back like he'd been shot. The rank scent of decay wafting from inside the hole turned his stomach, which was saying something for a man who barely smelled raw refuse.

Moonlight angled through the trash, and stars sparkled overhead as Oscar considered calling the boss and letting him and the Army handle this crap sundae. But if he'd learned anything from his fall, he'd learned that if he wanted something done right, he had to do it himself.

10

Oscar entered the rubbish realm, that graveyard of forgotten knowledge where the breeze whispered of what was. His heart raced as the trash blocked the moonlight, the beam of the Maglite bouncing off glass in dazzling starbursts that drove away the shadows.

Dirt, time, and weather had compacted the pile of phones along with earth, grit, and an uncountable number of pieces of windblown trash. The stratified layers were mostly black, but here and there a patch of green plastic bled through like an open wound. Old-style handsets hung from the tunnel's rough-hewn ceiling by twisted wires like seedpods, and Oscar eased around them as he carefully made his way down the narrow passageway.

He had been taught that an animal could fit through any space its skull could fit through, regardless of the creature's overall size. So he wasn't surprised that the tunnel was only eight feet high and ten or so feet wide, despite the creature being three times that size. The beast tracks were old and muddled, and they backtracked over each other.

The tunnel turned sharply downward, the path descending through levels of garbage strata, the junk dating the American eras like tree rings. As he trekked deeper underground, the tunnel walls shifted and changed. The sides of the passageway became rougher, and huge hollows and cracks and gaps appeared where pieces of ancient trash had totally decomposed, leaving an air pocket or a fossil-like depression in the plastic-laden sedimentary-like ground.

Oscar judged he was ten feet underground when the overlapping footprints ended, and the tunnel floor gave way to a series of mesa-like pillars that stretched into the blackness ahead. The flashlight only penetrated twenty yards into the syrupy darkness that filled the chasm, and the gaps between the earthen columns revealed a bottomless hole.

He had no rope, no supplies to help him get across safely. Phone cords with attached handsets hung from the ceiling, and the walls were loose and powdery and were comprised of an amalgamation of garbage that looked like it would come apart like rice under the stream of a power washer.

Without thought, Oscar stepped on the nearest pillar. It was stable. He moved around and jumped up and down. Nothing. Still… He should go back.

As if in answer to that thought a hollow clicking that transformed into a chicken-bark echoed down the tunnel.

Tension stomped up Oscar's spine and settled in his neck like a jackhammer going full tilt. The primeval call had come from behind him.

Oscar cast the Maglite's unflinching eye down the tunnel in the direction he'd come.

Nothing.

On an impulse driven by the lizard side of his brain, he jumped to the next pillar. It was rocksteady.

More catcalls and bellows and shrieks and hisses carried down the tunnel.

He was almost halfway across when the Maglite illuminated the finish line, the undisturbed tunnel floor trailing into darkness. That was the good news. The bad news was that several of the pillars had fallen and there was a twenty-foot gap between the last pillar and the end of the abyss.

Oscar pivoted on his column and turned around, preparing to head back, but instead, he froze.

A mutant sat in the tunnel opening at the edge of the void, its nictitating membranes open, its bright eyes focused on Oscar. A long serpentine tongue flicked in and out of the creature's narrow jaws, lashing the air. Its tail lifted and swayed as if searching for a target. The tail held no weapon, but it curled, flexing in and out, as if searching and wanting to grab something to throw or swing. Oscar saw no blood and the mutant had no wounds.

That observation made Oscar sway on his feet as his head clouded with the idea that he hadn't shot this creature and therefore there was more than one.

He lifted the shotgun and leveled it at the giant lizard. A thought occurred to him as he stood there and steeled himself to fire his last shot. There were no five-fingered footprints on the pillars, and there were no signs the beast had climbed along the walls. That could mean only one thing. Where he was headed had more than one entrance, and the beasts had abandoned the tunnel when the floor collapsed.

Oscar aimed the shotgun at the mutant, sighting the weapon on its mouth, waiting for the creature to shriek so he could blow the back of its skull out.

But the beast only watched, slowly swaying and shifting, its loose skin rippling. The thwap of its tongue jetting out of its mouth and the whistle as it sucked it back in carried through the mutant's subterranean lair.

The creature's eyelids closed, its eyes darkened, and the gigantic lizard didn't move.

Tapping sounds resounded through the earth and the beast cackled, the cry of aggression almost a laugh as its mouth slid open, revealing sharp teeth.

Oscar fired his last bullet, his ears ringing as #4 turkey shot streaked from the shotgun's barrel and sprayed the creature's face. The barrage of tiny round shot impaled the beast's eyes, and teeth broke off as dots of blood appeared all over the creature's head. With a pop and squish of flesh, a spatter of blood, bone, and brains splattered the tunnel wall.

The giant lizard surged forward in this madness and landed on the earthen pillars at the edge of the gap in the floor. Wind hollered as it twisted down the tunnel and clouds of dust filled the air. The beast was ten feet from Oscar, where he stood on the last pillar, a gap of blackness at his back.

But the beast was too heavy, and the pillars of sedimentary garbage stone cracked and shook and broke. Clouds of dirt and grit carried up from the void, and the lizard shrieked. As it fell the creature's arms thrashed wildly, its tongue lashing out, looking for anything to grab hold of.

Oscar got low, protecting his face with his arms, and when he looked back, the mutant was gone and all that was left was the fading shrieking of its death call.

He stood there for several minutes, panting, his mind cycling through what he'd just seen, adjusting the order of events, making sure he wasn't living a chaotic dream. But it had happened, and the fact that there were no pillars left behind the one he stood on was evidence of the fact.

Dust swirled above the gap in the tunnel floor, and Oscar panned the flashlight around and examined the walls.

There were deformed items of trash jutting from the walls, and there were plenty of handholds and places to notch his feet, but he didn't know how sturdy they were.

Only one way to find out.

Oscar coiled to jump to the pillar on his right but paused. He shined the light right, then left, and though his muddled brain admitted it wasn't sure, Oscar thought the wall on his left looked more climbable, whatever the hell that meant.

He jumped to the pillar directly to his left, and to his surprise the column swayed, but didn't break. Oscar wasted no time as he jumped from pillar to pillar until he came to the tunnel wall.

There he paused and pulled off his belt. The black leather had a stainless-steel buckle at its end and he threaded the belt through it, making a small lasso-like loop. It wasn't much of a safety line, but it would have to do. He swung the shotgun onto his back and secured the flashlight in its holder, but left it on, its glow still supplying ample light.

Oscar wore his dress work boots, and though they weren't steel-toed, they were sturdy. He swung his right leg and buried the tip of his boot in the wall. Dirt and small pieces of detritus rained down into the abyss.

A cracked and melted phone handset jutted from the wall like a climbing piton. He gripped it to test its strength, and it broke away. With that failure fresh in his mind, he swung his belt loop and managed to secure his safety line on a deformed piece of trash that looked to have once been metal. Then he worked the tips of his fingers into the wall and took a leap of faith.

Oscar swung his left leg and planted his foot in the wall as he stepped from the column of earth. He clung to the wall like a spider, his face pressed to dirt, the earthen scent of moisture and rot filling his nostrils.

Inch by inch, foothold by foothold, he worked his way along the wall. Using the belt for leverage, he was able to swing the final five feet to the edge of the hole. There he landed on his hands and knees, his neck and back screaming, spittle leaking from his mouth, though he felt like he hadn't had anything to drink in hours.

He got to his feet, dusted himself off, and pulled the Maglite. Dust hung in the air, and the faint scent of burning gunpowder tickled his nose.

Oscar didn't have to go far before he found the mutant's burrow.

He was aware that typical Gila monsters spent about ninety percent of their lives underground, taking refuge in burrows or rocky shelters that offered a favorable microclimate and sufficient humidity. They relied on these shelters and often chose rocky locations, such as sandstone or basaltic lava flows. Despite their preference for sheltered environments, Gila monsters also required access to water and were often observed near puddles—Oscar had seen it with his own eyes—and he knew they avoided open areas like flats and grasslands. The dump was the perfect spot for them to call home.

Oscar also understood that the lizards would relocate to different shelters every four or five days to optimize their microhabitat.

But one thing was certain: these creatures weren't standard Gila monsters.

Like the tunnel, the walls of the burrow were a stratified mess of trash that had broken down, most of the items no longer recognizable.

The ground was a mosaic of cracked natural tiles clearly molded by intelligent life. All the stones were triangular, though they were slightly different shapes, and there was gray mortar in between each that made the ground look like an Italian piazza. Many of the stones were marked with pictograms and writing Oscar believed to be of Native American origin.

Oscar had found paint pots and arrowheads out on the desert, and he knew the Native American tribes that had lived in the Sonoran Desert were renowned for their intricate pottery and finely woven baskets.

Despite all this, it was the nest-like den at the center of the space that drew the eye.

Like a bird's nest that's been constructed from pieces of its surrounding environment, the mutant's burrow was decorated with an assortment of trash that told the history of the United States and its decor and construction.

A knot of varied refuse was woven together like a basket, and its wide ends were attached to the ceiling and floor, the structure's length narrowing at its center where there was a dark hole that opened into a den.

Oscar inched forward, the huge hourglass-shaped heap of trash towering over him as he aimed the flashlight into the den.

Six large white eggs sat atop a bed of wires, paper, and cardboard stripped into long lengths and woven like a basket.

His brain staggered. Female Gila monsters laid one clutch of eggs per year, and he knew the number of eggs in a clutch could vary but was generally between two and twelve eggs.

If the mutants had similar reproductive patterns... He didn't want to ponder on it for too long because he didn't want to think about the answers to the many questions that knotted his head. He'd already known there was more than one mutant lizard on the loose, and now he knew there might be many more.

Tension rippled through him, and Oscar felt the urge to get out of the burrow. There were more creatures, beasts he hadn't wounded, and they could return home at any time.

It was then Oscar noticed two more tunnels and his suspicions of alternate entrances were confirmed. But which one should he use?

Oscar headed for the closest tunnel but stopped and looked back at the eggs. Should he destroy them? Heat spread through him as he considered. Mothers didn't usually appreciate their offspring being messed with, and that included eggs. What wrath would he unleash if he destroyed the eggs? When mother-mutant found her eggs ready for the frying pan, who knew what she would do?

No. He'd turn the entire thing over to the boss in the morning.

The tunnel he took was similar in construction to the other, except for the fresh five-toed footprints that covered the sandy ground.

As he retreated out the closest tunnel, his thoughts drifted to Tank and he wondered if he'd made things better on this night, or worse. Most living things didn't abide by intruders in their homes, and Oscar hoped he hadn't unleashed some terror by probing into one of the mutant's burrows. The six large eggs filled his mind's eye, and again he asked himself if he should have destroyed the eggs.

Did the eggs have value? That thought stopped him in his mental tracks. From the beginning, he'd suspected the mutants were the result of fallout or unforeseen consequences of the Army's experiments, and it had never occurred to him that the mini-Godzillas had been intentionally created to be used as weapons. Bomb delivery devices? Something worse? If so, the eggs could be valuable to the Army, and Oscar knew what the greenies were capable of when it came to getting what they wanted.

The tunnel was wider than the one he'd used to enter the burrow, and in many spots, the compressed junk pile above had settled, and there were large lobby-like gaps and thick cracks that trailed up into darkness like narrow ravines.

There were also signs of the creatures. Several sections of the cave had been nothing more than drain channels for rainwater that had been widened by claws and teeth, and there were also a couple of cave-ins where debris had been cleared with what Oscar had to assume was the creatures' dexterous tails.

The tunnel was much longer, and it wound on for several hundred yards as it curved steadily left before turning sharply up.

A sliver of pale light marked the end of the passage.

Oscar doused the Maglite because he didn't want to announce himself, and jogged the last stretch of tunnel. He emerged on the dark side of the Grassy Knoll into a pile of large boulders that had been pushed into a pile when the area was cleared.

He sucked in air, not caring about the smell. He had no corpse, but there were no longer any doubts that the local population of Gila monsters was being transformed and distorted, either intentionally or by whatever the Army was dumping in the Fill or whatever nightmare they'd recently created out on the testing range. Not surprising, but worrisome. He knew better than most that the greenies couldn't be trusted, and they'd do anything to cover their asses.

He gazed east, the bright lights of the Cactus Ridge Proving Ground main base burning away the night. Oscar had failed, and it was time to go find out how big the bill was for that failure.

11

Night clung to the road and wrapped it in syrupy darkness, the pickup's headlights piercing the gloom, revealing sand, dark mounds of devil grass, and the writhing and twisting shadows of storm-swept trees. Wasten's knuckles tightened around the steering wheel of his new pickup as he peered through the dust-covered windshield, his evening meal of pasta and store-bought sauce sitting in his stomach like loose concrete.

In the distance, the glow of the Fill drove away the blackness, a fuzzy white halo floating at the center of the perimeter lights. The chirping and bleating of the creatures of the night leaked into the cab through the open windows, and the scent of mesquite mixed with smoke carried on the gentle breeze. He liked having AC, but there was nothing like fresh desert air at night, even if it was tinged with trash.

Wasten licked his lips and bit his lower lip as he caressed the silver Colt .357 Magnum that sat on the seat beside him. Anger stirred his stomach with resentment, but it faded fast. He'd been home, chilling, three drinks and a joint past caring, when the boss sent him an SOS.

"Thank the lord you picked up," Trash-master had said. "The admin building alarm at the Fill tripped about half an hour ago and the law isn't responding. Surprise, surprise. Some shit about the dump being a low priority on a Friday night. Anyway, I'm tied up… literally, ask me at work… and I can't go check things out and reset the alarm. Oscar's not picking up and I can't send Alice down there alone at night in the dark."

Wasten had said nothing. If the boss needed a favor, he could ask. Just like Wasten had to when he needed something.

"Oscar really should do it," Trash-master said. "But you kind of owe him, right?"

Wasten knew about the bullet Oscar had taken for him concerning the brass they'd left behind the recycling building. It had been nice of Oscar to take the hit, but how had the boss found out? Wasten kept his mouth shut.

"Can you go?" Trash-master asked. No, please. No, I owe you one.

"Sure thing," Wasten said. So he'd splashed water on his face, sprayed deodorant under his arms, and drove nice and slow to the dump like he was on his way to church.

The Fill's entrance appeared undisturbed. Wasten slipped out of his truck, unlocked and opened the gates, and pulled through.

As he closed the gates a thunderous blast shattered the stillness and an unmistakable gunshot echoed through the Fill. The booming report reverberated off the mountains of garbage, making it impossible to discern its origin. Panic surged through him, a jolt of adrenaline stinging the tips of his fingers and toes.

Wasten grabbed the gun and locked the pickup, the sounds of the night creatures buzzing in Wasten's head. There had been no more gunshots, but Wasten held the Colt at the ready as he walked across the dirt parking area before the admin building.

Usually a desolate wasteland, the landfill felt different on this night—like a living entity pulsating with energy and secrets. The solitary hum of the power transformer and the desert breeze rattling trash broke the silence. A sense that he wasn't alone filled Wasten with caution, and he shook his head to shake the alcohol-induced haze.

The sharp tang of decomposing waste clawed at his nostrils, but there was something else, something metallic and acrid. Wasten's breath caught in his throat as he approached the admin building, the single light above the entrance a beacon in the vast expanse of darkness that engulfed the interior of the dump.

A distant wail carried on the breeze and the air crackled as Wasten made his way to the rear of the building where the power, security, and communication panels were housed within a large metal box affixed to the side of the building. He fumbled with his keys, got the lock open, and sure enough the security panel was pulsing red, ZONE 3 DEFAULT. All the cameras were also down, even the gate which normally worked.

Wasten strolled around the structure, flashlight ablaze, visually checking windows and doors. Sometimes when the wind gusted and rattled the windows the old alarm contacts separated which triggered the system. He examined the ground all around the building, and other than a series of trampled footprints, nothing was out of place. When he'd circumnavigated the building, he typed in his code, reset the panel, and relocked the control box.

Something within the jungle of trash clanged. The sound rang over the Fill like a bell, and it was followed by a low-cackle chicken-bark that made Wasten grip the handle of the Magnum even tighter as he headed for the source of the noise.

Wasten had no business tracking the coyote or Gila lizard or desert rats partying in the trash. Still… if whatever was lurking in the Fill had set off the alarm it was sure to happen again as soon as his taillights dimmed, and he had no desire to make a return voyage.

Chaotic shadows argued and fought within the fresh refuse pile. Wasten cut between the newly dumped junk and a plowed area he'd been working on earlier in the day. His dozer sat atop the dirt pile, blade up, scraps of paper, plastic, cardboard, and fabric sticking from the tiled soil like horrific blades of garbage grass.

It was then that Wasten noticed one of the Fill's work trucks was gone. The old pickup that the crew used to get around the dump and haul small items like air conditioners and chemical drums. He licked his lips as he considered. The boss hadn't mentioned that someone had borrowed a truck, but clearly, it hadn't been stolen. What kind of thief steals a broken-down old truck and then locks the gate on the way out? But the system being down...

His thoughts strayed to the military entrance, which he couldn't see from his position. Wasten pulled his phone to call the Trash-master, but froze with the device halfway out of his pocket.

A giant shadow fell over him, a writhing patch of blackness hiding from the moon's glare.

Wasten got low, brought the flashlight to bear as he aimed the revolver, and fired three times at the hulking blackness inching toward him. Bullets pinged off metal, plunked into rubber, and shattered glass, but there were no wails of pain.

A creature peeled itself from the trash, its grotesque form revealed in streaks of green nuclear light. Wasten stared transfixed as the beast materialized from the garbage into the moonlight. Akin to a colossal Gila monster that had undergone a severe mutation, the creature had large spines and bony protrusions all along its legs, tail, and back. Its torso was thick and muscular, and the pearl-shaped bones that covered its skin had evolved into an intricate fusion of organic-like armor.

Bioluminescent patterns adorned its body, creating an array of green streaks that made it look as though the creature's skeleton was glowing. Its flat, triangular head featured a long snout with narrow jaws lined with teeth. A python-like tail swayed as the beast came on, its single eye an orb of wet light.

Then the monster doubled its pace as it cut through the shadows, flashes of green streaks moving through the darkness.

A nasty trash-laden wind gusted over Wasten.

With a cackle-bark of anger, the mutant lizard was upon him, the shadow to his right giving way to a scaly missile with a nose cone of teeth.

Wasten swung the Colt and fired, pulling the trigger as fast as he could until the gun clicked empty.

A shriek pierced the dark, and the creature flew past and skidded to a halt within the flashlight's cone of light. The mutant was injured, badly, but Wasten could tell from the wounds that most of the damage hadn't been caused by him.

Black oozing dots that could only have been caused by a shotgun shot covered the front of the beast, and the monster limped forward on three legs, its front right paw lifted. One of its eyes was dark and hanging from its socket, and black gaps stood out within the creature's jaws where teeth were broken off at the base.

None of this made Wasten confident. Fear surged through him, transforming into raw, primal survival instinct. He stumbled backward, his gaze darting around for anything that could serve as a makeshift weapon, his gun empty.

Despite its injuries, the creature's movements were sinuous and unpredictable. Its venomous tail sliced the air as the beast came forward, its tongue cracking like a whip.

The monster was twenty feet away when Wasten picked up a flash of metal in his peripheral vision. He stuffed the Colt in his waistband, put the flashlight in its holder, and gripped the gleaming metal handle of a vacuum cleaner. The thing was old and heavy, its brick-like silver end embedded in the trash pile.

The mutant shrieked and let loose with a growl-bark that made the hair on the back of Wasten's neck stand at attention.

He clutched the handle as tightly as he could, and threw himself backward, pulling the vacuum from the refuse pile and using his weight and momentum to swing the unit.

If the monster knew what was coming, the beast did nothing to stop it.

The heavy end of the vacuum smacked the side of the creature's head, and the thump and accompanying wail of pain rose above the wind and his raging heart.

Stunned and shaking its narrow head, the creature backed off, using the extra reach of its forward legs and tail as weapons.

Wasten's heart pounded in his ears as he dodged the creature's tail strikes, each of his movements a desperate attempt to survive. He stumbled as his foot caught on a stray cable.

With a screech, Wasten went to the ground in a tangle, eyes wide with terror, his muscles protesting, his stomach a failing nuclear reactor. The crunch of the flashlight breaking brought stabbing pain and the air thickened with the stench of desperation, the chorus of impending death ringing in his ears as Wasten pressed to his hands and knees.

The wounded mutant lunged at him, its jaws flexed open, its remaining teeth dripping cloudy fluid.

He rolled, narrowly avoiding a bone-crunching bite, but though the mutant was staggering toward death's door, it was still bigger, stronger, and better equipped.

Wasten tugged on the vacuum as he attempted another swing, but the creature knocked the machine away with its tail. Pain surged through him, a searing agony that clouded his mind and slackened his muscles.

Like one of the largest apex predators to ever walk the Earth—the T. rex—the mutant lizard used its best weapon and swung its head around, jaws opening.

Wasten dodged, but he was too slow.

Teeth found flesh and bone as the lizard's jaws clamped down on his torso. Wasten lost all feeling in his legs and a wave of searing heat burst through him like his blood had transformed into lava.

But he didn't fall. The monster held him upright like a marionette, the beast's teeth sinking deeper into his body as the creature's jaws squeezed the life from him.

A loud snap reverberated over the Fill and the lizard's jaws opened. Then Wasten was falling, the ground racing up to greet him. He gritted his teeth as he hit the hardpan, suppressing a scream, his body aflame. His vision grew blurry, and he felt tired, so very tired.

The lizard backed away, and in that moment Wasten knew he was going to die. He could no longer move, and he recalled that Gila monsters of the non-mutated variety produced toxic venom, which normally isn't fatal to healthy adult humans. But there were cases where intoxicated bite victims had succumbed to the lizard's poison.

Excruciating pain paralyzed him as his arms and neck turned to stone. Wasten's heart raced, and he felt faint, blackness creeping in around the edges of his vision. He was certain now that the mutant's venom was spreading through his veins like a corrosive tide. The world grew gray, and his wife's face ran across his mental screen as he fought against the encroaching darkness.

An ominous silence settled over the Fill, broken only by the distant hum of the power transformer, the mumble of the wind, and the occasional rustling and hissing of the beast, its tongue lashing in and out.

Not how he'd wanted to go out. Wasten tried to get up, and his mind tantalized and tricked him because for a heartbeat he believed he was making progress only to discover he'd been unable to move.

The prophets say the final moments of one's life are the most joyous, but if that was the case, Wasten was going to hell because all he saw was failure and imperfection. A cynic he'd always been, but he'd always been good at paddling the river of denial and few acts of stupidity or poor judgment could toss him from his boat.

Darkness pushed out the light, the world draining away until there was nothing left but a single glowing eye growing in size as it advanced through the shadows, and Wasten screamed.

12

The Fill on Saturdays was Oscar's castoff companion, his love for the landfill a painful reminder of his social standing. He knew he had a long day ahead thanks to the prior night's events, but the heavy motorcade of trash-laden vehicles streaming away from the dump told him this particular Saturday was going to be his worst yet.

Turned out to be the worst ever.

Wasten's chewed-up corpse had been found at the Fill.

Oscar arrived to find the deputy sheriff's patrol car angled across the Fill's entrance, gates closed, a large crude sign of black marker on cardboard proclaiming, "Dump closed. Sorry for any inconvenience." He chuckled at the misspelling of inconvenience, but the humor fell dead.

Inside the Fill, the Army crawled over the restricted area and soldiers patrolled around the Grassy Knoll.

Oscar's first thought upon arrival at work was that he should turn around and head home, but the Trash-master spotted him getting an update from a turned-away customer and waved him through the gates.

He had planned to arrive at the Fill early and clean up his mess from the prior night, but he'd overslept, and that turned out to be a lucky break. He'd intended to tell the Trash-master a modified version of why he entered the landfill after hours, what had happened to Tank, the canine's current condition, the location of the dump's pick-up, and if things were going well, he'd resolved to show the boss the burrow.

But what was it the prophets said about best-laid plans?

"I assume you heard?" Trash-master said.

Behind the boss, the crew waited patiently like a flock of lost doves. Moxie and Alice stood huddled together, and Curby and Roy "Refuston" Thorton stood off to the side sucking on old-school burners, white smoke trailing away into the trash.

"Yeah," Oscar said. "You found him?"

The boss nodded. "You know I'm always in early on Saturdays."

Oscar did, that's why he'd planned to get in earlier.

"I saw the crowd of buzzards dive-bombing something out by the Wasteland, so I investigated and…" He threw up his hands and sighed.

"Do you know what he was doing here?" Oscar asked.

The boss said, "I asked him to come in and reset the alarm. Where were you last night? I tried calling you."

Oscar heard the messages on his phone, but not until morning. "I hit the rack early," he said as shame washed through him. He'd killed his friend. Oscar had disabled the alarm and the camera and that's why Wasten had come to the Fill on a night Oscar and Earl had been chasing monsters. He'd forgotten to reset the panel after Earl left with Tank. Sweat dripped down Oscar's forehead as he thought about Tank, the missing pickup, and he felt the eyes of every Army soldier on him.

"Tank is nowhere to be found. There's blood all over the place, but the Army and the cops think it's Wasten's. Our pickup is missing and get this... the thief locked the gate. No idea how they got in, but there are several holes in some of the interior barriers."

"Amazing," was all Oscar could push out.

"And since the camera was down at the gate we've got no security footage," Trash-master said. "Can't tell me that's a coincidence."

With his plan to come clean going off the rails, Oscar didn't know how to deal with Tank being missing. The canine was resting comfortably at the clinic, and perhaps when he was well enough Oscar could "find" the dog wandering out in the desert. Then there was the truck. Earl had been smart enough to abandon it, and it would eventually be found and assumed stolen. But that was the least of his problems. What was important now was that the Army mustn't find out he'd been at the heart of the mess, maybe even the cause of it.

"What happened to Wasten?" Oscar asked because he couldn't think of anything else to say.

"Go home," Trash-master said. Then he turned to the crew. "All of you. Go home and report Monday morning."

Curby said, "What about our pay? I need—" A man was dead, but that didn't stop the rent bill from coming.

Trash-master put up a hand. "You'll each get six hours. Fair?"

Nobody spoke as they shuffled toward the exit.

When the audience was gone, Oscar said, "So what happened to him?"

"Oscar, I know he was your friend. But all this will keep. Go rest and we'll—"

"I will. Tell me." Oscar had a good idea of what happened, but he needed to hear it anyway.

"The cops and greenies don't know, but whatever got him tuned him up real good," Trash-master said. "Gashes all over him from what looks like long sharp talons, and there were bite marks and missing chunks of flesh all over the corpse. An arm and half a leg were chewed off, and his head was crushed." Trash-master shook his head.

"Could have been me... or you," Oscar said.

The boss's eyes shifted to the ground. "Well, it wasn't. You know what I always say—"

Oscar didn't give the man a chance. "Yup. If the big man opens his book and your name is on the page, nothing else matters."

Trash-master nodded.

Oscar fished for some information. "There's no sign of Tank at all?"

Trash-master shook his head no.

"Probably ran off," Oscar planted. "Hopefully none of the desert beasts get hold of him."

"Or whatever got Wasten."

"What do you mean?"

The boss hiked his shoulders.

Oscar said. "Where is Wasten's body?"

Trash-master pointed his chin toward the restricted area where the Army soldiers still crawled over the mountains of garbage.

"Say no more."

"They said there'll be a service. They went to see his wife first thing, so we'll see," the boss said.

"Yes, we will," Oscar said.

With free time on his hands, there was only one place Oscar absolutely needed to be. By Tank's side. He called Earl, who picked him up down the road a ways from the Fill's entrance.

Roscoe was with him. "I figured you might need a woman's touch," she said.

Oscar shot Earl a withering gaze as he jumped in the backseat, but he wasn't really angry. Though he and Earl had agreed to keep their escapades of the prior night a secret until they felt spilling everything was safe and served some purpose, he knew it was only a matter of time before he confided in Roscoe. He told her everything, and with good reason. The woman had helped him out of many binds with her well-reasoned solutions.

Aunt Sue's MS looked like a dated T.V. set from an 80's sitcom. It was all mauve and worn wood laminate surfaces and prints of Saturday Evening Post covers and basic floral watercolors adorned the walls. There was a waiting area with old metal furniture, a reception counter with a window, and a hallway that led to three exam rooms, a storage room, a private office, an all-sex bathroom, and a room labeled lab. The establishment's main function was to fill the gaps between the military's services and to help servicemen and women get through sticky medical situations that Uncle Sam might find objectionable or job-threatening.

It was Saturday and the clinic was packed so Oscar and his partners used the back entrance, where they were met by Dr. Shelly DiBard, the local Nightingale.

"Hi, Shelly," Oscar said. "Thank you so much for doing this."

The doctor's long spiral-curled hair was pulled back in a ponytail, and her thick glasses made her beautiful hazel eyes look twice their size. She wore a lab coat over jeans, a plain dress shirt, and old running shoes. There was a barely noticeable sheen of makeup on her face, and her eyeshadow was dark, the way Oscar liked it. She said, "I'm out on a limb for you, Oscar, and... Well, not for you, for Tank, but still... If the bigwigs find out I treated an animal in here I can get in big trouble."

"Isn't Jay Dingman a patient?" prodded Roscoe. Jay was so hairy people called him the Wolfman.

"Not funny," Shelly said, but she was smiling. "Come this way." As she led the party down the short hallway she said, "I'm not sure I want to know why all this must be a secret. Lucky for you Deputy Sheriff Kendra hasn't been by."

Oscar hadn't thought of that. With Tank missing Kendra would be searching, but the overworked cop had a huge patrol area.

Shelly reached a door labeled Supply Room, and the four companions slipped inside.

Tank lay on a gurney, an IV pole beside him, several bags hanging from the rack, clear tubes running to a large bandage on the canine's side. His broken leg was splinted and wrapped, and his ear had been bandaged. The red inflammation around his wounds had diminished and no longer looked infected.

Tears welled in Oscar's eyes. He couldn't shake the idea that this was all his fault.

The canine didn't open his eyes as Oscar stroked his friend's head. "Is he going to be alright?"

The doctor nodded in the affirmative. "I think so, but it was a close thing. Whatever attacked him poisoned him. I hit him hard with antibiotics and a series of antivenin treatments, though I normally use the antivenin for rattlers, but he came around. Any clue what got him? I've taken some samples and I'm going to try and determine what type of venom took him down."

Oscar's tongue was frozen to the bottom of his mouth, and he said nothing. He'd been prepared to tell the doctor what he knew if it would help Tank, but with the canine on the mend Shelly was on a need-to-know basis, and she didn't need to know. Not yet, anyway.

"Earl saved his life by rushing him here and, well, being very persistent," Shelly said.

"Sorry about that," Earl said.

She waved him off. "No harm, no foul."

The group stared at Tank, the gentle push of air escaping the ceiling vent and the whimpers of a cat the only sounds.

"When can he come home?" Roscoe asked. The plan was to bring the dog back to Twilight Dunes until he was healthy enough to wander the desert so Oscar could guide the canine home to the Fill, but that was for another day.

"He can go home tomorrow if he continues to improve," Shelly said. "And there is the matter of payment?"

Earl had promised her fee plus fifty percent for breaking the rules and keeping it to herself. Oscar couldn't afford to pay, but he would even if he had to start selling off possessions. "No worries," he said. "I'll have full payment when I pick him up."

"You don't even know how much you owe?"

Oscar licked his lips.

"A grand will cover it," she said. "Cash."

Oscar's face hurt from suppressing a frown and all he could find to say was, "Thank you."

Back in the car, Earl said, "Just so you know, that's probably the standard price. The drugs alone were three or four hundred bucks out of her pocket."

"Shotgun," said Oscar.

On the drive back to Twilight Dune's Oscar told Roscoe everything, Earl listening intently and filling the gaps in what he knew.

"You took a big chance taking on the creature alone," Roscoe said.

Oscar wanted to tell her his dead wife had urged him on, but that hadn't been the entirety of it. It had been his drive to avenge Tank that had spurred him on.

"You're still taking a big risk," Roscoe said.

"We didn't do anything wrong," Earl said. "It was barely breaking and entering."

"That's not what I mean, and you know it," she said. "You need to tell the police, the Army, anyone who will listen, what you saw."

"And other than a dead body, what proof do I have?" Oscar said. "I'm not exactly an upstanding citizen in the eyes of the greenies, and from what I saw they were crawling all over the dump, so they'll figure it out. Why do I need to go down?"

"What about Deputy Kendra?" Roscoe said. "She likes you and you trust her."

"Maybe," Oscar said. "You are right about one thing. We need to warn someone."

As Earl made the right into Twilight Dunes and passed under the ramshackle portcullis, he brought the car to a stop.

The Pride blocked the road.

"Maybe we should tell Shelly everything," said Roscoe. "She might know what to do, and if we have a problem, a medical situation like Tank, it's always good to have a doctor in your corner."

Earl inched the car forward and the Pride parted like the road was the Red Sea and Earl's ride was Moses, but they took their time, tails up.

Oscar watched the cats as they stared at the car. He knew most of the felines, but as he counted, he realized three cats were missing. Not unusual, but given the situation he made a mental note to speak with Ms. Perriweather.

"They're such a tight group," Roscoe said of the Pride.

"Like the folks that live at Twilight Dunes," Oscar said. Seeing the clan of cats had sparked an idea.

His entire life Oscar had tried to tough things out on his own. Even after he'd found Monica, he tried to spare her from his daily problems and insecurities. When he'd arrived at the Dunes a broken man with a broken wife, he'd wanted nothing from anyone. Even talking to others made him angry.

The folks at Twilight Dunes had yanked him from his cocoon of pity and self-loathing and insisted on helping. He'd fought them, but the people of Twilight Dunes had won, and he was better for it.

It was time to put aside his ego, his propensity for trying to protect everyone all the time and ask for help.

13

The council of Oscar wasn't a lavish affair, but it was well attended, and all the participants managed to keep straight faces as he recounted his story for the third time in recent memory.

Roscoe, Earl, Toby, his wife Paula, and Deputy Sheriff Kendra Iquiro sat around a table at the back of Toby's joint. The speakeasy was closed for the night, though the crew was paying for their beer. The eyes of Oscar's neighbors and friends never left him as he spoke, their faces stoic blank canvases as they sipped their beers.

Kendra had been lured with the promise of a drink, which Oscar delivered, but when she discovered the purpose of the meeting Oscar was surprised to see she was happy to be included. Oscar decided not to invite anyone from the dump because he never defecated where he slept, and Shelly had been benched along with Mr. E and Ms. Perriweather, all of which Oscar could bring into the fold at a later date if necessary.

When Oscar finished telling his tale, Toby said, "You weren't kidding. That's a rough tuna sandwich to swallow."

"Granted, tuna salad is smelly and nasty, but this sandwich is fresh," Earl said. "I was with Oscar for a good chunk of it. I saw what happened out at the dump, even though I didn't see the burrow."

"And we've all seen and heard tell of the strange happenings around the Dunes," said Roscoe.

"I guess it's time to be blunt," Oscar said. "Does anyone here doubt my story? Or, maybe you believe my imagination and eyes played me for the fool? Because I would understand, but it would probably be best if you left now if you feel that way."

Nobody spoke or stood, and as Oscar met the eyes of each of his companions none of them looked away.

"What's your working theory? Where did these things come from?" Toby asked. "Genetic mutations from experiments at the base? Mutations from bombs detonating out on the range? Poison from a bioweapon? Did I miss anything?"

"All viable options," Earl said. "But what about the eggs?"

Oscar hiked his shoulders. "It seems clear that some of the local Gila monster population has mutated. How, why, and whether it was intentional are all open questions. We know Gila monsters lay eggs, so that's nothing new…"

"You're saying the greenies might want the eggs?" Paula said.

Earl said, "It's possible, whether they helped make them or not."

"Gila monsters move around, and have several burrows," Roscoe said. "They may only stay in one for a few days at a time, remember? They're kind of like nomads, and they'll come back to places they've previously stayed."

"You're thinking we could make a trap?" Earl said. "For proof?"

"Maybe," Roscoe countered.

"Truth is, we don't know shit," said Oscar. "And we need to change that."

Kendra hadn't spoken throughout the exchange, and when Oscar tried to catch the deputy's eye, she wouldn't look at him.

"You've been quiet, Kendra," Oscar said.

The deputy sheriff blew out a long stream of air and cleared her throat. The room was heavy with tension, a palpable fear that clawed at the edges of her words.

"I got the call around midnight eight days ago," Kendra began, her eyes darting around the table as she spoke. "Dispatch said there was some kind of collapse at the Thompsons'. I figured it was just a sinkhole or something. But it was no sinkhole."

Nobody made a sound as Kendra spoke, and Oscar felt a chill sweep through the air as she recalled the unsettling feeling that crawled through her as she'd surveyed the scene.

"Mr. Thompson was a wreck—he's barely normal when he's not stressed. I arrived to find him standing on his stoop, in his robe, sleep clawing at his face." She threw up her hands. "He's babbling about a strange barking sound, and then he says there was a crash like the entire Earth caving in on itself. I followed him around back, the guy blathering nonsense the entire time about a huge shadow, how his cat is missing."

Kendra's eyes glazed over as she took a sip of beer and examined the table. "The pool, or what was left of it, was a black hole, a void of cracked tiles, broken concrete, and torn plastic. Half the pool had crumbled as if the earth itself had turned against it."

"Not uncommon when the desert dries out and gaps form around the pool," Earl said.

"Yup. That's what I thought at first," Kendra said. "I approached the edge of the crater and shined my flashlight down. That's when I saw it— there was a tunnel opening that..." She paused, drained her mug, and poured another beer from the pitcher at the center of the table.

"What?" Toby pushed.

"I felt like Oscar. That feeling he described. The tunnel had a... a haunted vibe, you know? Like it was whispering secrets from the past.

Like there was something there. Something old and dangerous that wanted…" She drank her beer.

"That wanted you dead," Oscar said.

She nodded. "The tunnel twisted and turned, a labyrinth of passageways, many of which crisscrossed over one another." She paused. "And then, I stumbled upon it—a massive, oversized burrow. There were thick scratches on the walls, and I knew something had clawed its way through the earth.

"The smell hit me like a brick—a stench of decay and the coppery scent of blood. There were dried splatters on the walls and floor, and clumps of rancid dried flesh littered the ground."

Paula cleared her throat, and a coyote tried to join the conversation.

"A network of veins spidered out from the burrow, but these side tunnels were different. There were no claw marks, and the walls were smooth as if they'd been made by a drill bit or a huge termite. At the heart of the space, there was a massive, abandoned nest. Like the one you described, Oscar, except there were piles of bones. The place looked like something out of prehistoric times, a breeding ground for nightmares." She shook her head and sipped her beer. "There was dust on the ground, no fresh tracks, and it was clear whatever had called the place home hadn't been home in a while, but its presence lingered. I felt it.

"The air down there was stifling, and as my flashlight played over the walls, I saw things I'll never be able to forget. Above the den, there was a grotesque sculpture of bones, hanging corpses, and discarded trash. Empty bags of lifeless beasts hung from the ceiling, their blood still oozing out and puddling on the ground."

Kendra's voice wavered, the weight of the horrific memory pressing on her. "The burrow was a feeding ground, a buffet for the creatures. Discarded trash littered the ground—personal belongings, torn clothing, and remnants of the creatures' thievery."

The coyote stopped bitching and Toby went to refill the pitchers. When he returned, he filled everyone's mugs as he said, "Kendra, your story certainly jives with what Oscar and Earl told us."

"What did you do, Kendra?" Roscoe asked.

"I cordoned off the area with hazard tape and told the family not to go near the cave-in, then I wrote my report," Kendra said. "I went back the next day and the ground had been turned under, the remnants of the pool taken away, and the tunnel entrance was gone." She paused and stared wistfully at her beer. "Mr. Thompson said the Army showed up. Offered to help."

"And don't tell me," Earl said. "Your report went missing, and the desk sergeant told you to forget about it?"

Kendra's eyes darted from her mug to Oscar and back to her beer, but she said nothing.

"The real question is," said Roscoe, "what do we do now?"

"Like Oscar said, the greenies are hiding something," Earl said.

"No doubts now," said Roscoe. "And whether they made the little Godzillas on purpose, or by accident, you know when it comes to the way they think that really doesn't matter. Does it?"

Roscoe and Earl had both served, and so had Toby and his wife, so they were all well-versed in the shady activities of the U.S. military, and they understood what the greenies were capable of.

Paula said, "So now we know how screwed we are."

"What's the plan, boss?" Roscoe said.

Oscar rubbed his chin as he considered, then realizing he was doing it, he let his hand fall to his side. "We need more information. I think it's time to go to Colonel Jeffries," he said.

Roscoe chuckled. "Have you lost your mind? What makes you think he'd even meet with us, let alone tell us anything useful?"

"Who is Colonel Jeffries?" Earl asked. "I don't recognize the name?"

"That's the way he likes it," Oscar said. "His nickname on base is Ghost."

"Seems like Roscoe is right," Paula said. "Guys like that don't even do pillow talk."

"And you're not… the greenies' favorite person," Earl said.

"He'll talk to Roscoe and me. I guarantee it," Oscar said. "We'll head out to the base tomorrow."

Roscoe harrumphed and crossed her arms over her chest, but didn't challenge Oscar.

"Next up is we need to recon the landfill," Oscar said. "Find out what the military guys are doing and if they've sealed up the tunnels I found or changed anything else that might be relevant to us."

Nobody volunteered as the wind gusted and sand scraped over sand.

"Earl, I can give you my keys," Oscar pressed. "You know the place, can handle yourself, and you've done it before. Are you up for a second trip?"

Earl said nothing as he studied the white layer of dead foam atop his beer.

"Look," Oscar said. "More people are going to get killed if we don't do something to convince the bigwigs. It's time to take some risks."

"Come on, Oscar," said Earl. He motioned toward Kendra. "Even the cops are backing off."

"That's why we need proof for the nightly news, the newspapers, and websites. That will force the powers that be to act."

Earl nodded. "But I'm not getting arrested by the military police. First sign of trouble I'm out, and if the Army is crawling around the perimeter, I'm walking away."

"Fair enough," Oscar said.

"I've got a buddy who has night vision binoculars," Earl said. "I'll borrow them so at minimum I'll be able to do some long-range recon. My nephew has a toy drone with a camera, but the Army guys would just shoot it down."

"What can we do?" asked Toby.

Oscar leaned back in his chair and took his time sipping his beer. He didn't want to appear to be in charge or to have all the answers, but given the situation and the fact that he'd been the driving force behind the meeting, he could understand why folks were looking to him for answers.

The wind whispered and complained, the group drank beer, and the low murmur of a T.V. carried over the Dunes.

"We need to fortify Twilight Dunes," said Oscar as he planted his elbows on the table.

"Care to be more specific?" Paula asked.

"Toby, we'll give you a list and money and you can run to the depot to stock up on ammunition," Oscar said. "Better to be prepared, than not, and you can never have too many bullets."

"Amen to that," Toby said. "Consider it done."

"Paula, I need you to go through the park. Casually talk with everybody without getting them nervous or scared. Tell them to stay alert, lock their doors and fence gates, shed doors, etc... Don't go out after dark at night alone. Stuff like that," Oscar said.

"And how am I to do this without telling them mutant lizards are running around eating stuff?" Paula asked.

Oscar rolled his shoulders and cracked his neck as he fought to keep his jumping nerves in check. "Just tell them there's a big rabid cat or something on the loose and it's taken pets and chickens. Make sure you use those examples. Everyone in the Dunes has heard the stories by now."

Nods and grunts of approval.

"Find Tommy, also," said Oscar. "Tell him I sent you. See what the clueless youth of America knows. Any questions?"

"Let's make sure we all have each other's cell numbers," Roscoe said.

"I have a question," Earl asked, and all eyes swung to him. "Any update on Wasten?"

Everyone's gaze shifted to Kendra and Oscar's stomach stopped churning.

The deputy sheriff said, "There'll be a memorial—without a body according to his wife."

"The greenies haven't released the corpse?" Oscar said.

Kendra shook her head no.

"I guess that's it then," Oscar said.

Deputy Sheriff Kendra cleared her throat.

"Yes?" Oscar asked.

"I, well," she stumbled. "Might be an odd question coming from me, but... Everyone else got a task, what about me?"

"I just assumed you'd want to distance yourself until we had something rock solid you can lay your badge on," Oscar said.

"Ass out of you and me," the cop said.

"I considered bringing you as muscle out to the base, but that would stir too much shit and get you in trouble. No. We need you to be working in the background. Our secret weapon if you will. Find out if there have been other calls of pets missing, damaged property, or anything that might be attributable to the creatures. Maybe we can use the information to find more burrows."

"So do my job," Kendra said.

Oscar nodded.

With that, the group finished their beers, chatted about nothing, and tried not to bring up the topic of mutants. Oscar knew they'd accomplished very little on this night except putting their minds at ease a little, but at least they were doing something. Whether that something was enough, only time would tell.

14

"When was the last time you spoke with the colonel?" asked Roscoe.

The early morning desert was dyed a dusky blue, the road's cracked pavement an out-of-tune band as the car bounced and bumped across the emptiness toward the Cactus Ridge Proving Ground. Nothing moved on the open plane, except shadows running for cover from the sun as it inched over the western horizon, the outline of the Big Horn Mountains towering over the desert.

"The day I got bounced," Oscar said.

Roscoe's eyes strayed from the road to him, and she stared for several uncomfortable seconds before returning her attention to the road. There wasn't another car in sight and Roscoe could probably drive with her eyes closed for miles, but Oscar didn't want to test the theory. She said, "What makes you think he'll talk to us? I knew you had something up your sleeve when you were so adamant last night, but for the life of me, I can't think of what."

"If you recall, I worked night security for a time," he said. "It was a kind of punishment for what my superior called 'a bad attitude'. That's what I was doing at the end when..." He trailed off. No reason to relive a very bad memory.

She nodded, her hands tightening on the wheel, her knuckles going red then fading white. The mere mention of the incident that completed Oscar's fall from grace created a toxic tension that stalled the conversation for a time.

Roscoe waited him out, and after several minutes, Oscar said, "Let's just say I have something on him. Something that would, let's say, put him on less than favorable terms with Mrs. Colonel and the Army. I'm figuring they wouldn't like knowing what was happening atop a million-dollar missile."

Her face scrunched in revulsion, but Roscoe didn't take her eyes off the road.

"I'd rather not say exactly," Oscar said. "That way you don't know. Plausible deniability and all that rot."

"In case they torture me," she said, sarcasm dripping from her tone.

"Yeah, in case they torture you."

The night he'd punched an officer still sat in Oscar's stomach like a bad taco. Yet even after rehashing the incident a million times in an attempt to change the memory of what he'd done and its outcome, he still couldn't convince himself he'd do anything differently. Thus was the price of the righteous.

"He handcuffed you, right?"

The memory of it still burned Oscar's stomach. It had been one of the most embarrassing moments of his life. "Yeah," he pushed out.

"It's been a few years, Oscar," she said. "I'm sure most of the people who were at the base at the time have moved on."

"If they're lucky."

The Cactus Ridge Proving Ground guard booth materialized out of the gloom. A series of fading floodlights on tall metal poles surrounded the gates and booth. A basic fence ran north and south into the desert, but both runs ended after five hundred yards. The fence was for show and anyone stupid enough to venture out on the proving ground without permission very well could get a missile up their ass.

What wasn't for show were the eight soldiers in full body armor loitering around the gates holding guns that looked straight out of a science fiction movie.

"This looks like it's going to be easy," said Roscoe.

Amazingly, it was.

Roscoe brought the car to a stop before the gates.

Oscar explained why he was there to the lead grunt, who made a phone call, and Oscar and Roscoe picked up a passenger.

The young female soldier sat in the backseat, staring forward through the windshield, her weapon at rest across her chest.

"How did you know the colonel would be awake?" Roscoe asked. "It's barely eight o'clock."

"He's always up early," Oscar said. "He's probably just getting off the bike to nowhere as we speak," Oscar said.

The soldier in the backseat cleared her throat.

"That not true, Private?" Oscar said.

The grunt didn't answer. If the Army was good at anything, it was following orders.

Their military babysitter directed them to a parking space on the side of a building that had no name and no number. The guard escorted the partners through several layers of security and deposited them in a small conference room that felt dangerously close to a cell to Oscar.

The greenie turned to leave, and Oscar said, "What? No offer of coffee? Water?"

A low chuckle echoed through the room as the soldier left, the door lock clicking behind her.

"Do you really think antagonizing them is the right way to go?" Roscoe said when the private was gone.

Oscar hiked his shoulders and said nothing.

The duo waited eighteen minutes before Colonel Jeffries swept into the room, closed the door with a little extra force, and planted himself in a seat.

The colonel had aged since Oscar had last seen him. Thick black eyebrows had gone gray, and he no longer wore the thin beard that broke every rule in the Army's book. His hair was shorter and slicked back, and he wore glasses with round lenses that made him look ten years older than he was. But he was still jacked. His arms pressed against his uniform shirt, and he wore his sidearm, an old .45, and he'd taken the time to pin his multi-colored fruit salad of honors to his pocket.

Colonel Jeffries stared at them for a long minute, his eyes lingering on Roscoe for several seconds before he said, "I don't recall your name."

"Sergeant Roscoe Bently, retired, sir." She started to stand as she lifted her hand to cut a salute, but the colonel pressed her back down with a wave.

Silence filled the room. Oscar could wait anyone out. Except maybe his dead wife Monica, who had been conspicuously silent since last night.

"I'll go straight at it, Oscar," Colonel Jefferies said. "Why the hell are you here?"

"Well, what kind of mood are you in?"

The colonel's face was a stone mask of disappointment and barely concealed anger.

"So, pissy as usual," Oscar said. "Got it."

Roscoe squeaked like she'd been poked.

The colonel said nothing as he stared holes into Oscar.

In a calm voice, as he had the night the colonel had handcuffed him and planted him in a cell, he explained what happened, every mind-blowing detail. He started at the dump, moved to the missing chickens, the burrow, and everything except the group's suspicions about the Army's involvement.

With Oscar's voice still hanging in the air, the story Kendra told at the meeting right there at the front of the line, the colonel said, "This better be a joke, Oscar. I really don't have the time."

Oscar was taken aback. The response seemed genuine. He knew the Ghost and the man couldn't play cards. He might be a sneaky manipulative bastard, but his emotions played on his face like it was a movie screen. The colonel was either telling the truth, or he had been prepared to answer this question. Very prepared.

"Yeah," Oscar said, the specter of his never-ending supply of anger raising its eager head above the calm. "I'm that stupid. I came out here to muddle your morning, because, you know, that would get me... what?"

Colonel Jefferies shifted his gaze to Roscoe, who wilted a little under the nuclear stare. Very little rattled Roscoe. "You saw all this as well?" the colonel asked.

Roscoe's eyes strayed to Oscar, then she began studying a smudge of dirt on the linoleum floor.

"What I thought," Colonel Jefferies said.

Roscoe found her voice. "It's not like that. We don't have pictures or a corpse, but a man has been killed. I know you're aware of that."

The colonel licked his lips, but didn't respond.

"Greenies are scouring the landfill," Oscar added. "Don't pretend not to be aware of wha—"

Colonel Jefferies slammed his fists on the table, and the air in the room vibrated and rose twenty degrees. "Who the hell do you think you're talking to, Private? Don't think because you no longer wear the uniform that you're beyond my reach."

Oscar stood and planted his hands on the table. "Don't threaten me. I'm trying to help and you're acting like an ass."

The colonel surged to his feet, but Roscoe was faster.

"Easy, easy," she said as she leaned over the table and wedged herself between the two giants. "You're both alphas. Yay for you both. Now sit down."

Both men complied like they'd been reprimanded by their grandmothers.

Silence filled the conference room, the sounds of air pushing through a vent and the hum of the building's lifeblood the only sounds.

After several tense minutes, Roscoe said, "I know you have no reason to trust us..." She looked at Oscar. "Maybe less than a reason, but we're trying to help. Something bad... multiple something bads are stalking the desert. If something's not done, it will draw attention."

Oscar saw the road Roscoe was on and he followed her. "Body counts always bring attention. Do you want the base on the nightly news?"

The colonel bit his lip and said, "I'm sorry, but I have no idea what you're talking about. I suggest your cop friend go to her superiors."

"I told you she already tried, but they did nothing," Oscar said.

Colonel Jefferies was an unmoving glacier.

"Fine," Oscar said. "I didn't want to have to do this, but..." He reached into a pocket and pulled a memory stick free. It was black with a red stripe. There was nothing on it, but the colonel didn't need to know that. Oscar placed the device on the table but said nothing.

The colonel stared at the memory stick, his face going red, crimson veins spidering his eyes.

"All I'm asking for is a little help," Oscar said.

If the colonel's eyes were guns, Oscar would've been a bullet-ridden corpse.

"I know you can't get directly involved," Roscoe said. "We'll do the work, just give us a lead. Tell us we're on the same side."

"Tell us you're not ignoring this and hoping it goes away," Oscar added.

"Do what you feel you must with that," he said as he pointed at the memory stick. "Just don't forget I was the only one who helped you, if you recall."

"I do recall. I also recall you hated every minute of it, but still, you did the right thing. That's why I believe you'll do the right thing now," Oscar pushed.

The colonel's face twisted, his inner battle featured on his face. He said, "I'm sorry." That also appeared genuine. "But I don't have a clue what you're talking about. Now I've got to start my day." Colonel Jefferies pushed to his feet, nodded at Roscoe, and left without another word.

"He's lying," Roscoe said. "He always bites his lip when he's not telling the whole truth."

Oscar nodded as he drove. They'd dropped their babysitter back at her post and the partners were cruising toward Aunt Sue's MS to pick up Tank.

"She's right," came the voice of Monica, his dead wife.

"I know," Oscar said.

"We didn't accomplish anything just now except bring on heat," Roscoe said.

Oscar saw his red anger-stained face in the rearview mirror as he glanced back the way they'd come. No tail yet, at least on the ground. He leaned forward and peered up through the windshield like that character in Goodfellas when he was looking for the helicopters following him down his suburban street. There was nothing in the sky that he could see, but he knew there could be drones, and there were plenty of long-range viewing options. Hell, he knew the greenies could take a picture of the mole on his ass from space.

"We're on our own," Oscar said.

"What else is new?" Roscoe answered.

Not much, and that ate at Oscar like a canker. All the local authorities appeared content to dismiss Oscar's claims, and this left him not only angry but even more determined to protect the landfill and Twilight Dunes. They were all he had.

"That's not true," came Monica's voice.

Wasn't it? He glanced over at Roscoe, who was staring out at the desert.

"Just make sure you don't get yourself arrested, or worse," added his dead wife.

Images of Monica during her healthy years rampaged through his head, the bump and rattle of Roscoe's car and the push of the wind fighting to get into the vehicle the only sounds. The road ran on, and in its faded and cracked matrix, Oscar saw a memory.

15

A determined breeze clawed at the edges of the winding blacktop road, the wind's mournful grumble poisoning Oscar's attempt to ignore the weight that had settled in his chest. The Pacific Ocean shimmered in the fading light, the sun sitting on the bruised horizon.

Oscar pulled into the Lobster Boat's parking lot, the thunderous waves exploding against the rugged cliffside pushing clouds of cool fog over the restaurant's weather-beaten exterior. Monica had requested the restaurant's best table, and as the couple was seated mist clung to the salt-crusted windows, blurring the line between inside and outside, between what Oscar knew to be true and the unknown.

Muted candlelight flickered in the heavy, salt-tinged air, and the scent of fish and charred beef filled the dining room. Monica ordered a vodka and soda and Oscar a Manhattan, straight-up with cherries.

"I thought we could use a night out," Monica said, her voice barely audible over the haunting melody of the wind forcing itself on the windows. "You know, just to forget about everything for a while."

That was the purpose of their trip to the west coast, Oscar's five day leave the longest he'd had in months. Their drinks arrived, but Oscar only swirled the brown liquid in his glass, unable to savor its sting.

Monica's eyes were clouded with approaching tears Oscar couldn't fathom as she sipped her drink.

He smiled and Monica looked away. Oscar sensed his wife's unspoken worry, a silent storm waiting to unleash its fury. Monica was burdened with a truth she couldn't bring herself to share, so she'd sought solace in the normalcy of a dinner date.

Oscar sipped his drink, the burn and rush of heat doing little to soothe his rising anxiety. He stole glances at Monica, searching for clues, any hints of what she was hiding.

Monica's gaze remained fixed on the menu.

The waitress arrived, interrupting the suffocating silence with a forced smile. Oscar looked at the menu, pretending to contemplate the choices. The words blurred, meaningless symbols in the face of impending doom. He ordered mechanically, a steak with a salad, and Monica asked for pasta with grilled chicken.

As the waitress retreated, Monica's fingers traced circles on the tablecloth. "Oscar," she began, her voice trembling, "There's something I need to tell you."

Oscar reached across the table, covering Monica's hand with his own. "Whatever it is, we'll face it together." Heat surged through him, worry eating his stomach. That was what you said, right?

"I went to the doctor last week," Monica confessed, her gaze finally meeting his. "I've been feeling... off, you know? And they found something. Something they're not sure how to fix."

The room tilted, and the muffled sound of the crashing of waves echoed in Oscar's ears as terror seized him. She'd had a miscarriage several months back and it had almost torn them apart, and now…

A mixture of sorrow and fear played across Monica's face as she fought to contain her emotions.

Sorrow, fear, and anger washed through him, threatening to engulf Oscar in a wave of despair. He needed to be strong. Oscar squeezed Monica's hand, the silent gesture an anchor in the tempest of emotions. Dread tightened its grip and Oscar's heart raced. He nodded, urging her to continue, though he feared the revelation to come, and he couldn't imagine what could be worse than losing your unborn child.

A tear escaped the corner of Monica's eye, tracing a path through her makeup and down her cheek. "Oscar, I have cancer."

The news hung between them like a specter. Loss, the silent assassin, had crept between them.

Time froze as Oscar absorbed the weight of those words. The sea roared in the distance, mirroring the conflict within him. The cliffside restaurant, once a picturesque retreat, now felt like the edge of a precipice, the abyss below waiting to claim everything he held dear.

As the couple waited for their food, the restaurant seemed to close in around Oscar, and the air thickened with unspoken pain, the weight of Monica's revelation.

The server returned and placed their meals on the table, asked a few questions, but neither of them answered. Reading the situation, the waitress retreated, and the steak, and pasta with chicken sat untouched.

Monica drew a shuddering breath, and her eyes locked onto Oscar's. "I didn't want to tell you like this, in a public place, but I couldn't keep it from you any longer," she confessed, her voice barely rising above a whisper.

Oscar gripped her hand like she was sliding away from him, and suddenly she was. He tightened his grip as if trying to anchor her in this new nightmare reality. Oscar's mouth fell open as he searched for words that could change fate and rollback time, if only a few minutes, but he found none.

"I have cancer, Oscar," Monica repeated, the words resonating with a finality that made Oscar's bones hurt. She swallowed hard, driving back the tears that threatened to overflow.

"How bad is it?" Oscar managed to say.

Monica hesitated, the weight of her truth crushing her. "Stage four," she finally pushed out, her voice cracking.

The revelation took Oscar's breath away and his heart pounded so hard it drove out the buzz of the static filling his head. Stage four—a dark pronouncement that whispered of inevitability. Oscar's eyes darted around the restaurant, fixating on trivial details—the worn edges of the menu, the condensation on his glass—as if searching for an escape from the suffocating certainty.

He said, "Monica, I can't accept this. There has to be something more we can do." His voice cracked under the strain of the emotions that threatened to consume him as he fought back tears, his throat tight with a mixture of grief and helplessness. "We'll fight this. Find the best doctors, and explore every option. We're not giving up."

His wife managed a weak smile, a fragile attempt to convey gratitude amidst her despair. "I know you'll do everything you can, Oscar. But we have to face reality." Monica's eyes flooded with a mixture of sadness and understanding as she reached across the table to cup Oscar's face in her hands. "I need you to be strong for both of us. We can't change what's happening, but we can choose how we face it."

A surge of frustration and helplessness boiled over in Oscar, his anger taking control as he realized he was powerless against the unseen adversary that clawed at the edges of his sanity. He pulled away from Monica, and surged to his feet, sending the chair scraping across the floor.

Silverware stopped tinkling on plates and the murmur of conversation died as the surrounding diners stole furtive glances at the unfolding drama.

"I won't just sit here and watch you fade away! There has to be a way, a treatment, something you haven't considered," Oscar's voice echoed through the restaurant.

Monica's eyes held a silent plea for understanding. "Oscar, I've spoken to the doctors. They've given me the options, and none of them guarantee a cure. I can't bear to see you suffer like this, too."

His frustration escalated into a maelstrom of anger. "We had plans, a life together. We were going to try and have another... a baby. You can't—" He kicked the chair, sending it clattering across the floor, drawing more attention from the onlookers.

The server, hesitant, hovered nearby, unsure whether to intervene.

Monica rose.

Shame, horror, and anger fought for control of the reigns that ruled Oscar's emotions. He saw Monica as a frail and broken woman, what she'd look like at the end. He wanted to kill himself. Right there and then.

"Oscar, please. We can't change what's happening. We can only choose how we face it."

Tears welled in his eyes. "I can't lose you, Monica. I can't." But he knew he already had, and pain knifed through his chest at the thought of it.

The truth hung in the air, a bitter pill neither of them wanted to swallow. Oscar's gaze shifted from Monica to the expanse beyond the restaurant's windows, the darkened sea crashing against the cliffs below.

His hands trembled. The anger, a visceral force, surged within him—an indignant protest against a fate that seemed unjust.

The tears came hard then, Monica's eyes spilling the vulnerability of her situation which had been laid bare to the person she loved most. She reached out for him, but Oscar recoiled.

"This is bullshit," he muttered through gritted teeth, his fists clenched.

Monica's face softened, and she smiled as she leaned in and kissed him on the lips. "I love you."

The anger within Oscar transformed into a mix of grief and acceptance. He sank back into his chair, defeated and depleted.

Monica sat and reached for his hand, a silent reassurance that, together, they could weather the storm.

As the waves continued their relentless assault on the cliffs, the partners sat in quiet reflection, the restaurant a silent witness to their emotional upheaval.

The evening wore on, and their untouched meals grew cold, forgotten relics of a life that had abruptly shifted course. The restaurant, once bustling with the clinking of glasses and laughter, now cocooned them in an eerie silence.

"I need you to promise me something," Monica said.

Oscar's eyes stung as he met his wife's gaze. "Anything, Monica. I'll do anything."

"Promise me that, whatever happens, you'll remember the love we shared, the moments that made us smile. Promise me you won't let this illness define our time together."

Oscar nodded, the lava rock in his throat making it difficult to speak.

In that dimly lit restaurant perched on the edge of the world, a pact was sealed, a silent vow to stand together through the impending storm.

Waves crashed against the cliffs in a relentless rhythm, a stark reminder of the passage of time, how that morning he'd had an endless supply, and how now he had none.

"Hey! You in there?" Roscoe asked. "You're not listening to a word I'm saying, are you?"

"Do you ever think about…" Oscar's heart was heavy, but with his trauma had come some wisdom. Heaping his insecurities, fears, and doubts onto other people—especially those he loved—was the height of cowardness. He stayed silent, marinating in the memory of the worst night of his life.

"What is it? You can tell me. Wasten?" she asked. "It's not your fault."

"I don't know, but that's not it," he said, and as soon as the words escaped his lips he wished he could have them back.

"Spill it!" she snapped.

"Do you ever…" He sucked on his lips. "Do you ever think about what your life would be like if Rick didn't come home?"

Silence filled the car, the thump of his heart galloping in rhythm with the pounding in his head.

"I'm sorry, I shouldn't have," he said. True to what he'd learned, unloading his fear had only made him feel worse, and now he'd dragged down his best friend.

Oscar saw Roscoe's face twist in the windshield's reflection. "I'd be lying if I said I never did. Everyone worries about losing the ones they love, maybe more these days than ever."

He said nothing.

"But you have to try and not dwell on it, Oscar," she said.

Oscar felt a hand on his shoulder. As always, the woman had figured out his puzzle with only a few pieces.

"I know you miss her, but that wasn't your fault, either," she said. "You got dealt a shitty hand, but from what I've heard of Monica, she wouldn't want you sitting around pining for her. She told you as much, didn't she?"

The sound of crashing waves soothed the nerves fighting to break through his skin.

"I want you to live," whispered Monica from beyond the grave.

Oscar smiled and said, "Take me home."

16

Oscar and Roscoe sat in a rear pew, hidden in shadow, the desert winds playing the old church like a broken bassoon. Stained glass windows cast fractured rainbows on the assembled crowd, creating an eerie mosaic that danced with the flickering candlelight. The air was thick with grief and the scent of desperation. Even the kids sensed it. This was a ceremony about an end, despite the priest's best efforts to put lipstick on the pig in the form of Heaven and meeting up with everyone again in the clouds.

A black wooden urn sat on an ornate table before the priest. Within were the remains of Wasten—ashes that whispered of a life cut short. Like Monica's.

The priest's soliloquy echoed through the chamber, each word a mournful cadence that reminded Oscar that one day it would be his turn. A stoic figure with sunken eyes and a demeanor as cold as the granite headstones that dotted the dusty churchyard, the priest appeared disinterested and bored. This irked Oscar, though he didn't know why. He didn't believe in God, not really, and if the Almighty did exist, he or she certainly didn't give two shits about Oscar. The proof was in the pudding.

"In the ashes, we find truth, the remnants of a life consumed by the fires of fate. May Wasten's soul find peace in the embrace of eternity," the priest intoned.

As the echo of the minister's words faded into oppressive silence, a cavalcade of questions clouded Oscar's head, the foremost being how was he going to stop the creatures?

Family members wept, their grief laid bare as the mourners bowed their heads. The landfill crew exchanged glances laden with unspoken dread. Oscar was caught in the undertow of his own sorrow, his heart heavy with the weight of unanswered questions.

The priest motioned toward the wooden box, and the mourners gathered around it. Each took turns placing a wilted rose atop the urn. Wasten's widow, with guidance and support from the Army, had stipulated that Wasten's ashes were to be spread to the desert winds.

Oscar placed his rose, recalling the scene in The Big Lebowski where Walter accidentally spreads Donny's ashes upwind of the Dude. He hoped the colonel caught a mouthful of Wasten when his buddy took flight. There was no military presence at the church, not surprising,

Wasten wasn't a military man, but Oscar figured the Army was watching.

As the mourners filed out of the church, the echoes of their sorrow trailed behind them like lingering ghosts.

Oscar and Roscoe hung back, the mysteries lurking in the shadows whispering, the voices reminding Oscar that if he didn't watch his back, he'd end up mixed in the desert sands with Wasten. The priest offered a sympathetic nod before gliding away to tend to the aftermath of the ceremony.

The heavy wooden door groaned as Oscar pushed out into the late afternoon sun.

Roscoe said, "Will you look at this."

Trash-master was holding court before the landfill crew. "I found him, you know," the boss said. "He was a real mess, I tell ya."

Trash-master's nonchalant tone made Oscar grind his teeth.

"Army called me. Me!" Trash-master intoned. "They said they were gonna bring his ashes to his wife. Least they could do for the poor bastard. I had to go up to the base and meet with the general and a bunch of folks. They were real nice. Thanked me a million times. Told me if I ever needed anything I should call."

"That what Colonel Jefferies said?" Roscoe said.

Trash-master only stared at her.

"No," Oscar said. "It was probably Ms. PR, Carol Devito."

"What the hell do you know of it?" the boss spat.

Anger assaulted Oscar, the incongruities in the boss's account setting his body aflame. "I never heard Wasten say he wanted to be cremated," Oscar said. He and Wasten had never discussed issues of the heart, but there it was.

Trash-master harrumphed and continued, his narrative a tapestry woven with half-truths, veiled secrets, and attempts at building up his own role. "Army said they owed Wasten a debt for some service he did back in the day. Something hush-hush. Can't say much about it, you know how it goes. Need to know."

Oscar's stomach stirred and his neck ached. "Do you believe everything the *Army* tells you?" he asked. The military's involvement in Wasten's affairs was worrisome and only added credence to the theory that the Army was behind the entire mess. Suddenly the Fill, normally a desolate expanse where secrets went to die, was the epicenter of a conspiracy. He tried to connect all the dots, but the pieces of the puzzle were scattered.

"Why don't you worry about things at your—level, Oscar," Trash-master said, his tone cold. "Like how much trash you can rake tomorrow."

Oscar licked his lips and said nothing.

As the crowd dispersed and headed for their vehicles, Oscar balled his fists and said, "We can't let them get away with this."

Roscoe placed a calming hand on his arm, her touch a grounding force. "I get it, Oscar. I want answers too, but fighting with the boss won't help."

Oscar's jaw tightened, torn between the urge to unleash his anger and the rationality that seemed a distant second. "He knows something, Roscoe. We can't just stand by and do nothing," he said, his anger fueled by grief and indignation and a dash of self-righteousness.

Roscoe sighed, her gaze rock steady. "We are doing something... things, but if we act recklessly, we risk making enemies we can't handle. We need allies, and information, not a fight... Though I agree that would feel great. I'd like nothing more than to punch that smug... But we need to dig deeper and find out what the Army's involvement is really about, and more importantly, what they intend to do. Then we can expose the truth like we've been planning and go back to our boring lives."

The comment was innocuous enough, but it had cut a bit too close to the bone.

A coyote's howl rose above the rumble of engines and the snap and pop of rubber rolling over sand and pebbles as the parking lot cleared out. Clouds of dust rolled over the lot, the sun touching the horizon, the sky on fire.

"I need a drink," Roscoe said.

Oscar smiled at her. No words were necessary.

The next two days rolled by without incident and Oscar lived in a world of denial where the mutated lizards didn't exist and the memory of Wasten began its inevitable fade to obscurity.

Shelly rarely made house calls, and Tank was well enough to travel, but the doctor offered to come to Tank. Treating animals at her clinic was an unnecessary risk, and despite the fact that the canine was cleaner than some of her human patients, she could be fined, and her license suspended.

Tank was moved to a lounge chair on Oscar's tiny screen porch, and he, Earl, and Roscoe drank beer as they watched the doctor work. She listened to Tank's heart, took his temperature, removed his bandages, and cleaned his wounds, all of which were healing well. She pulled off her gloves with a snap and proclaimed, "He's doing great. A few more days and I'll take the bandages off so the wounds can get some air, and soon he'll be good to go."

"Did you hear back on the venom samples you took?" Oscar asked.

Shelly shook her head no. "The state lab is really slow."

"Even with a man dead?" Oscar blurted.

"The staties are unaware of a possible connection," Shelly said, sarcasm dripping in her tone. "Is there one?"

Silence fell over the assembled, the gentle breeze stirring the desert sands.

"I haven't earned any trust?" the doc said.

Oscar's stomach burned as he glanced around at his partners in crime. Shelly had no idea how Tank had been hurt and why his condition and location were a secret.

"I went out on a limb, here," Shelly said. When nobody spoke, she chuckled. "O.K., then."

"It's just…" Oscar couldn't find the words.

"If you tell me you'd have to kill me?" Shelly joked.

"Not that extreme, but you don't want in on this. Trust me," Oscar said.

"Fair enough," Shelly said as she stuffed the tools of her trade back into her medical bag.

"There is one thing you could do," Roscoe said.

Tank licked his lips and chirped.

Oscar tossed the dog a treat as he stared at Roscoe.

"Keep an eye out for any unusual wounds that come through your place. Stuff like Tank here," Roscoe said.

"Cat bites?" Shelly probed.

Seeing where Roscoe was headed, Oscar added, "Anything unusual that comes in. Let us know, will you?"

"What are you guys chasing?" the doctor asked.

Another surreal silence engulfed Twilight Dunes.

Shelly nodded, got to her feet, and said, "I'll be back to see Tank in a couple of days. Finish off the antibiotics and make sure he eats and goes to the bathroom."

Oscar and the assembled all nodded as if Shelly was their teacher and their graduation depended on following the doctor's orders exactly.

"Thank you for coming out here," Earl said. "It goes without saying we owe you."

"Big time," Roscoe said.

Shelly nodded solemnly and said, "Yup."

Oscar felt horrible about deceiving the doctor and once again he considered telling her everything. But what would that accomplish? He said, "We're just trying to protect you. Really."

"Do you know what would happen to the area if you weren't around to patch everyone up?" Roscoe added. "You're too important to this community to be messing around with our stupid shit."

"I doubt it's stupid, but clearly you're operating outside the law, and that would be a problem for me, but…" Shelly examined a bug crawling across the screen.

"If we need you, don't doubt for a second that we'll call you," Earl said.

"Sure," Shelly said as she left.

The group sat in silence, Tank resting his head on his folded front paws as his gaze shifted around the assembled.

It was Earl who broke the silence. "Speaking of the law, has anyone heard from Kendra?"

"I haven't," Oscar said.

Nobody else offered anything.

"I've got a report if you guys are up for it. Nothing new, really," Earl said.

"Go. It might spark an idea," Oscar said.

Earl took a long pull off his beer. "As we thought, the greenies have put extra patrols on the Fill at night when Oscar and crew are gone. There's been a guard stationed at their gate twenty-four hours a day since Wasten was killed and they're patrolling the perimeter at night, and not just the restricted area. The entire Fill."

"You haven't gotten inside?" Oscar said. He and his fellow workers hadn't been allowed beyond the fresh refuse dumping area in days, and Wasten's dozer sat where he'd left it, atop a fresh section of tilled earth.

"Haven't tried," Earl said. "Like I told you, I borrowed night vision goggles and that was enough."

The wind sang and sand sifted through the screens wrapping the porch, the faint tinkle reminding Oscar of rattling palm fronds.

Earl continued, "The Army plowed under the entrance to the burrow you found, Oscar. I mean they leveled it. You won't recognize the area when you see it."

"Not surprising," Roscoe said.

"It certainly proves the greenies know something," Earl said.

"Has that ever been in doubt? The colonel basically confirmed our suspicions by lying to us," Oscar said.

"The tunnel entrance where you came out, Oscar," Earl said.

Oscar sucked on his lips.

"There's a huge pile of stones there now. More than before and there's no sign of the entrance to the tunnel any longer from what I can tell."

"Does any of this matter?" Roscoe said. "We've rehashed this several times. Normal Gila monsters don't stay in a single burrow. They move around. So what have the greenies accomplished?"

"They took control of the dump, the creature's nesting area," Oscar said.

"What about trapping one?" Earl said.

"If they already have a specimen, they wouldn't care about trapping one," Oscar offered.

To that, nobody had anything to say.

"Paula and I made the rounds," Toby said. "We didn't have to sell very hard. Everyone senses something is up. Even the Pride is acting weird. And I stocked up on bullets like you asked. Do you want me to hand the ammo out or keep it in my gun safe?"

"Let's keep it together under lock and key," Oscar said. He stood up. "I'm bushed. Anything else we need to handle tonight?"

Nobody spoke, and that was the cue for everyone to move on. "I'll call Kendra, but I doubt she's got any news, or she would have called."

"No news is good news, right?" Earl said as he finished his beer, got to his feet, and tossed the empty in the trash.

"I suppose." Oscar hoisted Tank and the dog moaned weakly as Oscar moved him inside to the couch.

It had been a long day, and though he was weary to the bone, he dreaded falling asleep. Recently his dreams had been haunted by giant lizards and Wasten's walking corpse. But it wasn't his friend's bloody face staring at him through the darkness, or the haunted eyes and serpentine tongue of the mutants that caused his dreams to go sour, but the feeling that everything that had happened was merely a prelude to disaster, a wave of horrors that he wouldn't be able to stop.

Oscar gave Tank his meds, and sat beside his friend, staring out the camper's window at the silvery moonglow that engulfed Twilight Dunes, thinking about the times he and the dog had sat atop the trash pile howling at the moon.

Soon Tank's snores and wheezes filled the darkness.

When the grayness of dawn filled the camper, Oscar got ready for work.

17

The Fill was inundated with excess garbage.

Not many people were brave enough to call Scorched Mesa home, and even as important as the military base was, there weren't many greenies stationed there. Still, humans generate an immense amount of waste. Oscar knew from safety training that the average American generated almost five pounds of trash per day, and with the Fill closed for a few days and running on a skeleton crew the garbage had piled up.

Oscar's lunch wrestled with his stomach as he raked trash that had blown off the main pile, his gaze constantly shifting to Wasten's pickup truck, which sat next to the administration building awaiting a tow to the dead man's house.

There was no friendly chatter on this day. The dump was an alternate version of a hair salon. Mostly men, but a few women, usually stood along the fresh trash line talking and gossiping about recent events, all of which amounted to not very much recently except Wasten's body being found at the landfill. The patrons looked at Oscar and his coworkers askance, as if they'd lost a family member, and the way Oscar saw it, they had.

Wasten hadn't been a good friend, but he'd been a friend.

The afternoon rush dwindled, and Oscar was ordered to rake the edges of the fresh pile as Moxie and Curby worked the machines. Moxie drove Wasten's dozer, the old, rusted machine whining, its engine knocking as if it missed its longtime operator.

Oscar worked absently, killing time and making sure he looked busy because these days the Trash-master was always watching. As the giant machines rumbled he scanned the Wasteland, trying to see what was happening in the restricted area beyond, while trying not to look like he was staring at the Wasteland and examining the restricted area.

Only shadows moved in the Wasteland, and there were no Army personnel at the edges of the restricted area.

He came across a pile of finely shredded detritus that had been scratched out of the sedimentary garbage heap. There were claw marks, and it was clear something big with long talons had dug its way into the garbage pile.

The newly created tunnel was five feet in diameter, and shreds of garbage marred its walls. A torn open bag of household trash that stank of spoiled milk and rotting meat marked the tunnel's threshold, but beneath the stink there was a chemical smell that Oscar associated with the sterile confines of a hospital, which was odd given the mountains of rubbish that surrounded him.

Oscar looked over his shoulder. The dozers roared, trash clinked and clanged as it was rolled under, and the Trash-master talked to patrons, most likely letting them know how important he was not only to the Fill, but to them because of it. He could almost hear the man apologizing, saying that he was sorry about the closing, and how it would never happen again. Wasten had literally and figuratively gummed-up the Fill's works, and the Trash-master, despite whatever feelings he may have had for Wasten, wanted the operator's death in the rearview as fast as possible. Sad thing was, Oscar couldn't say he blamed the guy for wanting that. Though it burned his gut, on many levels, so did he.

He dropped to a knee and stared into the opening. The tunnel twisted and turned like it had been made by a worm on crack, the walls a rough display of postmodern trash art, its floor a muddy, wet, slimy mix of crimson water, thick white fluid, dirt, and what looked to be pieces of cracked eggshell. He didn't have his flashlight on his belt, and as he stuck his head into the tunnel, he knew there was no way he was going inside, not this time. With some of their burrows cut off or destroyed, the creatures had delved into the trash to make a new home, and there was—

Two eyes appeared in the depths of the tunnel, and the hiss and slap of a tongue lashing out and a tail knocking trash from the walls chanted from the tunnel.

Oscar stepped back, a plan forming. Maybe he could set a trap here.

The mountain of garbage with the newly created tunnel in its side shifted, and smaller pieces of trash fell and filtered through the larger items like a pinball bouncing off point obstacles.

Darkness filled the tunnel as the glowing orbs jerked into the trash heap. The creature was on the move.

While he didn't have his flashlight, Oscar was carrying. He pulled his Smith & Wesson .38 revolver from where it was concealed in the small of his back. Trash-master didn't approve of staff carrying guns at work because he was afraid an employee would shoot another employee, possibly even accidentally. But given recent events, Oscar didn't think the boss would mind, though he hadn't asked permission. He'd rather ask for forgiveness.

Seconds dripped away, a minute, as Oscar stared into the refuse pile, searching for a target, but there was none to be found. That was probably for the best. Shooting into a pile of garbage was asking to get caught with a ricochet.

The *boom* of something large and metal falling shook the air, and everything went still for a heartbeat before a primal scream, not of a mutant creature unknown to man, but of a woman, broke the stillness.

Oscar knew immediately who it was. Alice. And she was screaming for help.

He vaulted to his feet and sprinted through the mounds of garbage, shadows trailing after him, the steady hum of an elongated hiss carrying over the Fill. There was yelling and screaming, then a gunshot.

Clouds of dust obscured the scene as Oscar broke free of the trash valley and skidded to a stop. A wake-like trail of dust led past the fresh garbage toward where Alice stood out front of the admin building screaming.

A gust of wind gathered the clouds of grit, twisting them together as they lifted into the sky.

Oscar's mouth fell open a crack as he aimed his gun, but didn't fire because Alice was in the way.

A huge lizard trundled toward Trash-master's assistant, tongue lashing out, its dark leathery skin decorated with lines of green bioluminescence. Gigantic claws dug into the hardpan, the beast's massive tail swinging and knocking over anything it came in contact with. The lizard wasn't as big as the one he'd tangled with, but it didn't take an expert to see this creature was no Gila monster.

The creature's limbs bulged with muscles, the armored skin tight, and rows of sharp teeth filled crimson gums.

Alice screamed again as the beast charged her, and despite the monster's staggering zigzag path, the creature's movements were sharp and well-coordinated which allowed the lizard to move with miraculous speed.

Oscar knew regular Gila's spent most of their time underground in the dark, and sunlight wasn't their friend. Despite this, the mutant appeared to be having little trouble navigating around the vehicles and piles of recycled trash that stood between it and its prey.

Alice, for her part, had moved beyond panic and she opened the door of the admin building, threw herself inside, and slammed the door behind her.

Patrons were bolting like rats when the lights came on, and trucks peeled-out, everyone heading for the exit.

Oscar caught sight of one customer wandering toward the admin building, phone out before him as he photographed the beast.

The lizard was non-photogenic because the mutant changed course and casually scooped the man up in its jaws. The beast threw its head back as it ran, jaws flexing and chopping on the man, legs dangling before being severed and falling to the hardpan.

The mutant lizard didn't slow. The corpse fell from its mouth, an arm stuck between two of its teeth, its eyes ranging around, eyelids opening and closing as they tried to protect the creature from the blazing midday sun.

Trash-master, along with three eager patrons, stood their ground along the fresh refuse pile, guns aimed at the creature.

Oscar resolved to join them, but he'd only taken two steps before the Trash-master and his posse opened up. The pop and crack of gunshots echoed over the Fill, and bullets slapped the admin building as the creature used it for cover.

"No! Hold your fire!" Oscar screamed as he ran forward, fear for his own safety forgotten. The admin building was nothing more than a temporary modular structure that had become permanent by virtue of it having been in place for more than forty years. The walls were paper thin, and it wouldn't take a cannon for bullets to pierce the sides of the structure, and Alice was inside.

Trash-master either didn't hear Oscar, didn't understand why he was calling for a ceasefire, or didn't care. The line of men continued firing, white smoke mixing with the clouds of dust and grit. Bullets thumped into the admin building, glass shattered, and the lizard disappeared around the building, its tail taking a chunk of wood from the corner of the structure.

Splinters flew, cinderblocks cracked, and a piece of the building gave way and crashed to the ground exposing the interior of the Trash-master's office. The gunfire stopped, and Alice screamed as the corner of the building began a slow-motion collapse, the roof sagging as the walls gave way.

The mutant roared.

Trash-master yelled orders, but suddenly his little army of volunteers wasn't so eager. The cab of Moxie's dozer was empty, but Curby still sat in his machine, staring intently at the melee playing out before him.

Oscar's skin crawled with inaction. He had to help Alice. If he did nothing else on this day, he would do that. He double-timed it to Curby's dozer. "Move in closer," he yelled. "I'll use the plow for cover." He held up his gun as evidence of his plan.

Curby's dirt-stained face turned in his direction, but he made no move to put the dozer in gear. The squirrelly old fart wasn't a licensed operator, but desperate times required desperate measures. Curby stared at Oscar with his owl-eyes like he didn't understand English.

Alice screamed again and that broke Oscar's paralysis.

He gripped the handrail on the side of the bulldozer's cab and hoisted himself onto the machine's metal tread.

Curby's eyes strayed from Oscar to the admin building, which was obscured by dust and smoke, the lizard's massive python tail wriggling above the maelstrom like Cthulhu rising from the underworld.

Frustration consumed him, and Oscar tore open the dozer's cab door, gripped the front of Curby's shirt, and jerked the man from his seat.

Curby screeched but didn't resist as Oscar tossed him to the hardpan. The man hit the ground hard, but he bounced to his feet and set off at a full run toward a cluster of parked vehicles.

Oscar wasn't an operator, but he knew how to handle all the Fill's equipment, and the dozers were no exception. The plow was stuck in a pile of refuse, and as Oscar worked the controls the machine backed up and the plow rose.

When Oscar was protected by the plow, he eased the gearshift into forward. The bulldozer creaked and swayed as it lurched into motion, its engines growling, the metal treads rolling over their metal drive wheels squeaking and chirping as the machine picked-up speed.

Oscar looked over his shoulder and found Trash-master and his merry band trailing after the bulldozer, using it for cover. He spared a glance east toward the Wasteland and the Army's restricted area beyond and saw the cavalry wasn't on the way yet.

The mutant lizard reared up, and its narrow head appeared above the smoke churning above the admin building.

There was no way this was the same beast that had been in the newly formed tunnel.

That thought brought rage, and with a scream of fury, Oscar pressed the dozer's throttle control to full. With a hail of kicked-up dirt and pebbles, the machine picked up speed, its plow raised, its three-inch teeth ready to bite flesh. Oscar rotated the dozer when he reached the building, making a hard right and following the southern wall until he got to the ruins of the structure's southeast corner.

Oscar kicked open the cab door and jumped down onto the machine's drive tread, staying low and using the lifted plow for cover as he aimed his gun.

In its fury, the massive lizard pounded the building with its tail, and Oscar caught a brief glimpse of Alice hiding between two metal filing cabinets.

He licked his lips, gathered his courage, checked the pistol again, and sprang from cover. Alice was his target. He'd swoop in, grab her, and then fall back and let Trash-master and the—

A great rending and tearing and squealing thundered over the Fill, and Oscar skidded to a stop as the roof of the admin building collapsed, burying Alice under an avalanche of wood, metal, and sheetrock.

18

Oscar's soul unwound, and his brain stopped issuing orders as Alice's death wail cut through the chaos. He skidded to a halt as a blast of hot air pushed over the dump and Oscar was pelted with tiny splinters, nails, broken glass, and shards of metal. He dropped to the ground, his arms wrapped around his head, eyes pressed closed.

Sorrow leaked through him, the persistent pain of loss stinging his chest. Like everyone at the Fill, Alice was a casual friend, a person he saw only at work. He did know more about her life than most of the others at the landfill because her domain was heated and air-conditioned. So it was that Oscar and Alice had many discussions about marriage, its futility, and its necessity. Those talks had helped immensely when he'd first arrived at the dump, and still did. Seeing the woman get crushed and hearing her die took a piece of him, and he wondered how many pieces he had left.

It wasn't the death. He had seen death and he had killed. Oscar did his best to bury those memories deep, but when he saw another suffering, especially someone or something he cared about, the old wounds opened, and guilt spilled out.

The mutant reared back, debris spilling from the building's wreckage toward the creature in a deadly wave. It swung its massive tail to balance itself as it rose on its hindlegs, front claws flexing, its narrow head ranging around, eyes searching. Green stripes shone through the dust and calamity as the beast screamed, its tongue lashing out, its fury rippling the air.

Flight didn't even let fight speak, and a tremor of fear tore Oscar from his fugue. He looked toward the exit. A packed line of trucks struggled to get out. He could work his way through the trucks, and… Do what?

Head back to Twilight Dunes? He recalled the U.S. military's motto, "it's better to fight them over there than over here." Would it be better to stop this now, right here? He looked west, searching in vain for greenies surging through the garbage, but there was nothing but the past and the writhing shadows of the future.

The monster dropped back onto all fours, scurried between two huge piles of garbage, and was lost from view.

Oscar's knees threatened to come unhinged, and he bent and put his hands on his legs, the gun digging into his kneecap, spittle leaking from his mouth.

It was then he saw Curby hiding under a pile of cars waiting to be stripped of parts and crushed. The little man lay on his chest, chin resting on his hands as he stared at the remains of bedlam, his big eyes aglow.

"Are you alright?" Trash-master asked. He'd arrived at Oscar's side along with old man Karver and two men Oscar had seen around the dump, but whose names he had forgotten or had never known.

Oscar straightened as he nodded, but he was far from O.K. "Alice… Alice…" was all he could get out.

In a rare display of humanity, the boss put a hand on Oscar's shoulder and said, "I know. But there will be time to grieve for her later. Now…" His gaze shifted to the garbage pile as he brought up his shotgun and aimed it east at the trash mountain.

Oscar caught movement in his peripheral vision, and he jerked his head around.

Curby crawled out from under the stack of vehicles, got to one knee as he brushed dirt and sweat from his face, and pushed to his feet.

A long shadow fell over Curby, and a giant lizard head knifed from a trash heap. Jaws extended, and tooth-filled red gums and wet eyes burned through the dust and grit. The beast's tail swung wildly, and garbage was batted and smashed as the creature came on, a slithering missile of fury in search of prey.

From what Oscar could tell, Curby felt the creature before he saw it because he broke into a run only to realize he was heading right at the mutant.

A cackle-bark echoed over the Fill, and the lizard's head darted forward, its greatest weapon leading the attack.

Curby ducked and covered his head with his arms.

The mutant lizard's jaws clamped down on Curby and the upper portion of the man's body disappeared within the beast's jaws. A horrible *crunch* reverberated over the dump, and blood squirted from Curby's crushed body and splattered the hardpan.

Trash-master screamed.

The fuzz of chaos filled Oscar's head, his grief and surprise rendering him speechless. Gunshots thundered, and Oscar absently lifted his weapon but didn't fire.

A hollow *pop* resounded over the scene and one of Curby's legs was severed and fell to the ground. The sound of cracking bones, tearing flesh, and Curby's dying wail rose above the snap of gunpowder expanding.

Oscar's eyes stung from the smoke, his throat was dry as sand, and his muscles ached from the stress of overexertion and the excess adrenaline.

Metal clanged and the ground shook as the monster moved through the trash field, the sounds of its movements like the passage of a broken train. The sun had started its dive to the horizon, and tall shadows stretched over the landfill.

Nausea swept through Oscar, and suddenly he wished he'd called out sick.

Trash-master took control. "Fred and Karver, you take the north, and Oscar and I will take south. Lester, stay here and watch our backs. Call out if the creature tries to backtrack."

"Shouldn't we wait for help? The law or the greenies?" old man Karver said.

"The law? You see any help?" Trash-master barked. "During the day the Army only has a few guys patrolling and they could be on the opposite side of the Fill." He shook his head in what looked to be a mix of anger and frustration. "Anyone who's afraid to go forward can join the rest of the escaping rats."

Oscar thought that was a bit much, but there it was, and it couldn't be taken back.

The guy the boss identified as Fred was a tall skinny dude that always came in with debris from his construction jobs. He said, "Karver's got a point. I've got three bullets left. Why should we risk—"

"Then don't," Trash-master said.

Fred looked around, got no support, and said, "Screw this." He stuffed his revolver in his waistband, spun on a heel, and headed for the exit.

"Stay alert," Trash-master said as he inched forward into a valley of garbage.

Oscar hesitated, but only for a second before falling-in behind the boss. It wasn't Trash-master's goading, or some primeval instinct or need to help his fellow man that drove him forward. It was Alice's final scream and the echo of her life being snuffed out that drove away rational thought and ceded control to the lizard side of Oscar's brain, which wanted revenge.

Dust painted the trash field in fading colors, and shadows flitted and danced within the garbage. The beast had gone silent, and Trash-master lost the creature's trail as he threaded through the destruction caused by the massive beast. Oscar and his fellow crewmates would never be accused of being neat, but the dump wasn't totally disorganized. Piles of separated trash had been knocked over, heaps of metal and rubber scattered, but there was no longer a discernable path.

A gunshot carried through the detritus, and Trash-master and Oscar swung their weapons toward the noise.

Only shadows writhed within the garbage, the scent of rot and chemicals filling Oscar's nostrils like smoke.

The faint glow of the landfill's perimeter lights coming to life brought a sense of urgency. From what he'd seen, the mutants didn't like sunlight, and he and the others still hadn't taken the beast down under the Sun's glare. How successful would they be in the dark, when the creature…creatures… had the advantage? Again, he considered bailing on Trash-master, but he saw no end in sight, nowhere to hide, so he stayed the course.

Old man Karver slipped from the trash and when he saw the boss and Oscar he raised a hand but shook his head in the negative. He hadn't seen the mutant.

The murmur of voices and racing vehicles had died away, and Oscar figured he was one of the last morons left at the dump. He'd learned nothing from his fall. That was the only conclusion he could draw. He was creeping into the unknown, with darkness settling on the desert, with a limited amount of ammunition, instead of waiting for the Army to show up. When had he been appointed Chief Asshole Whisperer and Creature Slayer? Had he gotten a pay raise he wasn't aware of?

"We need… something more," Trash-master said as he held up his shotgun.

"Like what?" Oscar was having trouble putting one foot in front of the other, and there was no strategic thinking beyond the next ten seconds.

"The gas cans are where?" Trash-master asked.

There were a variety of gas supplies around the landfill for the various pieces of equipment, many of which required different types of fuel; diesel, ethanol, regular gasoline, and gasoline mixed with oil were all used to some degree. Oscar said, "Do you think lighting the dump on fire is a good idea? It could get out of control fast."

"You got anything better?" Trash-master challenged. "We can't let this thing—"

A series of staccato gunshots, followed by an extended wail of pain filtered through the trash to the partners' left.

Oscar aimed at the trash pile, but the boss gripped his arm.

"Save your ammo until you can at least see it," the boss said.

The man wasn't wrong. Bullets might not be doing much, but he had no desire to deal with the mutant with zero ammo.

Twilight raged across the land, and the lights and sounds of commotion and gathering men came from the Army's restricted area. Finally, the cavalry.

At the base of a stack of refrigerators, their doors off and Puron drained, the partners found Karver.

The old guy's body was twisted like a pretzel and his spent gun lay by his side. One arm was severed at the elbow, the other bent and looped around his head. An eye hung from its socket, and the exposed cheekbone had been crushed. His legs were splayed out at odd angles, but none of that was what had killed the man.

A narrow gash that ran from his neck to his balls spilled entrails onto the hardpan, a crimson pool spreading out around the corpse.

"Shit!" Trash-master yelled as he fired his shotgun into the sky. So much for saving ammunition.

A loud *boom* thundered through the dump, and the partners got low as they peered into the garbage. In the failing light, shadows took control, but the creature couldn't hide from the glowing green stripes that marked its movements.

The ratatat of gunfire erupted and bullets thumped into trash and ricocheted off metal.

"Here!" Oscar yelled as he took cover inside one of the refrigerators on the bottom of the stack.

Trash-master hesitated as he pointed his gun at nothing and scanned the garbage. The commotion in the Army's area had died away, but that didn't mean the greenies weren't coming. It only meant that whatever they were up to they didn't want the creature to know about it. With a nod the boss squeezed into the refrigerator next to Oscar, the two men standing side by side but separated by six inches of metal, insulation, and plastic.

A primal squeal of pain carried over the Fill, and Oscar allowed himself a moment of hope. Yes, this day had been bloody, but there was nothing left to prove. He didn't know how many patrons had seen the giant lizard, but he knew some had, which meant the tale of what had gone down at the landfill on this day had most likely already infected the entire town. The coconut telegraph was so fast that he wouldn't be surprised if the colonel and Ms. PR weren't already aware of the situation.

But did any of that matter? He knew from firsthand experience that the greenies couldn't be trusted. Shoot—that was why he and the others were trying to get proof, and—

The others. His thoughts strayed to Twilight Dunes and Roscoe, Toby, Paula, and the entire gang. He needed to get word to them. Tell them to get indoors and load their weapons. He reached for his phone, intending to send a text to Roscoe, but the huge leathery leg that appeared before him froze his movements.

Foot-long talons clawed the hardpan, muscles rippling as the monster ambled through the growing darkness, its green bioluminescent stripes blazing in the half-light and illuminating the interior of the refrigerator with an eerie green glow. The mutant paused, its leg blocking Oscar's escape.

He held his breath, and looked to his right, looking for Trash-master, but all he saw was the dirty and cracked white plastic of his fridge coffin.

The evening breeze rattled and stroked loose trash, but still, the beast didn't move. Instead, it settled onto its stomach, and a wrinkled patch of brown and black skin blocked the front of the fridge.

Oscar was encased in impenetrable darkness. He could reach out and touch the creature, it was that close. He held his breath, his heart hammering so hard he was sure the giant lizard could hear its thumping.

He heard Vincent Price reading the famous Poe lines, "—tear up the planks! —here, here! —it is the beating of his hideous heart!" Oscar brought up the gun and pointed it at the creature, the gun barrel's tip inches from the mutant's flank. He wanted to pull the trigger and never stop, but he had to be smart, or he'd be dead.

Oscar let out a slow breath as the creature pressed to its feet and moved away. Claustrophobia had taken control, and as soon as he was able, Oscar inched out of the refrigerator and sucked in a deep breath.

Indecision clawed at his senses because Oscar knew that as darkness came, so did the hour of reckoning.

19

Monica's insistent voice filled his head. "This is over. Over! Time for you to get out. You've done all you can. Oscar, I'm talking to you. Oscar!"

His dead wife was right. It was time to make like a tree and leave. Oscar searched for a path to retreat, but then the boss was next to him, blathering about not having any shells left and urging Oscar on into the chaos.

"Come on," Trash-master said as he darted between two piles of garbage.

Moonlight painted the world in black and white as a primal roar echoed over the Fill, and with an onrush of falling garbage a mutant burst from the trash. It was twenty feet long if it was a foot, its jaws agape, claws raking the hardpan. Ribbons of garbage and tinfoil clung to the many spikes and protrusions that covered the creature's body, and its whip-like tail knocked over refuse, leaving a trail of scattered garbage in its wake.

The mutant was wounded, and blood streamed down its right flank, but Oscar hadn't seen this particular monster before. He'd known there was more than one creature, there hadn't been any doubt, but now the question was how many of the goddamn things were there?

Trent "Trash-master" Masterson was known for poking his nose where it didn't belong. The crew talked about it often. About how one day he was gonna say the wrong thing to the wrong person who would stop his clock. Knowing all things were inevitable, Oscar took pleasure in knowing this, but he took no pleasure in knowing that it was going to happen now.

The boss dropped to a knee, put the stock of his gun to a shoulder, aimed, and fired until the gun clicked empty.

Smoke filled the air, and the report of the gunshots was like explosions inside the mountains of garbage, and the cloud of buckshot streaked through the air and peppered the front of the creature.

With a searing screech, the lizard doubled its pace.

Oscar stepped back into shadow.

Trash-master ran for cover behind a giant metal dumpster stuffed with old insulation. Pink cotton candy clouds made of deadly fiberglass spilled from the rusty box, and Oscar saw a field of glowing eyes beneath. The rats were staying out of the fight.

Gila monsters are slow and sluggish animals. Their mutant cousins weren't. The monster moved with an elegant grace, its legs short and stumpy, yet they churned quick and steady. Tail smacking trash, tongue leaking in and out of its mouth, eyes focused, the beast moved with incredible speed.

He had to do something, even if his actions didn't change the ultimate outcome. Oscar brought up his gun and fired twice into the beast's back as it ran toward the boss. The hope was the shots might distract the creature and buy Trash-master the precious few seconds he needed to reach the dumpster.

If the mutant even noticed the shots, it gave no sign and continued in its singular pursuit of its prey.

Trash-master, realizing he wasn't going to reach the dumpster, flipped the shotgun in his hands, and skidded to a halt. He spun around and planted his feet like a batter standing next to home plate looking to take a crack at a fastball.

But he was too small, and the gun-bat was like a metal toothpick.

The mutant launched like a cat, jaws flexed, tail straight back in attack position.

Trash-master screamed as he swung his gun.

Trent Masterson vanished as the creature snatched the man in its jaws. Then like a bird that's stolen a breadcrumb, the mutant moved into the nearest trash heap to dine.

Oscar stood in stunned silence, white moonlit clouds of grit obscuring the scene, his heart fighting to escape his chest.

The greenies had gone silent, and Oscar didn't know what scared him more, the lizards, or the Army being stealthy? The greenies didn't want to alert the beast, which likely meant they were trying to capture a mutant. If they wanted the creatures dead, there would already be choppers hovering over the dump, and missiles would be streaming toward the landfill. But that wasn't what was happening.

Monica's voice rang in Oscar's head, issuing a constant warning. "This isn't how I want to see you again. This isn't how it's supposed to end for you." Over and over and over, the words ringing in Oscar's head like an alarm klaxon, yet still he didn't comply.

"What the hell are you waiting for?" Monica asked.

That was the question. He decided not to wait any longer.

Oscar left Trash-master behind and though he had no love for the man, and his fate was out of his hands, Oscar felt a pang of sorrow as he headed for the southern section of the Fill.

The plan was to go to the spot where he and Earl had entered the dump under the cover of night over a week ago. He would rip open his repair and sneak across the desert, and when he was home, he'd gather his troops, dig in, and prepare for the worst. The Army was going to do whatever it wanted, and there was nothing Oscar could do about that except not become collateral damage.

"Oscar?"

The voice was hesitant, and Oscar stopped walking and ranged his gun around, searching the area.

A hiss, followed by a low growl-bark carried over the dump, and a mutant appeared on the path before Oscar.

In the glow of the moonlight Oscar saw that this monster was smaller than the others, a youngster, and the bumps that covered its skin were underdeveloped. There were no bioluminescent streaks, and for a heartbeat, Oscar thought perhaps the creature was an unusually large normal Gila, but when the animal flexed open its jaws, revealing oversized teeth, he knew that wasn't the case.

Oscar pressed his back to a plastic container filled with an unknown liquid and aimed his gun at the creature.

The voice came again, this time louder than before. "Oscar? Is that you? Oscar?"

Head down, the mutant shuffled forward as if the animal was sniffing the ground and following a trail. It hadn't seen him yet.

Since the start of his current odyssey, Oscar had done some internet research. Standard Gila monsters had a well-developed sense of smell. Like many reptiles, they used special organs to detect and analyze chemical cues in their environment. He knew Gila monsters didn't possess keen eyesight, which made their sense of smell crucial for finding food, locating mates, and navigating their environment. Their forked tongue also helped as it collected scent particles from the air. Even though when it came to the mutants all bets were off, Oscar had to assume there were some shared traits.

"Oscar!" The voice was more adamant now, and the monster stopped moving, its head ranging around, searching.

Finally, Oscar recognized the voice. It was Lester. The guy the Trash-master had assigned to watch their backs. With all the commotion, the man was investigating, and that was about to cost him his life.

"Take cover! Now! Take cover!" Oscar yelled, and he fired into the sky.

The creature's long head turned almost a hundred and eighty degrees as the beast scanned the dump. When the beast saw Oscar, its eyes widened, and its right front claw raked the hardpan as if spoiling to run.

"Oscar?" Moonlight illuminated the scene as Lester materialized out of the trash like a wraith, his Glock nine out before him in a doublehanded grip. When he saw Oscar, he relaxed and straightened.

"Look out!" Oscar yelled, but his warning was too late in the coming. He aimed his gun, recalled he had only three bullets left, and held his fire. Shooting the creature from afar would do nothing except waste precious bullets.

The monster pounced on Lester.

Oscar dropped and rolled, coming to a stop beneath an old table that the Fill's crew sometimes used as a workbench. The old furniture was at the edge of a refuse pile where semi-useful items were stored for future pickers, like a landfill thrift shop.

As the creature's teeth sank into the man, Lester screamed as bones snapped and flesh tore.

Lester didn't give up until the very end. With the beast's jaws noshing on his torso, blood spilling from him like a sieve, the man pressed the tip of his Glock into the beast's eye and pulled the trigger.

Gunshots roared through the garbage, a fountain of blood, brain, and bone spraying from the back of the lizard's narrow dome. Eleven shots rang out before Lester gave up the ghost, and he, along with the monster, fell to the hardpan, dead.

Oscar stood rooted to the ground, staring through the gloom at the pile of flesh that had once been a man and a freak of nature. He let the pistol fall to his side as his adrenaline fled and his muscles turned to stone. He wanted to sit down, go to sleep, and never wake.

A raucous chicken-bark broke the peace, but still Oscar didn't move. He was transfixed by the river of blood leaking from the carnage, his mind lost in the horror, moonlight painting the madness silvery gray.

"Move it, soldier. Now!" Monica screamed, and it was enough.

Oscar jerked into motion, sweat dripping into his eyes, pain searching for the limits of his extremities.

Ahead lay the barren dirt field that would become the new trash field once the current dumping site was transformed into Grassy Knoll number two. To the west was a fresh refuse pile, but nothing moved within the mountains of detritus. The eastern horizon was a dark expanse of emptiness.

Oscar paused at the edge of the trash, staring over the dirt field that stretched to the perimeter fence.

A giant monster blocked his path.

As he considered another way to flee, he saw a sight that made his nerves jangle.

Under the glare of the perimeter lights, Tommy and his buddy Jesse hid within a patch of sagebrush just beyond the fence, watching the battle unfold. This wasn't what he needed.

Oscar wasn't sure if the boys saw him, and he certainly didn't want to draw the monster towards the pair, so he went east, following the edge of the trash field, using the darkness and garbage as cover.

The massive mutant's head swung in Oscar's direction after he'd taken ten steps, and the beast roared as it gave chase.

A bang of metal rang out like a noon bell, and Oscar ducked as he looked back.

The creature had paused in its pursuit and was staring toward Tommy and Jesse, who were hurling rocks at the mutant.

"Shit!" Oscar yelled, but then he realized what the kids were trying to do. They were trying to distract the creature so Oscar could cross the open field to the fence.

Oscar ran, legs pumping, lungs burning as he crossed the dirt field that Wasten had created the prior year. He'd only gone twenty paces when the lizard shrieked and charged the fence, which was exactly what Oscar didn't want.

He changed course, but when he saw that Tommy and Jesse had fled, and were nowhere to be seen, his head stopped hammering and he slowed.

The beast, recognizing that its opportunity had passed, looked toward Oscar as he ran, but decided the small morsel wasn't worth the effort and wandered back into the trash field.

"Over here!" It was Tommy, and he'd opened a gap in the fence for Oscar.

Oscar muttered his thanks as he dove through the hole, rolled onto his feet, and bolted toward the glow of Twilight Dunes on the southern horizon.

Yelling and screaming filtered from the dump as he ran, then an earth-shaking thump thundered through the night and a massive fireball rose above the Fill. So much for the greenies wanting to capture the creatures.

"Thanks," Oscar said as he ran.

Tommy and Jesse jogged alongside him.

"You shouldn't have come, though," he said, but the boys weren't listening.

Devil grass and stunted trees cast undulating shadows over the bleak terrain, Oscar's feet slipping in the sand, his heart slowing as the adrenaline fled and his muscles protested.

The trio ran on, and then Tommy was gone. With frustration and hunger dulling his awareness, Oscar looked for Jesse and couldn't find the boy.

With a shriek of moving sand, the ground beneath Oscar's feet collapsed. There was no crack of rending stone, just the rush of sand as Oscar was sucked into the hardpan.

20

Oscar grasped franticly for purchase as he fell, but there was nothing to hold on to. He didn't plummet far, and jolts of pain spidered through him as he crash-landed atop a pile of sand. A field of stars dotted the darkness above, and he clawed and dug at the shifting soil as it sucked him into blackness. Oscar came to a stop, shifted his position, and sand slid, but he didn't slip any farther.

"Tommy? Jesse? You there?" Oscar called out as he spat sand from his mouth.

Both kids answered in the affirmative.

The ground shuddered, and sand and stones fell from the tunnel ceiling and walls. He wanted to help Jesse and Tommy, shelter them, but he was half-buried himself and there was no time. Oscar pressed his eyes shut as he waited for tons of dirt and sand to suffocate him.

Buried alive fifteen feet deep.

But the tunnel ceiling didn't give way, and when Oscar opened his eyes and saw the star-dappled sky, he was filled with a new sense of urgency.

"You boys still with me?" Oscar asked.

Double chirps of yes.

"Start digging yourselves out as slowly and easily as you can, and then we're going to climb up the cave-in and out of here. Nice and slow and careful." Oscar paused for questions, but all he heard was the gentle push of sand being moved as the boys dug themselves free.

The ground trembled like it had a heartbeat, a rhythmic thumping that got louder and more powerful with each passing second. Dirt, pebbles, twigs, and roots fell from the ceiling, and cracks formed in the tunnel walls. Oscar didn't want to think about what was causing the disturbance and he focused on freeing himself without triggering a landslide.

Slowly the cave filled with LED light as Jesse dug the flashlight from the sand.

As harsh light filled the tunnel, Oscar's nerves ceased waging war on his skin. There was a steep mound of sand, dirt, and dead vegetation beneath the hole, moonlight leaking through the gap into the tunnel. He figured the trio was no more than fifteen feet underground. An easy climb, especially with the three of them helping each other.

Oscar freed himself and helped Tommy, who was buried from the waist down.

Jesse got to his feet and stood on the side of the cave-in pile, holding the flashlight, his eyes gleaming in the half-light.

As if a ceasefire had been reached, the ground stopped beating and an otherworldly roar pierced the night.

Pebbles, sand, and dirt poured over the edge of the hole, and Jesse trained the flashlight on the source of the chaos.

A huge lizard head was backlit by the moon, its narrow shape filling the hole and blotting out the stars. A hollow clicking filled the cave as the beast stared down at the companions, its mouth hanging open, sharp teeth glinting in the gloom.

The monster's forked tongue lashed out and plucked Jesse from where he stood on the cave-in pile, the red serpent curling around the boy as the teenager let loose with an earsplitting screech that would have broken glass had any been in the vicinity.

Jesse dropped the flashlight as he was pulled from the cave with a whip of the monster's tongue.

Oscar and Tommy stood frozen with shock, their escape blocked, their legs no longer following orders.

Cracks appeared in the ceiling as the mutant pounded the hardpan with its tail and clawed at the edge of the hole with its talons like a squirrel digging for a nut.

Panic filled Oscar as he felt for his revolver, and relief washed through him when he felt it still lodged in the crack of his back. The relief faded when he remembered he only had three bullets left.

A drip of hot blood landed on Oscar's face and he screamed, all the anger and frustration coming out in a fury. He drew the gun and pointed it at the writhing shadow above, but didn't fire. Jesse was dead, and though it hadn't been Oscar's fault, he was the only adult for miles, so once again he'd been in the wrong place at the wrong time, and he had blood on his hands... his face.

Oscar lunged for the dropped flashlight, and as his fingers curled around it, an explosion of sand erupted on his right.

Tommy wailed as he dove down the side of the sand pile and rolled into the blackness of the tunnel.

The monster's tongue had lashed out searching for prey and had missed Oscar by two feet. With a smack and whistle the tongue retracted like a yo-yo, coiling for another strike.

Oscar pushed off with both arms, threw himself down the cave-in pile, and tumbled to the tunnel floor where he was met by Tommy's helping hand.

The mutant cried out, its form filling the hole above.

Oscar and Tommy stumbled away from the shower of earth, the harsh LED light driving away the solitary blackness.

The mutant lizard wailed and bitched, and the ground shook, but as the partners got farther away from the cave-in the sand and stones pouring from the ceiling lessened and finally stopped.

When Oscar deemed the pair had gone far enough, he turned off the flashlight and stopped to rest.

Impenetrable darkness filled the tunnel, but the beast above had either gone silent, or had moved on.

Tommy's whimpering carried through the tunnel.

"What happened to Jesse wasn't your fault, Tommy," Oscar blurted. He knew better than most that not all baggage weighed the same, and size had nothing to do with it.

Tommy said, "But still…"

"I know."

"Do you?" Tommy snapped. "You know what it's like living at the edge of nowhere with no car and about five other people your age within a twenty-five-mile radius? My social circle was just cut in half!"

Oscar said nothing as he stared at a bug crawling across his boot.

"It's not your fault, either," Tommy said between bursts of contained sobbing.

That was a bit more complicated. Oscar sat down and pressed his back to the roughly hewn walls, a root digging into his back, the air filled with dust and grit. He'd have to explain what happened to Deputy Sheriff Kendra. She'd believe his story, but what would it matter? It would be yet another stain on the quilt of his life that had more holes than thread.

Oscar stuffed the gun in his waistband and turned the light back on.

The tunnel looked to be a crack in the land, perhaps an arroyo covered by earth and time. Unlike some of the tunnels he'd seen at the landfill, this tunnel appeared at least partly a natural formation. He panned the light in both directions and the underground passageway ate the light and revealed nothing.

"These don't look like tunnels made by the lizards," Tommy said as he wiped tears from his face with the back of his hand.

Oscar looked at the boy but said nothing. He recalled some of the odd tunnels he'd seen at the Fill and remembered telling himself they looked like they'd been made by a termite or a worm on crack.

"What the hell are those lizard things, Mr. Rayos?"

Oscar was still trying to clear his head and calm the ringing that was rattling his brain, and for an instant, he didn't recognize his own last name. Everyone he knew called him Oscar.

The question sparked an inquiry. "What were you two... you doing there?"

Underground, wrapped in the desert, Tommy had no answer.

Oscar licked his lips and reined in his anger. The kid had just experienced a major trauma. He'd fallen into the Earth and watched his best friend get eaten by a creature striving to be Godzilla's replacement, but still, Oscar couldn't let the stupidity go. "Tommy, after all the talks we've had. After all the times you've almost gotten hurt. All the times I've bailed you out. You promised me you weren't going to go in the landfill anymore."

"I wasn't in the landfill," Tommy said.

Technically, the kid was right. He'd been outside the fence line watching, but no way Oscar was acknowledging the small semantic victory. "You knew what I meant. Does that small detail mean anything now?" That hurt to say, and Oscar was sure it was hard to hear, but some of the most important things in life are. "What were you doing out there?" Oscar asked again.

Tommy looked at the floor. Tear channels marred his dirt-covered face like tributaries of an ancient river, and the boy looked much older than his sixteen years.

Oscar's neck tightened. This wasn't the time or place to press the kid, and what was the point? What was done was done, and there was nothing to be gained by rehashing events that couldn't be changed. He'd resolved to let his question go unanswered when Tommy started talking.

"You know how it is around the Dunes, Oscar," Tommy said. "Even us younger folk hear stuff. See stuff."

"What did you see, Tommy?"

"I saw Earl watching the dump like a hawk," the kid said. "That's one thing for sure. We figured if Earl was watching, there must be something to see, but that was only part of it."

"Part?"

Tommy coughed and cleared his throat. "Deputy Sheriff hanging around at the Dunes. When do cops ever come to the Dunes?"

The kid had a point.

"Jesse heard tell that the military was up to something no good at the Fill. Hiding some experiments or something, and we..." Tommy sputtered to a stop.

Oscar, realizing that was all he was going to get and knowing he needed no more, said, "You wanted to help?"

"Sure." Tommy chuckled. "I guess that was some of it, but we were bored. There's nothing to do out here except stare at the walls. So when the opportunity to see something exciting came along..."

"Exciting? That's not what I'd call it."

"You know what I mean, but I guess…" Tommy's gaze strayed back down the tunnel in the direction they'd come.

When Jesse didn't materialize out of the darkness, Oscar said, "There's got to be a way out of here."

Tommy looked up at the ceiling and said, "Can't we dig out?"

"Too risky. We'd most likely cause another cave-in, and I'm not willing to try my luck twice on the same day."

Oscar pressed to his feet and checked the revolver. He inched out the cylinder and spun it. Additional bullets hadn't magically appeared, and as Oscar snapped the cylinder closed, he turned it so there was a bullet on deck. He dusted himself off and said, "Are you O.K. to continue?"

Tommy didn't answer, but he got to his feet, brushed off his jeans, and fell in beside Oscar.

Flashlight in one hand, the gun in the other, Oscar inched down the tunnel. The unforgiving LED light drove away the darkness but did nothing to ease the penetrating cold that chilled Oscar's bones despite the sweat rolling down his back. It was cooler underground, but it wasn't the temperature that drained his will to go on, it was the dead teenager he'd left behind.

He shook his head, willing the thoughts to go away. Oscar and Tommy hadn't left anyone behind. Jesse had been killed by a mutant, just like Wasten, Alice, Curby, Trash-master, and Lester. Random acts of violence by creatures that didn't know love or mercy, only hunting prey. Anger filled the empty spaces, a rage that brought him back to the here and now.

The duo had only gone half a mile when the walls of the cave fell away revealing a large natural underground chamber. No bats clung to the smooth ceiling, which was pocked with thousands of tiny holes. There were piles of dried blood-darkened bones scattered about the chamber, but there were no other signs of life.

Oscar thought he stood in a burrow, but it certainly wasn't home to the mutants. There was no nest, no den, and the marks that decorated the walls and tunnel openings were small, almost as if they'd been scratched out by something other than a talon, something much smaller and softer.

"Rats?" Tommy half asked, half stated.

Oscar shone the flashlight on the largest pile of bones.

Though there was nothing human-sized, or even bobcat-sized, there were bones that looked too large to have been stripped clean of their meat by desert rats, but he didn't know. One rat couldn't take down a bobcat. But a horde? "I don't know Tommy, but I think—"

A hollow gnashing sound, like the largest sheet of aluminum foil ever made was being crumbled into a ball, filled the space and echoed off the walls. The ground didn't tremble, but a rank breeze that smelled of rot and chemicals pushed into the chamber.

Oscar panned the flashlight around. The partners couldn't go back the way they'd come, there'd been no side passages and even if the beast was gone, the cave-in had blocked the tunnel.

The stark burrow got smaller on its opposite end and scaled back down to nothing more than a four-foot crack in the land.

There were two other passages dug through the desert by the creatures that used the chamber as a dining hall, but one was only a couple of feet wide, and the other had a five-foot radius. Still, there was no way he was crawling into either tunnel.

That left forward. "Let's go. Hurry," Oscar said.

Tommy said nothing as the intense grumbling filling the tunnel went silent.

21

The steady buzz of the desert night symphony penetrated the ground and filled the tunnel with faint static. Roots hung from the ceiling like hair, and a field of eyes appeared in the darkness ahead as the tunnel turned precipitously downward. Ant channels and stones slick with moisture decorated the walls, and the rotten scent of stagnant water filled the cave.

As Oscar and Tommy pressed forward the desert rats scattered, the scraping of their tiny feet and the titter of their constant bickering carrying through the subterranean passageway. Doubt plucked Oscar's nerves. He figured he and Tommy had walked about a mile, and though he believed they were moving southeast, he wasn't confident in the estimate. The tunnel had dipped and twisted and turned, and he had to admit to himself that he had no idea where he was other than that he was beneath the desert.

The passage widened, and the crack in the land that was the tunnel faltered and was replaced by a smooth washed-out sand floor and walls that looked to have been molded by water in the distant past.

"There should be an outflow and we might be able to get out," Oscar said, but he wasn't certain. He was trying to stay positive for the kid, but it was work.

As the partners walked, Tommy blurted, "Jesse and I stole beers from you and the others last week. I assume you didn't know?"

With all the pain filling Oscar's veins he still couldn't help but laugh. Those in the know said teenage boys had one-track minds and only thought about sex, but Oscar felt beer was the flip side to that single. "No, I didn't." Oscar tried to sound angry, but it came out goofy, so he added some bluster. "If I had known, I would have…" What? Whipped his ass? No. Gone to his mother? No, she didn't care what the kid did. Call the cops? That would only lead to more dysfunction, and Oscar didn't need the bad karma.

"I just wanted to say I'm sorry," the kid said.

"When?" Oscar was curious, and talking made the time go by and distracted him from the idea that he and Tommy weren't getting closer to an exit but instead delving deeper into the Earth like Professor Otto Lidenbrock.

"Paula was busy, and all you guys were talking," Tommy said. "Remember when I showed up and you came out to talk to me?"

Oscar nodded. The little shits had created a diversion.

"Jesse snuck around back, and when you were out front with me, Earl was in the can, and Toby and Paula were shuttling drinks, he slipped behind the bar and grabbed three Blue Ribbons."

"Three." Oscar whistled. "When did you drink them? After you sent me out into the desert?" He recalled the dance with death that had almost gotten the best of him and Tank.

The kid nodded. "I didn't know you were going to do that."

"How could you."

"That's not why I'm telling you though," Tommy said.

Invisible mice clawed their way down Oscar's spine and settled on his lower back, the stress of the impending revelation churning his insides.

"Jesse told me…" The kid studied the ground. "His, mom, well she… has a lot of boyfriends."

Well done, kid. In Oscar's day, the term slut would've been used.

"There was this one guy, made Jesse call him Big T or some shit…. Sorry," Tommy said. "This guy sleeps over, and you know how thin the walls are in these campers. It's like sleeping in a tent."

More than half of what Oscar knew about the people of Twilight Dunes he'd learned from the muffled screams of arguing neighbors, a thin sheet of aluminum, some balsa-like wood, and the thinnest paneling ever constructed all that separated their rage from the outside world.

"Jesse's room is right next-door, lucky him, but one night the guy starts yelling and screaming like a madman. It's the middle of the night, and Jess wakes to hear his mother wailing and this guy raging and yelling.

"Turns out the guy was dreaming, and when Jesse burst into the room his mother told him you should never wake someone in the middle of a dream, so they didn't."

"Jesse was afraid the guy would hurt him?"

"A little. The guy was thrashing around, kicking and punching the air, but it was what he said that really scared Jesse."

Oscar's stomach overheated.

"He went on and on about how the Army had opened a can of worms they couldn't put the lid back on. Jesse was never accused of being smart, but he wasn't stupid. He knew stuff. Said the guy mentioned a rift in the fabric of existence, whatever the hell that means. Science run amok."

"Anything about the… lizards?"

"Not specifically, but when the guy settled down, he murmured for several more hours, most of which were numbers and formulas and all kinds of weird shi—stuff Jesse didn't understand."

"Who was this guy?"

Tommy hiked his shoulders, the flashlight wavering in his hand. "All Jesse knew was the guy was a greenie."

Two words stuck in Oscar's brain like fishhooks: rift and amok. The greenies had broken something, and now it was out of control. Somehow that sounded worse than his darkest predictions. "We'll have to talk about this more when I can think straight."

Tommy said nothing.

"Why did you tell me this now?"

"Thought it might be important. Especially now…"

Oscar understood. When people die things get real very fast.

With the guilt lifted, Tommy seemed to perk up. His shoulders went back up, his chin lifted, and the flashlight ceased trembling in his hand. "Do you still think we're going the right way, not that we've got any other options," the kid said.

The lack of options was exactly the problem gnawing at Oscar's insides as the partners walked side by side into a wide natural cavern that would've made the creators of Pennsylvania Station proud. An itch started in the back of Oscar's head, crawled through his face to his ears, and transformed into a steady hum. He stumbled to a halt and gripped Tommy's shirtsleeve. "Do you hear that?"

The ground was steady and sand didn't sift down from the ceiling. All was still except for the pair's ragged breathing and the heartbeat of the desert. Even the static of the creatures of the night chirping, bleating, and buzzing had gone silent.

A tremor rolled through the land, a hollow rending and ripping that sounded like a massive shovel digging through dirt.

Hope surged through Oscar. He and Tommy were being rescued. But no, that wasn't possible. Nobody knew where the pair was, and there hadn't been enough time to move heavy equipment to their location even if said location was known.

His second thought was the mutants were somehow tracking them from above, but that made even less sense. Oscar had seen the massive lizards chew through the ground like a backhoe, and there had been nothing subtle about the process. No, this was something new, and Oscar couldn't come up with a scenario where that something was good.

"Should we… run?" Tommy said.

"You hear it now?"

The kid nodded.

Running posed a series of dangers, and without knowing what the odd sound was, how did they know they weren't running toward danger? But they had to do something, and they had to do it fast.

The noise grew in volume and pitch until a sharp whistle filled the cavern.

Oscar checked the revolver for the hundredth time and cocked back the hammer. With only three bullets in the cylinder, Oscar wanted to make sure one of the bullets rotated into firing position. He'd set it at the ready, but there was nothing worse than having a weapon that didn't work when it was needed most.

A thunderous cacophony of sifting sand, smacking stones, and crumbling earth erupted into the cave.

Oscar and Tommy ran. What else was there to do? But they'd only gone a few steps before the wall to their right exploded.

A screech, like a dolphin being tortured, echoed through the cavern as a groundswell of earth swept into the cave, driving Oscar and Tommy forward like the push of a tidal wave. The tsunami of sand, dirt, and stones broke over the floor, and under the shaky light of the flashlight, a new horror was revealed.

A giant desert millipede was at the crest of the onrush of earth, its two cable-like antennas rising above the tumult. The creature was huge, at least fifteen feet long, and the slithering and shifting segments of its elongated, cylindrical body each bore two pairs of legs.

But it was the monster's vibrant coloration that dazzled the eye. The beast's exoskeleton was decorated in a range of hues, including shades of red, orange, pink, and brown. All the colors were arranged in an intricate pattern that resembled a puzzle, and as the creature wiggled and slithered the design shifted, disguising the beast. There were no teeth visible—that was good, but the two shining eyes driving from the wave of earth made Oscar skid to a halt and point the revolver at the beast's swaying head.

Anyone who lived in the desert had encountered the annoying pests. Standard desert millipedes only came to the surface once annually to feed voraciously to store energy, and they were only eight inches long. The vivid coloration served as a warning to potential predators, signaling that the millipede wasn't a suitable meal. Oscar knew desert millipedes secreted a liquid with a pungent odor that acted as a deterrent against predators, but it wasn't poisonous to humans.

But neither was the venom of normal Gila monsters.

The tide of earth spat Oscar and Tommy out, and they hit the sandy floor in a tangle. Sand pressed up Oscar's nose, and as he struggled to get to his feet, he was knocked over by the knot of earth rolling before the mutant millipede.

A mutant was what it was. Scientific study wasn't necessary, and as the monster came on, antennas swinging and batting the walls, Oscar forced himself to his feet.

It was then he remembered the Smith & Wesson.

Tommy lay twisted on the ground, and for a horrifying instant, he thought the boy was dead and Oscar saw himself ending his own life. But then Tommy squirmed, spat sand, and rolled onto his side.

The roiling knot of earth slowed, and the monster slithered onto the ground.

Oscar gripped Tommy by the shirt and jerked the skinny kid to his feet. "Run. Run like your life depends on it. Because it does."

"What about—"

Oscar tossed the kid behind him and turned to face the beast.

The creature's many legs churned in perfect coordination as it lifted its forward sections, antennas flailing, beady eyes aglow, the mosaic of colors covering its body shifting and changing in the fading light.

Tommy retreated with the flashlight and shadows waltzed on the walls.

A thin wail leaked through the cavern, and beneath it the sound of liquid spraying.

Oscar aimed the pistol between the beast's eyes and pulled the trigger.

With a cry, the beast stumbled.

The shot hit the mutant between its eyes, and a sickening *crunch* reverberated through the cave as the bullet cracked the beast's exoskeleton.

He fired again, holding back the urge to squeeze the trigger until the weapon was empty.

The second shot hit the creature below its cycling mandibles, and the front sections of the millipede stopped moving and its head flopped to the ground as if the beast was dead.

Sensing his final opportunity, Oscar fired his last bullet.

The creature screamed and reared in its death throes, liquid spitting from between its segments as its head smashed into the tunnel's ceiling, antennas falling back. The poison-like fluid jetting from the monster sizzled and smoked as it splattered the walls and floor, missing Oscar by mere feet as he crab-walked backward.

With a final exhalation and a fading squeal, a rank breeze gusted through the cavern and the creature went down. Its antennas got caught up for an instant in roots hanging from the ceiling, before the dead mutant flopped onto the ground, its head landing ten feet from Oscar.

He pointed the .38 at the beast's dead eyes and pulled the trigger, over and over, the tap and pop of the hammer hitting spent cartridges and empty chambers echoing through the devastation.

Screeching and howling from down the tunnel.

The anger subsided, he stopped pulling the trigger, and he let the gun fall to his side.

Tommy had followed orders and was nowhere to be seen, the glow of the flashlight a far-off beacon on a distant horizon. He staggered away from the dead creature, the corpse's scent sticking to him like glue.

Pain jarred his muscles, and twisted thoughts filled his head. Mutant Gila monsters, mutant desert millipedes? What other species had the greenies bastardized, and what other horrors had they created?

A cloud of light appeared in the darkness ahead.

22

Ahead the LED light narrowed to a slender hole as the cavern tapered back to a tunnel that had been clawed through the loose sedimentary sandstone. The unnatural tunnel connected to another natural cave that looked to be the result of ancient runoff.

The cavern filled with light as Oscar and Tommy approached one another.

"Thank God you're O.K.," the kid said.

"Thank Mr. Smith and Mr. Wesson." Oscar raised the weapon as a visual aid.

"Is it dead?" Tommy asked.

"Deader than disco."

"Disco?"

"Forget it. Why did you come back?" Oscar asked.

The kid didn't answer right away, but after several long moments, he said, "Not sure really, but I think it's because I know that's what you would have done for me."

Oscar harrumphed. That might just be the smartest thing he'd ever heard the kid say. Could it be that the washwomen were right? Had his male influence rubbed off on the kid? He'd thought about joining the venerable Boys Club of America and agreeing to mentor a fatherless child, but the idea of him life-coaching another human being was too ridiculous to contemplate.

"You will make a good father," came Monica's voice from the void.

Will make? Oscar shook his head as the elephant in the tunnel occupied his thoughts. Where there was one massive mutant desert millipede, there were two. Probably more. The good news was he hadn't seen any side passages, which was also bad news because that gave the duo no options. Of course, none of that was significant because the monster dug its own channels.

"There are more of those things, aren't there?" Tommy said.

It was a good question that filled Oscar with hope for the future. Like every generation before him, he saw the people who would soon be in charge as misfits, at best. They had no experience and little knowledge about the hard knocks that would eventually come. But again, that wasn't his problem. The kid's insightful question only stoked his fears, but there was nothing he could do. He had an empty gun and only one path.

"Yeah, that's what I thought," Tommy said.

"Look. Just because I don't answer all your questions doesn't mean that I agree with you. All it usually means is I have no idea. I don't know. No clue."

The kid's pace slowed. "Well, not no clue," he said.

"Not a great moment to be a smartass."

"No." Tommy raised a hand and repeated the question Oscar had asked right before they were attacked. "Do you hear that?"

The pair stopped walking. Oscar did hear something, but it didn't sound like a large animal digging through dirt. This sound had a cadence, hollow deep echoes that rose and fell in rhythm. It didn't sound like a bird or desert rat.

"Is someone calling your name?" Tommy asked.

Oscar's head still rang, and the cracked egg of his brain was finally congealing, but he didn't hear his name being called. But he did hear something. He tried to block out the hum of the Earth, the gentle brush of sand blowing in the wind, and… He heard it. Someone was calling out Oscar's name, the faint warble of the voice distorted by its subterranean passage.

"Yeah. Yeah. Yeah!" Oscar shrieked.

The partners fist-bumped, hugged, and pushed away from each other awkwardly like some invisible barrier had been breached.

Tommy pointed the flashlight at the ceiling, and a cloud of dust floated just below the hanging roots, and sand sifted down to a growing pile.

Oscar gripped the kid by the shirt and tugged him down the tunnel away from the falling sand. "Whatever they're digging with could cause a cave-in and we don't want to be caught in it," Oscar said.

Then the spilling sand stopped.

Oscar felt Tommy staring at him in the darkness, the flashlight angled up at the ceiling.

Shadows fought in the grayness beyond the flashlight's reach, and a sense of urgency consumed Oscar. "Stay here," he said.

Tommy didn't protest as he handed over the flashlight.

Thoughts of a massive millipede waiting to break through the ceiling and splash him with its poison cajoled the lizard side of Oscar's brain as he inched down the passageway, nerves jangling, sweat soaking through his t-shirt.

When Oscar reached the small drift of sand, he angled the flashlight straight up.

At first, Oscar thought he'd lost it. Done. Fini. Because what his mind told him he was seeing couldn't possibly be.

Snot dripped from a black nose that wiggled through the dirt, a sniffing sound filling the tunnel.

Oscar laughed as he stepped back.

The digging resumed; scratching, clawing, panting. Dirt and dead vegetation fell from the ceiling, and the LED light revealed two glowing eyes, whiskers, and a black snout tinged with bronze.

Tank's head burst through the tunnel ceiling and the canine barked, the sound like music. Heavy metal, but music all the same.

Screaming, yelling, shouts of joy, and then Dr. Shelly DiBard's head appeared in the opening, stars twinkling behind her. "Oscar?"

"In the flesh."

"Who's with you?" Shelly asked.

"Tommy," Oscar said. His heart darkened at the thought of Jesse.

"Back up and give us a minute," she said.

"Go slow, we ended up down here becau—"

"We know. A cave-in," a second female voice said. It sounded like Roscoe.

Oscar and Tommy retreated and waited as the hole in the ceiling grew and moonlight leaked through the void. A yellow rope snaked into the tunnel, and it glowed under the harsh stare of the flashlight.

Shelly yelled, "Tommy first. He's lighter and can help us pull you up."

Tommy gripped the line and started to climb. The kid needed little help and was soon pulling himself over the lip of the hole into darkness.

Oscar spared a brief thought for those gym days of long ago when the class would gather around the climbing ropes in the gym to embarrass the athletically challenged among them. He figured Tommy had no such issues.

Neither had he, but Oscar was no teenager, and it had been a long time since he completed the advanced expeditionary obstacle course the greenies used at the Cactus Ridge Proving Ground.

Sand and dirt sifted down into his face as he climbed, and when he reached the top, Roscoe and Shelly pulled him the last few feet. Oscar rolled onto his back and stared at the stars as Tank licked his cheek.

"What are you doing out here?" Oscar asked the canine as he rubbed the dog behind his ears. The bandage on Tank's side was stained red, but otherwise, he looked O.K. He'd gained some weight, the splint had been removed from his leg, and the bandage covering his torn ear was gone.

"It's my fault, really," Shelly said.

"Your fault?" Roscoe said. "If you hadn't come by Oscar and Tommy would still be…" She looked at the ground.

"About that," Oscar said. "How the hell did you find us?"

"One question at a time," Shelly said. "Are you thirsty? Hungry?"

Oscar and Tommy both said yes.

"Let's head back to the Dunes," said Roscoe as she handed out water and granola bars.

Darkness hung like a shroud over the land, moonlight and starlight painting the desert silvery white. A rolling storm of black smoke embroiled the landfill like Mount Doom, the explosion coming back to Oscar like a bad dream. The lights of Twilight Dunes sparkled in the darkness about a mile to the southeast, and a line of headlights trailed out of the east, presumably from the base.

"I came out to see Tank," Shelly began as they walked.

Tommy sniffled and Roscoe pulled a crumbled paper towel from her pocket and tossed it to the kid.

"Tank's doing great, as you can see," Shelly continued. "We were just sitting and watching the sunset, Roscoe and I, when Tank gets up and starts growling. I asked him what was wrong, and he barked, hard, and started clawing at the door." Shelly paused and looked at Roscoe as if handing off the baton.

"I'd seen him act like this before when you'd brought him home for long weekends," Roscoe said. "The chirp of every bird, the moan of every lizard, and the howl of every coyote disturbs his peace."

"I opened the door, and he bolted outside," Shelly said. "I was a little concerned he might open the wound on his side, and he was still limping, but he was moving fast. He had a real sense of urgency that worried me."

"So, we followed him," Roscoe said.

"We were out in the desert, Tank's nose pressed to the hardpan when a huge explosion rocked the Fill. Roscoe and I felt its hot breath two miles away," Shelly said.

"Were you in the landfill when that happened?" Roscoe interjected.

Oscar shook his head no. "Almost, though, and I might have been if it wasn't for Tommy and Jesse's help."

Wind drove sand into Oscar's eyes, a tear leaking out.

"Jesse?" Roscoe said.

Oscar licked his lips and prepared to take his medicine, but Tommy jumped in, and Oscar took this as more proof of the growth caused by his slight influence on the kid.

Tommy told of how he and his friend had snuck across the desert. He listed all the reasons he'd given Oscar, and when he got to the part of the story where Jesse died he paused, and said simply, "But he didn't make it."

"A lizard… A mutant?" Shelly said.

Tommy said, "That's the general consensus."

"Consensus?" Oscar said.

The kid shrugged.

"We saw blood around the cave-in site," Shelly said. "Must've been his."

"You found the cave-in?" Oscar said.

Shelly nodded. "After the explosion we backed off, but Roscoe and I both agreed that you'd most likely head for home, so we scoured the desert just beyond the Fill's fence line to the south, and we found the cave-in."

"From there," Roscoe picked up the ball, "we walked a grid pattern across the desert, but we were ready to give up when Tank bolted into the darkness. We chased him down, but by that time we knew what had spooked the animal. The ground was vibrating, and sinkholes appeared to the southeast, so we went that way."

"Toward danger?" Oscar said.

The doctor and Oscar's best friend said nothing.

"And my boy here sniffed us out?" Oscar said.

Tank chirped.

"More or less," Shelly said.

The warm desert breeze soothed Oscar's bitching nerves as the companions made their way across the desert, the lights of Twilight Dune's growing in the blackness.

Oscar's glowing watch revealed the time to be 10:19 PM. It felt like days had passed since he'd fled the carnage at the landfill, and his muscles ached, his heart hurt, and despite the granola bar, his stomach campaigned for supper.

Roscoe inched up beside Oscar, put an arm around his shoulders, and whispered in his ear, "Is he O.K.?" She pointed covertly at Tommy, who was stumbling along in a zombie-like daze.

He hiked his shoulders. Childhood trauma and loss were tricky things. That which hurts us makes us stronger, but that adage didn't apply to young children, and it only applied selectively to teenagers and adults. Some of those things that hurt also kill, and young minds can be easily damaged. Oscar didn't think Tommy was a wallflower—to the contrary, the kid had handled himself well—but seeing your best friend get eaten by a giant lizard placed a veil over the remainder of his life, regardless of how well-adjusted and productive he became.

"He's going to need counseling, of course," Oscar whispered. "But I think he'll be O.K."

"What about you?"

Oscar sighed. That was a bit more complicated. With the adrenaline subsiding, guilt tore at him. Jesse was dead, and soon he'd have to tell the boy's mother what happened, and respond to the litany of questions, not the least of which would be, "Why didn't you do something?" The explanation that he'd been half buried wouldn't fly. Hell, it didn't even fly with him. He said, "I'll be O.K."

"That's not an answer," Roscoe said.

"I know."

Roscoe let out a long stream of air and said, "Jesus. You're worse than Rick."

A cackle sounded over the desert, and it was answered by another.

Darkness consumed the company as they walked, all the flashlights extinguished for fear of drawing attention. Was he O.K.? Was he ever? He wasn't sure what being O.K. meant. In his experience, every day brought a new challenge, and the challenges never ended until they put you in a box or burnt you out. Oscar had never given much thought to his mortal remains, and he didn't plan to. Who cared what happened to his body after he died? Oh, right, all the folks that would get his organs if they didn't mind them being marinated in alcohol, that's who.

More screeches and howls, and a field of eyes appeared behind them.

"What are they?" Shelly asked.

The doctor was still clueless about the big picture, so Oscar spun it out fast, furious, and without sugarcoating.

"Mutant lizards?" Shelly said when he was done.

"And millipedes," Tommy said. "The greenies did it."

One of the creatures out in the desert roared, a mournful cry of pain, frustration, and hunger. The field of radiant orbs advanced through the darkness, sets of eyes appearing out of the gloom, some close to the ground, some hovering in the blackness fifteen feet above the hardpan.

"We better pick up our pace," Roscoe said.

23

Six minutes short of midnight, the moon glaring down at the unforgiving desert, the night creatures screeching full blast, Oscar and the others arrived at the cut in the hedgerow at the edge of Twilight Dunes. Oscar's stomach protested as he entered the park, memories of the blood trail and the slaughter at the landfill reasserting themselves on his mental priority list.

The Dunes was dark, save for a few lights that stubbornly pushed away the blackness, illuminating outlines of the campers and doublewides that ran along the dirt streets. It wasn't that late, but on this night the murmur of T.V.s and music didn't pollute the natural chorus of the desert, which sang with an eerie intensity that buzzed in the back of Oscar's brain like an alarm klaxon that just wouldn't stop.

Tank nudged Oscar's leg and whined.

"Hungry, boy?"

Tank chirped.

"I've got a couple of things to deal with first, buddy," Oscar said.

"Do you want me to take him to the trailer and feed him?" Shelly asked. "I don't mind."

Oscar was sure she didn't. Losing a child is a crushing blow that many never recovered from, and he guessed the woman had no desire to see another human break. She probably saw enough of that on a daily basis. He said, "Sure. You know how to get in."

She nodded. "Come on, Tank."

The big dog looked at Oscar.

"Go ahead."

Tank bolted into the darkness and Shelly followed.

Earl's trailer was dark, but buttoned up, as was Ms. Perriweather's place. As instructed, their storm shutters were closed, gates locked, and Oscar spotted a tripwire running across the front of Earl's small yard.

Not a bad idea. Oscar said, "Roscoe, do you see what Earl did there?"

"The tripwire? Sure."

"Do you know how to make one? We could set them up around the park."

"I know how, but a desert rat can set them off, so they're only useful for close-quarters work," she said. "I figure it's only a warning signal, though, because I doubt he'd risk hurting a neighbor by using explosives."

That brought a new thought. "Do you think he has some?"

"What do you think?"

Oscar said nothing.

"You think they're going to attack?" Tommy asked.

Roscoe chuckled.

Oscar shot her a "not appropriate given the kid's recent trauma" look and said, "All past evidence points in that direction, yes."

The Pride appeared in the darkness ahead, a field of glowing eyes, and Oscar tried to count sets of eyes, but the felines were constantly moving and rubbing and hiding, and it was impossible. Ms. Perriweather had told him Ditz, Chrome, and Fred, three prominent alphas and members of the Pride hadn't been seen in days.

Oscar couldn't help but think he'd seen the bones of the three cats either in the landfill burrow or in the mutant desert millipede hole.

Mr. E's house was silent and dark, and the red indicator light on his doorbell camera and the green light atop the alarm panel knifed through the gloom.

The narrow arroyo that housed the forty-eight mobile homes that made up Twilight Dunes was surrounded by a thick hedgerow, and though it would provide a warning system via sound, it wouldn't stop even the smallest of the mutants from entering their little compound. It was time to set up patrols and guard posts. The idea of it made him sick to his stomach.

Jesse's trailer loomed in the darkness and the companions stopped in the middle of the road.

Tommy stared at his feet, and Roscoe looked longingly up the street toward Oscar's place where cold beer and a chair awaited.

"I'll do the talking," Oscar said.

A coyote howled, insects buzzed, lizards bleated, but Oscar's companions made no sign.

The trio approached Doris Grape's dilapidated trailer with caution. Startling someone from sleep, especially after all the recent warnings, could prove deadly. Oscar didn't know Doris, but he knew many women told their kids their fathers died doing something important for the military when in fact the kid was the product of some other short-term relationship. He didn't know if this was true in Jesse's case, but when the kid talked about how his father had died out on the range, he never seemed to truly believe it himself.

The few youngsters that called the park home had many surrogate parents, and Doris did her best, but working two jobs to put food on the table didn't lend itself to being an involved parent. Add to that the rumors of depression, drug abuse, and a less-than-stellar track record with the opposite sex, Jesse, God rest his soul, never had a chance.

Roscoe rapped on the screen door and its rattle carried through the Dunes.

No answer.

Oscar peeked through the front window. The digital clock above the stove illuminated the small space, and nothing moved within.

Roscoe knocked harder.

Nothing.

"This isn't unusual," Tommy said.

Oscar and Roscoe exchanged glances. "What do you mean?" Roscoe asked.

"She's gone for days sometimes," the kid said. "Stays at her boyfriend's house, or at least that's what she says. Jesse doesn't... didn't mind having the place to himself. Said it made things easier for himself."

The odd adage that a person needed a license to drive a car, catch a fish, and go to the park, but any dumbass could have a kid planted itself in Oscar's frontal lobe.

"I'll leave a note for her to contact you," Roscoe said.

Oscar nodded.

The next order of business was Tommy, but like teenagers worldwide, the boy had better instincts than his elders gave him credit for.

"I want to stick with you for now," Tommy said.

Oscar considered the boy's motivation. His mother was going to be very upset when she found out about Jesse, and how Tommy had almost bitten the donut because he hadn't listened to her, or Oscar's warnings. He also might want to help, but Oscar was done babysitting. He said, "Not happening."

"I can help," the boy whined. "After everything, you don't trust me? You don't think I can help?"

"I do think you can help," Oscar said. "Your mother. She's home alone and you've seen what these things can do. Do you want her to be alone?"

Tommy licked his lips and looked over his shoulder in the direction of his camper. "I guess not."

Time to play surrogate dad. Oscar put a hand on the kid's shoulder and said, "Do you know how proud I am of how you handled yourself today? When the time is right, I'll tell your mother everything. All the good things you did. But now, right here, tonight, I need you to be her protector. Can you do that?"

"I can try."

"That's all we can ask," Roscoe said, seeing an opportunity to support Oscar.

Tommy nodded.

"See you in the morning. O.K.?" Oscar said.

"Sure," the kid said, and he headed home.

Toby's was closed until further notice, and Toby and Paula's doublewide was dark. Lights blared from Oscar's trailer, and shadows danced in the windows.

Oscar arrived home to find Tank watered, fed, and content. Roscoe and Oscar joined the pair on the screen porch but there was no sipping whiskey or beer on this night. An urn of coffee sat on a table along with an array of guns, ammunition, and knives, that would've impressed Rambo.

Oscar cleaned and loaded his Smith & Wesson and the Benelli. On the table his Bowie knife sat next to Roscoe's field knife, along with one grenade she'd pilfered, her service weapon, an M4 carbine, and an Army-issued .45 that had been her father's. There were several boxes of ammo, but the bulk of the Dune's ammunition was still locked in Toby's gun safe.

Shelly took a long pull of coffee and said, "I haven't had a chance to tell you yet, but I had visitors at the clinic yesterday."

"Do tell," Oscar said.

Tank sat on the couch with Roscoe, his huge head in her lap, his eyes straying to each person as they talked as if the canine was following the conversation, and Oscar believed on some level the dog was.

"That lovely greenie stopped to see me with four military cops," Shelly said.

"Civil Affairs Officer Devito?" Oscar asked.

"Yup," Shelly said. "She marches in with her goons and starts asking questions about the sample I sent to the state to be analyzed."

Darkness leaked into the camper like oil, the sounds of the night creatures filling the stillness.

"Started making threats about what would happen if I didn't tell her where I got the sample."

"That's not good," Roscoe said.

"No, it isn't," the doctor said.

Oscar rubbed his hands together to drive back the anger. "What did you tell them?"

"Nothing," Shelly said. "I told them someone brought in a dead desert rat because it looked odd so I took a sample. When they asked to see the carcass, I said it had been destroyed."

"They bought that?" Oscar asked.

"No, but they had no proof otherwise," she said. "I came to see Tank, but my main reason for coming was to tell you face to face."

"We better call Deputy Sherrif Kendra," Roscoe said.

"Good idea." Oscar tried her cell number, got no answer, and left a message for her to call him back.

Oscar's nerves crawled with indecision. He needed to do something. Sitting around waiting to be attacked seemed like the worst possible plan.

"Should I try the colonel?" Roscoe asked.

"Why not."

The colonel's voicemail picked up and Roscoe didn't leave a message.

A jet streaked overhead, the static of its passage like distant thunder. The far-off sound of helicopter airfoils slicing the air made Oscar think of the Fill.

"Hang here a bit," Oscar said as he grabbed the night vision binoculars Earl had borrowed and Oscar had borrowed in turn. "I want to see what's happening at the Fill."

Oscar made a quick trip to the northern edge of the park, and everything was still. Back at his camper, he said, "There was nothing to see but a black smoke cloud enveloping the landfill. Plus, with the dark…" He put the binoculars next to the guns, grabbed more coffee, plopped into a chair, and hung his head.

"You O.K.?" Roscoe asked.

"I don't know," he said. Oscar had never been in battle, but he'd seen his share of deaths, but nothing like he'd experienced in the last twelve hours. His boss, Curby, Alice, Jesse… The list was getting longer and the blood on his hands was getting thicker, despite Oscar being responsible for nobody but himself, and maybe Tank. "With the Fill closed until further notice, everyone dead… I kind of feel like shit."

"That's to be expected, right?" Shelly said. "I mean, after everything you've seen, I can't imag—"

A deep chicken-like roar carried over the park, and it was answered by two others close at hand.

"That was a little too close for comfort," Roscoe said.

"Stay here," Oscar patted Tank on the head, grabbed his Benelli, and chambered a shell.

More odd braying and wailing, and it sounded to Oscar like the calls were coming from all directions.

Roscoe snatched up her rifle and fell in beside Oscar. When the pair went to investigate Tank barked.

Oscar slammed the screen door behind him and said, "You stay and protect Sherry."

The dog looked at the doctor, then back at Oscar, and a low growl leaked from between bared teeth.

A medium-sized mutant lizard trundled down the road, tongue lashing the night.

The few lights of his neighbors that were still shining winked out as the beast came on, which told Oscar the folks of Twilight Dunes were paying attention. At least there was that. They were a tough lot, and suddenly he felt proud, which was a feeling he was unaccustomed to.

Oscar and Roscoe took cover behind a parked car.

"What the hell are you doing?" came Monica's voice through the void, but the primal side of Oscar's brain silenced her.

The mutant lizard's head swung in Oscar and Roscoe's direction, the beast's eyes aglow, its thick tail cracking against an old cottonwood tree.

With a howl of rage, Tank burst through the side of the screen porch, diving through the thin barrier as if it wasn't there.

"Tank! Stop! Stop! Drop! Heel!" Oscar shouted every dog command he knew.

None of which worked. The canine shambled toward the beast, barking furiously, and looking for payback.

24

Tank howled as he broke into a run, the canine throwing himself forward in an awkward gallop, the wound across his torso slowing the beast and making him veer left.

The mutant reared back, the shadow of its narrow head lifting into the air, teeth glinting as jaws slid open, the glow of eyes cutting through the blackness. Green luminescent stripes wiggled and raced in the darkness as the creature sprang forward, tongue lashing the air, an earsplitting hiss rising above the growl of Tank and the arguing wind.

Oscar chased after Tank, Roscoe at his side.

The ground trembled as Tank and the monster played a deadly game of chicken.

A *crack* reverberated over Twilight Dunes as the creature's python-like tail took out a short wooden fence that ran along the road, sending a hail of splinters, wood, and nails in Tank's direction.

"Tank! Stop!" Oscar screamed as he skidded to a halt, brought up the shotgun, and sighted the weapon. The gun was loaded with #4 turkey, and while Tank wasn't directly in the line of fire, shotguns are imprecise weapons, and Oscar held his fire for fear of hitting the dog.

Oscar screamed, "Roscoe!"

"On it," she said. "Light it up!"

A cloud of LED light pushed away the blackness as Oscar turned on his flashlight. Dust filled the air and visibility was low. The outline of the beast rose through the clouds of grit, but Tank was nowhere to be seen.

Roscoe dropped to a knee, aimed, and fired.

A staccato burst of gunshots tore away the night followed by the plunk of bullets punching through skin, tearing muscle, and cracking bone.

In the harsh light, the blood spurting from the beast's wounds looked black, and the creature's eyes dulled as its protective membranes slid closed. The green stripes running up and down the lizard's torso grew in brightness as if the mutant was on fire, but its huge form slowed as its mouth fell open and its tongue flopped out.

A gust of wind tore away the dust shroud and Tank changed direction as some primal instinct told the animal it was time to call off the assault. The canine dug in and made a hard right, and the sound of tearing fabric followed by a wail of pain made Oscar wince. Tank's bandage had ripped.

The mutant came to an awkward, wobbly stop, lifted its head, and cried out, a desperate failing howl that started at breaking glass levels and fell to a hollow gurgle before falling still. A great exhalation of nasty air pushed down the lane as the beast deflated and toppled onto the dirt road, its skin sagging over bones and trembling muscles.

"Nice shooting," Oscar said.

Tank appeared from the gloom, panting, but the canine appeared no worse for the wear. The dog chirped as he jogged down the center of the road, and pride surged through Oscar. He and this mutt had a special bond, and if—

The dead lizard's corpse spasmed, its brain sending out its final command, and the monster's tongue lashed out one last time.

Tank dropped to the ground and the tongue flew inches above him before connecting with a parked car. A hollow boom carried over the park as the tongue retracted, but the thick rope of flesh didn't make it back into the lizard's mouth and fell to the ground like a bucking loose hose when the spigot was turned off.

Oscar dropped to a knee when Tank reached him. "You've got to start listening to me! Do you understand? I can't lose you too." He was hugging the animal when he felt Roscoe's eyes on him, and he realized what he'd said.

Tank whimpered in acknowledgment.

A series of cackle-barks echoed over the park, and it all sounded too much like communication for Oscar's liking.

"Holy shit," said Toby as he inched out his front door, flashlight blazing as he stared at the fallen lizard. "I only half believe it." His gaze shifted to Oscar and Roscoe. "I mean, I believed you, but…"

"Seeing is truly believing," Oscar said.

Toby nodded, his eyes once again locked on the creature's corpse.

More braying and shrieking and the calls sounded closer.

"Let's get indoors," Roscoe said.

"Yeah," Oscar said. "I think you're right. Lock yourself down, Toby."

The part-time bar owner didn't respond as he slipped back into his trailer and locked the door behind him.

Oscar's nerves were hammering and there was only one medicine that could calm them. Back at the trailer he took a shot of whiskey, and the burn eased his mind, if only for a minute.

"Are you two alright?" Shelly said as she stroked Tank and examined the large blood stain on his bandage. The doctor led Tank to the couch, which was covered in towels, and instructed him to lie down on it.

The dog grumbled, but complied, and Shelly set about stripping off the blood-soaked bandage.

Oscar cleaned himself up and ate a few slices of bread. He'd been going nonstop all day and into the night and the end was nowhere in sight. He took a second shot of whiskey to steady his nerves, which were still attacking the underside of his skin. "Roscoe, is your car gassed up and ready to go?" Oscar's old Ford hadn't run in over a year.

She nodded. "You want to hit the road?" Roscoe sounded disappointed. Or was it shame?

"Not yet," he said. "We need to call the greenies. Kendra."

"Do you really think there are still deniers?"

"No, but…"

"What else can we do?" Shelly said as she tended to Tank.

The wound on the dog's side had torn open, and the thin scab had given way all along the length of the gash. But there wasn't much blood, and the dog made no sound as the doctor cleaned the wound and replaced the bandage before proclaiming, "You're one lucky mutt."

Tank barked softly.

"No signal," Oscar said as he stared at his phone. "You guys?"

Roscoe and Shelly checked their phones.

"Nothing," Roscoe said.

"The cell tower must be down," Shelly said.

"That's not unusual on a normal day," Roscoe said.

That thought hung out there like a fart in a packed train, and Oscar's mind conjured up an image of a massive Gila monster taking down the tower with a flick of its bullwhip tail.

"Is it time to load everyone up and get out of here?" Roscoe said.

Oscar had done some preliminary calculations and he'd concluded that he could fit everyone at Twilight Dunes into the eighteen vehicles available if they packed themselves in, but where would they go? Then there was the fact that when he'd floated the idea of leaving to his neighbors, he'd received a less-than-positive response. "Over my dead body" was the overriding sentiment, but as the bodies piled up would his neighbors' bravado fade? He said, "We'd have to leave many people behind."

"I'm not into dying, Oscar. I want to see my husband again, you feel me? It may not seem like it, but we've got plans. I owe him. What do I owe…" She let her voice trail off as her gaze strayed to the trailer's living room window and the park beyond.

Outside the night symphony had gone still, and the calls of the mutants peeled through the darkness.

"I do think you should leave, Shelly," Oscar said. "And take Tank with you. He's done enough for king and country."

Tank squeaked and whimpered.

Shelly looked up in confusion. "Me? Why? I don't want to be alone."

"You're too important to lose," Roscoe said, jumping in to support Oscar.

"Well, that's ten kinds of bullshit and I'm not going anywhere until you do," Shelly said.

Oscar said, "That's not—"

"You brought me into this, remember?"

He nodded. "Well, if you're staying, you better take this." He lifted his Smith & Wesson .38 revolver, spun the cylinder, and handed it to the doctor. "You ever fire one of these?"

Shelly accepted the weapon and hefted it in her hand. "No," she said. "Never a handgun, but I've fired rifles and shotguns."

"Basically, the same thing," he said. "The revolver is easier. Just hold the gun with two hands, aim, and pull the trigger. No chance of jamming. No need to chamber a round. No safety. Easy-peasy."

Shelly's eyes strayed to Roscoe's old Army issue .45.

Roscoe chuckled as she lifted the old gun. "This baby jams about ten percent o—"

An explosion rocked the night and the camper's windows rattled.

"What the hell was that?" Shelly asked as she pointed her gun in the direction of the sound.

Oscar gently pushed her arm down. "Sounded like Earl's tripwire."

"Oh, poo," Roscoe said.

Oscar grabbed the Benelli and pushed out onto the screen porch.

Earl's camper was six trailers down on the same side of the street, but Oscar couldn't see it. Plumes of thick white smoke rolled through the darkness, obscuring the scene.

Oscar rushed across the porch and out into the night, but he stopped when he hit the road.

"Wait here," Oscar said when Roscoe, Shelly, and Tank arrived.

Tank barked.

"Especially you," Oscar said.

The dog made a strange gurgle-squeak sound but planted his butt on the ground.

Roscoe said, "I'm coming." And that was that. Oscar didn't have the sharpest of intellects, but he wasn't a complete dumbass and knew when to keep his mouth shut.

"Don't need to tell me twice," said the doctor as she dropped to a knee next to Tank. "I'll keep an eye on my patient here."

Oscar put the Benelli's stock to his shoulder and ranged the gun around as he inched forward into the smoke, Roscoe watching his back. The smoke irritated his eyes, the two shots of whiskey were waging war in his stomach, his joints ached, and in that moment, Oscar felt a hundred years old.

"It's not the years, it's the mileage," came Monica's voice through the void.

Oscar chuckled. The quote from Raiders of the Lost Ark never failed to make him smile, its simple truth having become one of the mantras of his life.

"Something funny?" Roscoe asked.

"Just wondering what the hell I'm doing out here."

Small orbs of glowing light appeared close to the ground ahead, and as the breeze massaged the smoke, he saw several members of the Pride standing in the center of the road. Most of the pack was there, but several of them were staring at the campfire-like blaze on Earl's lawn.

The cats fell in behind Oscar and Roscoe like a rearguard, and relief flooded through him when Earl slipped cautiously from his trailer, a double-barrel shotgun leveled at the world. He didn't see Oscar and Roscoe because he made no sign, and all his attention was focused on the miniature crater in his lawn where something had set off his tripwire.

Smoke eddied and cleared, but there was no beast, no giant lizard parts strewn about the yard, and no blood.

Oscar lowered his gun. "Earl, did you see anything before the explosion?" he yelled.

Earl turned toward Oscar and his eyes grew wide as he pointed. "The ground... The ground lifted. I saw it. Like a wave of sand. I swear."

"No need to swear," Oscar said. He opened his mouth to ask Earl if he had any more tripwires set up, but before he could get the words out two mutant lizards sauntered out from behind Earl's trailer, crunching through the sparse vegetation and knocking over garden statues and rusted lawn furniture.

Green lines undulated in the darkness and all flashlights were trained on the monsters, which were about half the size of the biggest mutant Oscar had seen so far.

Earl stood rooted like a shocked oak, his gun pointed at the ground.

Roscoe yelled, "Earl!" But her warning did more harm than good.

The narrow heads of both creatures swung in Roscoe's direction, and they caught sight of Earl, who stood ten steps beyond his front door. He looked at his double barrel, back at the creatures, and sprinted for the safety of the trailer.

Oscar and Roscoe laid cover fire, the crack and pop of weapons discharging drowning out all other sounds. Sand pelted Oscar's face as he pulled the trigger, the Benelli autoloading shells into the firing chamber and spitting out red empty cartridges. When the gun clicked empty, he took cover behind Earl's shed.

Roscoe's M4 roared, and the beast nearest to her was peppered with bullets.

But the pearl-shaped bones that covered the lizard's skin had evolved into an intricate mosaic of hardened plates, like armor, and though dark blood dripped from many of the bullet holes, the creature hardly slowed.

Earl was three steps from his front door when one of the creatures' snake-like tongues lashed out, its forked tip curling around Earl's legs and jerking him to the ground. The man screamed, a wail that knifed through Oscar and forced him into motion.

The monster's tongue retracted and released Earl as he clung to a half-dead bush next to his rusted metal stoop. He hit the steps hard, and a sharp *ring* resounded over Twilight Dunes.

Roscoe slapped a new magazine into her rifle, but she was too late.

The mutant's tongue lashed out again, this time wrapping around Earl's waist and drawing him toward the monster's open maw.

A death cry rose above the tumult as bones cracked and muscles were torn as Earl was crunched within the monster's jaws.

The massive creature shook its narrow head and shuffled off into the darkness, leaving a trail of blood and chaos in its wake.

25

Oscar's ears rang with fury as he broke into a run, intent on chasing down his dying friend, but Roscoe's screaming M4 carbine made him pull up short.

Gunshots peppered the mutant's tail and hindquarters as the beast fled with Earl. When the creature disappeared behind the camper, Roscoe shifted her aim to the second creature, but the lizard had slid into the shadows dancing behind Earl's beat Nissan Sentra. The brown vehicle looked like a toy next to the monster, the glowing green lines racing along the creature's body visible above the roof of the car, the beast's tail exposed.

Another explosion rocked the night, and a tiny orange fireball puffed over Earl's camper. Dirt and debris rained down on Oscar and Roscoe, and Earl's final cry rose above the clamor like the last note of a grand finale.

Slimy hot liquid splattered Oscar's face and he felt something in his hair. He reached up and pulled a leaf from his tangled mop, but as he tossed it to the ground, he realized it wasn't a leaf, but a piece of bloody lizard skin.

"Ahhhhh," yelled Roscoe as she clawed at her face with her hands, desperately trying to clear away a series of dark dots.

Oscar swiped his finger across his cheek. Blood.

The lizard hiding behind the Sentra lifted its head and shrieked, a weak attempt at a dinosaur wail that came out more like a dolphin call mixed with a bull giving birth.

Roscoe swung her rifle around and opened up, the gun spitting .45 MM rounds at the rate of ten per second, the gun's muzzle flash a foot long, the weapon's suppressor long lost. The gun clicked empty, and Roscoe slammed home a fresh magazine, but the monster once again took cover behind the Nissan.

She put the stock of the rifle to her shoulder and aimed at the creature's tail which trailed behind the small car like a twenty-foot tailpipe.

"Wait," Oscar said as he killed his flashlight. "Let your eyes adjust."

Roscoe's eyes looked like they were doing everything but adjusting. Her face was twisted in confusion, and she stared at Oscar like she didn't know him.

"How many more magazines do you have?" he asked.

She licked her lips. "I've got plenty of clips."

"On you?"

She lowered her weapon as her gaze strayed in the direction of Oscar and Toby's trailers where more clips waited.

The creature whined, its breathing ragged, and it didn't move, though Oscar saw the scaly protrusions all along the beast's spine rising and falling as the beast breathed.

"We hit it," Roscoe said.

Oscar took a deep breath, closed his eyes, and let the air slowly escape his lips. "A bit lucky."

"Not Earl," she said.

A red-hot ember formed in Oscar's stomach. Another death in a growing pile of lost lives, and this one he really cared about. Earl was a friend and ally, and Oscar could count on one hand the people he'd trust in a pinch, and Earl had been one of them. He lowered his head and said, "Godspeed, my friend."

Overhearing his sentiment, Roscoe said, "We'll..." But words failed her. What was there to say? Earl was gone. Yes, there would be a time to mourn, remember him, and put him to rest. But that day wasn't today.

The creature grumbled as if reading Oscar's mind, and its tail thwapped against Earl's camper, and a *gong* reverberated over Twilight Dunes.

"Oscar!" came a shrill cry from up the street.

"Shelly," Roscoe said.

The mutants were an afterthought as the partners turned on their heels and bounded up the road toward Oscar's place.

A clicking rose above the wind and Oscar looked over his shoulder and saw a large shadow rising from behind Earl's car.

Oscar yelled as he ran, "Roscoe!"

Roscoe glanced back, spun around, and brought up her rifle, all in one smooth motion that reminded Oscar of a ballerina.

The tap and crack of gunshots, then the roar of the creature as Roscoe's shots struck home.

His legs screamed, his head throbbed, and Oscar's mouth was dry as paper. He saw Toby and Paula watching from the large window at the front of their trailer, the glow of a light painting an ethereal visage of the couple.

Oscar slowed when he saw Shelly had retreated into his screen porch. She held onto Tank's leash as the beast barked and fought to get through the hole he'd made.

Tank saw Oscar and stopped barking, and the beast's ass hit the ground as if he hadn't disobeyed Oscar's prime directive.

"He wouldn't listen," Shelly said when Oscar arrived at her side. "So I tried to get him into the camper, but he's a strong and stubborn SOB."

A gust of wind slammed the screen door and Oscar jumped.

"Really?" Roscoe said when she arrived at Oscar's side. "Giant lizards and mutant millipedes don't get you, but the bang of a door rattles you?"

"I'm on my last nerve," Oscar said. "So stay off it!" He knelt next to Tank and stroked the animal. "You've got to learn to listen, buddy, or you're going to get yourself killed."

"He wanted to get to you. That was all he cared about," Shelly said.

A cackle howl carried over the dunes and was answered by a second, and then a third.

"Come on," Oscar said. "We need to hunker down."

No sooner had the echo of his words faded when Toby and Paula emerged from their trailer armed to the teeth.

A pump action shotgun was slung over Toby's shoulder, and there was a semi-automatic handgun of indeterminate age and make on his hip. He wore a chest belt filled with shotgun shells, and there were four leather pouches on his belt that Oscar assumed were filled with loaded magazines. Brown desert fatigues completed the ensemble, his hair tied back in a tight ponytail. He carried an Army green ammunition container.

Paula had a long gun—looked like a five-shot Ruger to Oscar, but the Glock on her hip was the real prize. A bulging satchel hung from her shoulder, her blue jeans were ripped, and an Army cap was slightly askew atop the knot of hair hidden beneath it. She also carried an Army green ammunition container.

Oscar and company loaded into his screen porch and when Toby arrived, he said, "Strength in numbers. And I know the fireworks usually come out at night, but given the situation." He lifted his ammo container as evidence.

To that, nobody had a response, and the small band of desert dwellers loaded into Oscar's trailer like clowns piling into a Volkswagen Beetle.

Everyone except Toby stopped at the camper's threshold and looked back. "I'll keep watch while you get yourselves together."

"That's not—" Oscar started, but Toby put up a hand.

"I've been sitting on my couch all night," Toby said. "You look like you've been to hell and back. Take a break. I got this."

Oscar nodded and wandered over to the kitchen sink in a daze. He washed his face and peered through the window above the sink, the faint glow of sunrise that was still a couple of hours off painting a purple-gray line across the eastern horizon.

"The new day will bring a new perspective," Shelly said.

"And Toby's right," Roscoe added. "You look shot. Rest and we'll keep an eye out."

Tank squeaked his agreement.

"Fine," Oscar said. He fell onto the couch. "Wake me if you need me or…" His eyes slipped closed, and sleep took him.

When he was woken by Roscoe, gray dusky light angled into the trailer. "Oscar. Oscar." She shook him gently.

Oscar sat bolt upright, alarm bells calling for all hands on deck, but when he saw Paula, Tank, and Shelly sitting quietly watching him, the panic fled and he said, "What is it?"

"Something is happening. It's dusk," Roscoe said. "Hunting hour."

"You've got to see this," Shelly added.

Oscar rubbed sleep from his eyes as he pushed to his feet and asked, "What time is it?"

"Almost 6:30 AM," Paula said.

Oscar felt like he hadn't slept at all, but a couple of hours was better than nothing, especially after the day he'd had. "Anything of note happen?"

"A lot of screeching, and it sounded like a few trailers were attacked," Paula said.

Roscoe added, "A couple of helicopters flew overhead, a jet, and we heard a series of distant explosions."

"O.K.," Oscar said. "Why did you wake me?"

Roscoe pointed at the large window at the front of the camper.

Through the grimy glass shutters, Oscar saw Toby's back, and two cats sat on the street like guards. He shifted his position so he could see through the window on the western side of the trailer, and three cats sat just beyond the screen porch keeping watch.

"They're all around the camper," Paula said.

"The entire Pride?" Oscar said.

"No, but a good chunk, maybe half," Roscoe said.

"They're watching over you," said Monica in Oscar's head. He almost responded but bit his lip instead. He'd never told anyone that his dead wife spoke to him, because he didn't think anyone would understand, and some might think he'd gone over the edge that he'd been tightrope walking since Monica died.

"When the sun comes up, we'll see what's up," Oscar said.

"Yeah, about that," Roscoe said. "From what I've seen these things aren't like normal Gilas that don't like the sunlight. These things…" She tossed a thumb toward the door. "They don't seem to mind the light too much."

No, they didn't. Oscar said, "That's why we're staying right where w—"

The cats surrounding the trailer all screeched at once, an earsplitting cry that sounded like a cloud of dying bats.

A rumble shook the trailer and the cats' shrieking rose in pitch and volume like a singer driving for the finish.

Gunshots rang out, and Oscar looked out the front window.

Mutant lizards filled the road, and Toby was holding them back, firing selectively.

The cats were nowhere to be seen. Warning provided, they'd apparently moved on to a less hostile environment.

Four hollow booms shook the trailer and a picture of Oscar and Monica on a beach in Florida fell from the wall, the cheap plastic frame festooned with oranges breaking as the photo slipped out.

Oscar stared at the picture as a low hum grew in volume, but was soon replaced by more explosions that were much closer.

"They're driving them our way, whether they mean to or not," Shelly said.

"There's too many!" Toby's faint call leaked into the camper and then there was pounding on the door and more gunfire.

The trailer rocked, and the glass dome covering the kitchen's ceiling light fell to the worn linoleum and smashed into pieces with a *pop*, shards of glass skittering across the floor.

More gunshots as Oscar rushed to the door and threw it open.

Toby stood there, his empty weapon across his chest. He smiled, and said, "Thank go—"

A thick black tail covered in pearl-shaped armored scales crashed through the screen porch and smacked into Toby. The blow propelled the bartender into the camper, and he hit Oscar like a two-hundred-and-fifty-pound shotgun slug. Both men flew across the trailer, crashed into the far wall, and fell to the floor in a tangle.

Shelly fired the revolver, screaming as she pulled the trigger as fast as she could. The flailing tail was only five feet away, and at close range all six of Shelly's shots hit home. With a squeal, the tail withdrew.

Oscar rolled onto his side, his shoulder bitching, knees unhinged, and the harder he sucked for air the less he got.

"That… was… close," Toby said. "I almost bought the far—" Toby's gaze fixed on the window above the couch.

A forked tongue thicker than any python Oscar had ever seen broke through the window, glass spraying the camper as the rope of flesh curled around Toby's waist and jerked him toward the window. The man fired his rifle, but it was empty, and he screamed for help as he slammed into the camper's wall, his body folding as the tongue tried to pull him through the narrow opening.

With a final inrush of breath, a loud crack reverberated through the trailer as Toby's back snapped, and his broken body crumpled as it was jerked through the window.

Oscar and the others stood rooted with horror, and Paula cried, slow, soft sobs at first, that built to a waterfall of emotion.

Shelly put her arms around the woman. Her mouth fell open to offer comfort but then closed. What was there to say?

Everything went still; the wind, the beasts, the scratch of sand pushing over sand, and the roar of explosions and helicopters and planes. It was like the world was on pause except for Oscar's pounding heart and the low murmur of his dead wife's soothing voice telling him everything was going to be O.K.

26

Roscoe vaulted across the camper and slammed the door. The trailer vibrated and shook as the creatures nudged and pawed at it, the twenty-two-year-old Sunbeam nothing more than a wooden box covered in thin corrugated aluminum.

The eruption of sound was like an explosion, a coordinated screech of fury that hurt Oscar's head. A mutant's underbelly covered the window Toby had been pulled through, blocking out the growing daylight. The creature's paws were on the trailer's roof, and the shriek and pop of flexing metal and breaking wood filled the camper.

Paula swung her rifle off her shoulder and put two bullets into the beast.

The lizard wailed and pushed away from the trailer with such force the Sunbeam was nudged from one of its foundation blocks.

Tank barked and growled, and Shelly screamed.

Oscar's ears rang as the floor tilted and shifted, then settled on its remaining supports. The trailer's wheels were nothing but rusted metal and dry rotted rubber, and the next journey the camper made would be to the Patriot Landfill & Recycling Center.

Creaks and pops rose above the steady hiss of the beasts, and one of the monsters was scratching at the aluminum with its sharp claws, the screech like fingernails being pulled over glass.

Then the clawing ceased, and the wind, the group's frenzied breathing, and the sounds of the camper settling filled the stillness.

"Are they gone?" Shelly asked.

"I don't—" Oscar's words caught in his throat like an unintended insult.

A tearing sound ripped through the trailer and two curved talons pierced the roof and dragged through the metal and wood, slices of pale light leaking into the camper. When the claws reached the end of the roof the beast began pounding the side of the trailer, and the old camper screamed as it swayed and rocked.

The ripping sound doubled, then tripled as more claws impaled the trailer. Cracks appeared in the walls, pictures fell, and the old TV crashed from its stand onto the buckling floor.

Shelly shouted something, the garbled sound a distant warning that Oscar's brain couldn't process.

The floor pitched as a violent strike knocked the camper off its remaining foundation stones and Oscar was tossed aside like his beloved garbage. Like an amusement park ride gone awry, the entire interior of the camper was in violent motion as it tipped over. A section of roof collapsed onto Shelly, and the doctor screamed as she was buried beneath a chunk of tar-covered aluminum and wood.

A torrent of sewage filled with globs of human excrement ran down the walls and the camper filled with a nauseating stink. As the foul water dripped onto his face, Oscar wished he'd been more diligent about emptying his waste tank.

Roscoe gagged and spewed the remnants of potato chips, then tried to pull the debris off Shelly, but the debris was too heavy.

Oscar pushed to his feet, the camper a cacophony of flying objects, breaking glass, and fury as the beasts pounded on the trailer.

The camper shook harder, the floor heaving up and down, shit water raining down on the companions. A smell so horrid it reminded Oscar of dead bodies and eggs baking in the sun filled his nostrils and he spewed the tiny bit of whiskey left in his stomach. The alcohol mixed with bile burned his throat like acid, and his eyes watered, his head still ringing so loudly it had become a steady buzz.

A mad pounding ran through the camper and shook the walls and rattled the floor like an insane work crew were all hammering the trailer at the same time. Metal snapped and tore, and the kitchen cabinets opened and spilled their contents onto a terrified Tank.

Over the cacophony a choir of screams swelled and ebbed, Paula being the loudest of the group. Roscoe struggled to uncover Shelly, but a steady stream of blood flowed from beneath the chunk of roof, and he knew the doctor had moved on from this world.

Oscar clung to the dining table's support pole, his heart racing so hard he saw starbursts at the edges of his vision. Sewage water dripped on him, and a cloud of dust and splinters and specks of metal pushed from the rear of the camper as one of the trailer's side panels was torn off.

The creatures shrieked and bellowed as if partying, the blows from their powerful tails hammering the camper to dust.

Roscoe yelled an order, but Oscar didn't understand and neither did Paula, because the woman stayed planted where she was, her arms wrapped around the corner of the couch.

Then the floor became a wall as the camper was tipped onto its side.

As Oscar was once again tossed like trash, he heard himself screaming. His leg got caught on the edge of a cabinet and he landed with a thud that drove his breath away and stifled his scream.

Faint rays of weak sunlight poured through the many rents and gaps in the trailer, and objects that moments before had rested on flat surfaces had all succumbed to gravity. Food, pots, pans, clothing, ammunition boxes, guns, and dogs had landed on the side of the camper all around Oscar.

Oscar rolled over and screamed.

Shelly's crushed corpse lay beside him, the right side of her head caved in, dark hair matted with blood. But it was her eyes that made Oscar shiver with fear and guilt. The dead woman stared at him accusingly, her fiery eyes fading as Oscar recalled why the woman was there, and whose fault that was. More blood. More blood on his hands. He turned away.

Tank whimpered and licked Oscar's face. Somehow the canine had gotten through unharmed.

"Roscoe? Paula?" Oscar forced out.

"Here," came the weak strangled voice of Roscoe.

Nothing from Paula.

"Paula?"

"She's over here," Roscoe said. "Unconscious, but she's coming around."

Oscar sat up and put his back to the camper's ceiling, which was now a wall. He closed his eyes, taking deep breaths of dusty air as he blocked out the creaking of the trailer, the push of the wind, and the sound of scouring sand.

Hissing and claws scraping over metal, then quiet.

"What... happened?" Paula asked as she regained consciousness.

Roscoe fell back against the wall, a loud sigh of relief escaping her lips.

Then she screamed.

Oscar jumped like he'd been prodded with a hot poker, and every bump, bruise, and contusion on his beaten body yelled and bitched.

"What the hell is it now?" Roscoe said, but before Paula could answer, the cause of her dismay became clear.

Tank pressed his torso to the debris-covered floor, a furious growl filling the crumpled camper.

At the head of the wreckage, where the large front window had been crushed into a narrow slit, two glowing eyes and a scaly snout packed with teeth filled the opening.

Oscar searched for the Benelli, any weapon, but his head was still ringing, his vision hadn't fully cleared, and a thick cloud of dust hung in the trailer like smoke.

A crackling and tearing echoed through the wreckage as Paula shifted her position and pressed herself to her knees. The satchel still hung from her shoulder, but her rifle was gone, and her Glock was missing from its holster. Her features darkened as a wicked smile spread across her blood and dirt-covered face.

Paula's hand snaked into her bag, and she pulled out a green egg.

Oscar's tired brain was a bit slow on the uptake, and as he realized the woman was holding a grenade, his heart sank with a finality that almost crushed his spirit. Almost.

The lizard's tongue probed the interior of the trailer, searching for prey.

Roscoe lashed out with her foot and pinned the writhing rope of flesh to the cracked wall. The forked tongue gyrated and bucked as Roscoe braced herself and applied more pressure.

The mutant wailed, and the tongue pulled back.

"We need to kill it. Kill it. Kill it now!" said Paula as she got to her feet. Her face was a torn visage of grief and revenge and despair. With eyes that were red with blood, she bit her lip and stared down the monster.

Time slowed as several things happened at once.

Paula pulled the grenade's safety pin.

Oscar sprang forward, arm outstretched as he reached for the grenade.

Tank cried out and cowered.

Roscoe dove for cover.

A mutant smacked the overturned camper, and the wreckage shuddered and shifted, a section of the wall giving way like a tuna can being peeled back.

Paula stumbled forward and the live grenade went flying from her grasp. It sailed across the camper, hit the closed bathroom door, and fell to the floor—the camper's side—with a thud.

The thumping stopped and the companions all stared at the bomb for a heartbeat, before they all dove for it.

Oscar smashed into Paula, their heads knocking like two infants wrestling in a playpen.

Roscoe was on her feet first, and she reached for the grenade.

As the camper was hit again it quaked. The grenade rolled down the slanted side of the camper, between Roscoe's legs, and came to rest against a crushed kitchen cabinet inches from Oscar's head.

His arms were pinned beneath him, and the heat of death spread through Oscar as he saw Monica in his mind's eye, dressed in her wedding gown. He wanted to go there so badly. To see and hold his wife again. He would give anything. Even his life if he believed seeing her again was possible.

"Get your ass in gear, soldier!" Monica shrieked. "You're not meant to go out like this, and neither is Roscoe. You promised Rick that you'd look out for her, even though she's the one who watches over you. Isn't that what friends do?"

Oscar jerked an arm free, scooped up the grenade, and tossed it through the broken window above him. As he watched the green metal egg sail toward the hole, a sense of relief flooded through his adrenaline-soaked body, and he surged under the dining table with a firm push of his knotted legs. Once again, he gripped the table's support pole like it was a life raft and he was tumbling on a storm swept sea.

The explosion cleaved the camper, and a hot cloud of splinters and shards of metal sprayed Oscar where he hid, his arms wrapped around his head.

Tank dove for Oscar, and as the ceiling came down and the camper was crushed like a tin can, he felt the dog's gentle lick on his cheek.

Mutants hollered and screamed as they pounded the trailer, the shrieking of claws tearing metal and the screams of Roscoe bringing the rage. His stomach went nuclear, and the crunching of cracking wood made Oscar think of Toby's snapped spine. He searched the chaos for Paula, but he didn't see the woman.

What remained of the camper rolled, and the screen house was pushed through the gap where the trailer's roof had been. The tabletop broke, and it, along with an assortment of metal, possessions, wood, and sewage buried Oscar. As the wreckage pressed the life out of him, Oscar caught sight of Roscoe through a gap in the destruction, and the anger became so intense he let loose with a battle cry that stung his throat.

Roscoe lay pinned beneath a mound of debris, but when Oscar tried to help her, he found that he couldn't move.

The destroyed camper moved like a living thing as the creatures poked and prodded the wreck. Forked tongues searched the cracks and crevices, and the ground shook as the mutants pranced about their prize.

A chorus of squeals leaked through the remains of the trailer, and a loud boom drove out all other sounds.

Then the camper was moving again, metal flexing as one of the mutants beat the trailer with its tail in an attempt to drive it through the earth.

The tabletop and debris atop Oscar compressed tighter, and the remaining sides of the camper gave way as the trailer was flattened.

Oscar was plunged into impenetrable darkness, and the last thing he saw before the world went black was the image of two yellow eyes staring at him through the darkness.

"Dance with the devil and you're gonna get burned," Monica said.

As blackness crept in around the edges of his vision, Oscar pictured the photo of himself and Monica on a beach in Florida, and then his eyes saw no more.

27

Oscar was in the bar across the street from the hospital when the call came. It was the on-duty intensive care nurse in charge of Monica's floor, and the woman said he should get back to his wife and he should double-time it.

It was 2 AM in Flanagan's Pub, an hour before the joint closed for two hours before opening for breakfast. It was between shifts at the hospital, so the place was dead, except for a few solitary drinkers like Oscar who awaited their ultimate fate via the destiny of someone they loved.

The gentle hum of smooth jazz that permeated the old place fell away, and a thick buzz filled Oscar's head as he closed his eyes and reached out with his mind. She was there. She hadn't died. Not yet. He thought his sixth sense connection to his wife was bullshit, but he'd prayed. When push came to shove, he didn't believe in God, and that made him a poser, but when there was nothing else left to do but bend over and kiss your ass goodbye one might as well say a prayer. Who knew? Maybe there was a God, and the entity would be benevolent and forgive his nonbelief. Based on what he'd seen of Christians, he thought the odds of that happening were somewhere north of Not Possible Town.

He downed the rest of his Jack Daniel's, pushed up from his stool, dropped money on the bar, and headed for the door.

"Good luck, Oscar," yelled Tom from behind the bar.

The sentiment made Oscar's stomach grow hot, but not because he'd probably never see the man again, but why.

Security waved him through like a VIP but Jenny at the desk didn't look up, but simply waved her hand, as if she didn't want him to see her face. He didn't blame her. People who worked at hospitals saw enough suffering. The lobby was quiet, the buzz of the tiny coffee shop a low murmur, and his ears rang with a finality that weakened his knees.

He was going to say goodbye to his wife forever.

The elevator ride up to the ICU was endless, and all the thoughts, fantasies, and horrors that he'd experienced since he'd learned of Monica's cancer diagnosis came rushing back like the onslaught of five thousand warriors. What was he going to do? How was he going to live? Where would he go? Could he take care of himself?

Of course, he could. But did he want to?

The elevator doors slid open, and Dr. Raynor stood before him. Her face told Oscar everything he needed to know. The doctor's bright eyes were dull with weariness and sunken deep within darkened sockets. Her normally tidy hair was ruffled, the clip holding the mop together askew. She had blood on her lab coat, and there were four metal clipboards under her arm.

"You made it," the doctor said. "She's asking for you, Oscar."

A tremor ran through him that threatened to shake him apart. Oscar looked at the floor as perspiration dampened his armpits and coated his forehead. Suddenly the black specks on the white tile floor were of particular interest. If he didn't go with the doctor, he could pause things. That was it. If he didn't go to Monica's bedside, she would keep fighting. For him. And eventually... eventually.

"Oscar," the doctor prodded. "There's not much time."

Time was the one thing Oscar had believed he and Monica had in plenty. Maybe the only thing other than their love, and now both were being torn from him.

The doctor took Oscar's elbow and tugged him into motion. Harsh LED light filled the hallway, and it felt like everyone was watching him as the doctor led Oscar to his wife's room. She held open the door and said, "Know we all did everything we could. This wasn't... isn't, your fault. Stop and see me after so we can talk."

"Talk? About what?" Oscar tried to keep the sarcasm from his tone but failed.

"Your future." She licked her lips, looked away, then sauntered off.

Monica had tubes running to both arms and an army of machines huffed and puffed but they just couldn't blow the cancer down. There was nothing left of his wife but skin and bones, and it broke his heart anew every time he saw her. Why hadn't it been him? He'd been the one hanging around nuclear weapons, working the bio range, and she was such a good person.

Only bastards live forever. Isn't that what the cynics said?

When he entered the room, the door swishing closed behind him, Monica opened her eyes. It was like a skeleton coming to life, and she lifted a bony hand and beckoned him to her side.

Oscar knew what was coming, and he didn't want to hear what his dying wife had to say because it would be the end. He'd do anything to stop time and keep that from happening, and yet he obeyed and took her hand.

She smiled up at him and squeezed his hand, but Oscar hardly felt it. "It's almost time, sweetie, and I wanted to say goodbye," she said.

The dam broke then, and the tears Oscar had been holding back for months erupted like a broken water main. He sobbed and wailed, Monica staring at him with pity-filled eyes the entire time, pain creasing her face.

When he got himself under control, she handed him a paper napkin and said, "First, and most important, is that none of this is your fault."

"Monica, I—"

"Shut it!" she shouted, her voice surprisingly strong. "I will talk. You will listen. There will be no question and answer period."

Oscar said nothing as he stared at the various fluids running through the tubes that were supposed to save his wife's life but had done nothing.

"You didn't give me cancer," she said. "One of your biggest faults— by far, on a lengthy list…"

Oscar laughed.

"You take burdens that aren't yours to bear," she pushed. "You take responsibility for things you have no business getting involved with. Please stop. You are the strongest man I know, but even you can't carry the weight of the world on your shoulders.

"Two, I know you love me, but the thought of you alone for the rest of your life brings more pain than the cancer."

Knowing what the next line was going to be, Oscar screamed, "No! There will never be another."

She sighed. "Never is a very long word. Try. For me. I'm not saying tomorrow, or the next day, but someday. Please. I know I'm the greatest, but there are other fine fish in the vast sea."

He chuckled.

"Promise me."

Then Oscar told the biggest lie of his life. "I promise."

"Kiss me."

Oscar leaned in and pecked his wife on cold lips, and when he pulled back her eyes were closed. Seconds later the steady beep of her heart monitor filled the room, and the only woman he'd ever loved was gone.

Oscar came awake to the sound of buzzing flies and Paula whimpering. The pests alighted on every blood and sewage-stained item, including his face. He tried to swipe the insects away but realized he was still buried beneath a pile of debris. Metal clanged and pieces of the camper toppled as he shifted position.

The crushed camper still moaned and creaked, but he didn't hear any lizards pawing at the wreckage.

Paula's wailing ceased, and Roscoe said, "I know it hurts, but we've got no choice."

Oscar blurted, "Tank? Where are you?"

A sharp bark came from nearby, but Oscar couldn't see the canine. Stray beams of sunlight knifed through the wreckage, illuminating sections of the crushed trailer. He saw Roscoe's back. She was buried in debris from the waist down.

"Help! Help!" Oscar screamed. He didn't know what else to do.

"Tried that already," Roscoe barked. "There's nobody around. Nobody alive, anyway."

The coppery scent of blood filled Oscar's nostrils and he realized Shelly's crushed corpse was still wedged into the debris at his side. The blood had congealed, and Oscar felt the sticky substance on his right hand.

"Hang on a minute. I'm almost free. I was just helping Paula. She's got a bad cut on her arm, and I had to stop the bleeding."

Dust and smoke filled what little space there was, and the smell of human waste pervaded everything. He slowly turned his head and started wiggling his legs, but it was no use. How he'd been compressed into such a tiny space without sustaining major injuries he didn't know. Luck had never been his lady, but maybe Monica was watching out for him.

Oscar's back was twisted, but the pain was minimal. He pushed at the tabletop, trying to make a little space to move, but it didn't budge.

A light appeared in the darkness, and he saw Roscoe's face through a gap in the wreckage. "I have to go slow. We're compacted tight, and I don't want to make things worse."

"Do you see a way out?"

"No," she said.

That was a problem.

"I'm free, but there's nowhere to go, Oscar. I'm afraid if I start digging out all this is going to come down on us."

"Do you see any water?" If they had some H2O, they might be able to hold out until someone found them. "There was a case of bottles on top of the fridge."

She chuckled. "I'm in a closet here," she said. "Do you want me to try and free you?"

The obvious answer was yes, but as she'd pointed out, the possibility that she could make things worse was very real and a cave-in at this point would mean certain death.

"The good news is I see a crushed ammo container and your Benelli."

"Yay." Sarcasm was in his blood, what blood he had left. "Get me out if you can."

Roscoe went to work easing debris aside as she tried to reach Oscar, who was only five feet away. More sunlight filled his small space, and the rubble shifted. Roscoe stopped working. This sequence played out several times over the next half hour as she carefully moved chunks of the camper and its destroyed contents. When she reached him, Roscoe planted a kiss on Oscar's forehead.

Oscar wriggled as Roscoe pulled, and after several minutes of shimmying through the wreckage, Oscar managed to free himself. He joined Roscoe in a tiny space that was created when a piece of the camper's roof landed on the upside-down refrigerator. The partners couldn't stand, but they huddled together, cold weakening Oscar's resolve despite the intense heat.

"I don't know how long I can take that smell," Roscoe said. "Is the—"

A siren rang through the stillness, but it was far off.

"Not loving the sound of that," Paula said. The woman lay with her left leg pinned under a crushed cabinet, her arm covered in a red bandage. Her face was powdery white, her lips pink and shriveled, and a thick layer of dirt covered her blood-smeared face.

Tank lay beside her.

The siren grew louder, and Oscar shifted his position, trying to stretch, but the companions were pressed into a space the size of a bathroom with a four-foot high ceiling.

With a suddenness that made Oscar draw in a deep breath, the klaxon ceased, and a muffled static-marred voice boomed from a bullhorn or speakers.

Oscar's nerves danced just beneath his skin, the primal side of his brain processing the garbled words as a warning. Tension rattled his nerves and sweat ran down his back. Not to be denied, his cuts and bruises fought for attention as he tried to block out the singing wind and the tinkle of sand scrubbing metal.

"Can you make out what they're saying?" Roscoe asked.

"No, but..." He heard a rhythm as if whatever the person was saying was being repeated.

Time dripped away, and the shouting voice grew louder as the thunderous roar and squeak of a large vehicle grew nearer.

"Oh, shit," Roscoe said.

Then Oscar heard it too, and suddenly he was no longer cold, but very warm.

"Immediately," yelled the mechanical-like voice. A brief pause, then, "This is the United States Army. By order of the President of the United States, you are hereby ordered to evacuate the area. Military personnel and vehicles are on hand to aid you. This is not a drill or a request. Staying in place is not an option. At noon today, the infestation will be eliminated, and this will pose a significant danger to anyone within the restricted zone. You must leave immediately."

The companions screamed, yelled, and banged on metal to catch the attention of the advance warning team, but nobody heard them.

A brief pause, and then the message repeated and faded until it was nothing more than a faint growl.

28

At first, Oscar thought he was hearing things. His vision had grown blurry, and he was tired. So very tired. His entire body ached and throbbed, the ringing in his head a dull roar. The pops and crackling got louder, and Oscar had visions of a steak frying in a skillet. He was starving and he tried to remember how long it had been since he'd gone twenty-four hours without substantial food. He'd eaten a couple of pieces of bread, but thrown up most of the whiskey, and his stomach was growling like it wanted out.

The snapping got louder, and the tinkle of stones hitting metal was added to the ensemble. The sound became the steady crunch of rubber rolling over the hardpan. Oscar jerked back, and he hit his head on the section of debris holding the advance of the destruction at bay.

There was a car rolling up the road. A car!

Tank barked like someone was trying to break into the recycling building to steal the mound of copper. The ferocious roar echoed through the wreckage, and that sparked Oscar.

"Help! Help! Please help," he screamed as loud as he could, releasing all his joy and frustration and fear.

Roscoe and Paula were chanting as well, the stridency of their pleas thunderous in the confined space.

A loud, elongated squeak cut through the chaos. Oscar thought it sounded like brake pads pressing on metal rotors.

The group went all out then, pounding on the wreckage and screaming with everything they had.

A car door slammed. "Oscar?" came a female voice.

"Under here!" He pounded on the upturned refrigerator, the hollow booms leaking from the destroyed camper.

"Got you. Stay still," said the voice.

Over the next several minutes Oscar and his companions waited as Tank whimpered and the clang and ring of pieces of the camper getting thrown aside dominated Oscar's thoughts. Who was digging them out? He had a guess, but if it was Deputy Sheriff Kendra Iquiro, what was she doing here? Surely, she had more important things to do with chaos in control.

"Yell again to give me a marker," came the voice.

The companions complied, and soon a piece of debris was lifted away, and Kendra's face filled the opening.

It was sketchy separating themselves from the rubble of the trailer, but Tank had no problem. When Oscar and Roscoe were free, they considered what to do about Paula.

The woman's leg was pinned under a metal support that had made-up the camper's frame.

"We could wedge it off her," Roscoe suggested.

"That could bring everything down on her," Kendra said.

"What other option do we have?" Oscar asked.

As if in answer, a lizard bleated and screamed, and the call was answered by another.

"Risk it," Paula yelled. "I can't stay awake much longer."

"Got it," Oscar said. He found a metal rod and Kendra retrieved a section of rope from her cruiser for a safety line. Oscar didn't think it would matter if it all came crashing down, but at least they'd be able to drag his corpse from the wreckage.

Line around his waist, Kendra and Roscoe watching his back, Kendra with her service Glock and Roscoe with his Benelli, Oscar wedged himself back into the wreckage.

Getting back in was easier than getting out, a path having already been cleared, but he went as slow as he could anyway. So it was that five minutes later Oscar had wedged the prybar under the support and inched it up just enough for Paula to pull her leg free.

As soon as Oscar had freed the woman from the flattened camper, Kendra went to work with the first aid kit. The cop managed to stop the bleeding and bandage the leg, but it was broken in several places, so she didn't attempt dressing the leg with a splint.

The ground shook and a screech peeled away the stillness.

A mid-sized mutant, ten feet from its teeth to the tip of its tail, surged from behind the destroyed camper, jaws flexing open, sun-dulled green stripes writhing all along the creature's bulging muscles.

Kendra fell backward onto her ass as she pulled her gun, but she was too slow.

The beast's tongue lashed out, and Paula was gone.

Paula screamed as she was dragged across the hardpan.

The lizard pulled the flailing woman into its jaws, and a loud *crunch* echoed over the devastation as her right leg was severed.

Roscoe wailed as she fired the shotgun. The air-shaking booms blew the mutant off its feet and splattered blood, brain, and bone over the remains of the camper.

What was left of Paula's corpse was impaled on the dead monster's teeth.

Oscar stared in shock. Paula had watched her husband die and came so close to death herself she'd kissed the black specter before flipping him the bird only to be taken down when survival seemed realistic. He emptied his lungs and dropped to his knees, his head falling into his hands.

Tank licked his cheek, whined, and sat beside him.

Kendra put a hand on his shoulder. "Do you know what the most common cause of suicide is?"

Oscar licked his lips and looked up at her like she was insane.

"I know, not a good time, but still," she said. "It's applicable. It's not desperation or money, though those are high on the list."

Oscar and Roscoe said nothing.

"It's surviving when those you love die, especially when the deaths happen in a tragic and unexplainable way."

"Unexplainable?" he said. "The greenies prac—"

"That's not what I mean, and you know it," Kendra said. "I know you questioned your own life when Monica died, so don't claim to not understand."

They weren't that close, and the woman didn't know him, but still... The comment cut too close to the bone and Oscar said nothing. She was right, but every ounce of his being told him not to admit it, though he had no idea why.

"Why are you here?" Roscoe asked.

"I was following the military advance team," said Kendra. "I assume you heard the warning?"

"We did," Oscar said. "What the hell did they mean by 'the infestation will be eliminated, and this will propose a significant danger to anyone within the restricted zone?'"

"A lot has happened in the last twelve hours," she said.

"We know," Oscar said. "I was at the dump."

"That was the start of it," Kendra said. "After the chaos at the Fill, there were attacks all around Scorched Mesa. Even the base."

"Ahhhh," Roscoe said. "That's why the greenies are pissed."

"They established a restricted zone, and at noon they're going to release a new bioweapon, some kind of poison mixed with a gas that's fatal to most living things, not including plants."

"What about people left behind, or hurt?" Roscoe asked.

"And the wildlife?" Oscar added.

"Anything below ground will be fine. The greenies say that because there's a liquid component to the weapon the air will clear fast," Kendra said.

"And you believe everything the Army tells you?" Roscoe pushed.

"Do you see another option?"

"How do they plan to deploy the weapon?" Oscar said.

"From the air, and there'll also be copters ahead of the planes to drive any land animals underground or out of the restricted area."

"The damage to the habitat is still going to be huge," Roscoe said.

"How large is the affected area?" Oscar asked.

"The weapon 'test' will extend well beyond the test range and our current position," Kendra said.

"And what about us?" Roscoe said as her glance strayed to the dead mutant with Paula's corpse still wedged in its jaws.

Kendra looked at her watch. "We've got roughly two hours to get the hell out of Dodge, so I suggest we get our asses in gear."

"Damn it!" Oscar yelled. "Did they say why? I knew they wouldn't admit to shit, but where did they say the things came from?"

"No surprises there," Kendra said. "As we've thought all along, the beasts are mutants that were created out on the test range due to some random mixture of biological agents. They claim it was unintentional, but that when they discovered the beasts the higher-ups wanted to figure out how they were created and if they could be used as weapons. That last part is widely accepted speculation."

"Same shit different day," Oscar said.

"That may be, but when things went sideways, and the bigwigs started having visions of brass being stripped from their chests, the tune of the band changed significantly."

Before hitting the road, Oscar and Kendra wrapped Paula's body and put it in the trunk of her cruiser as Roscoe and Tank scavenged the wreckage.

Shelly's corpse had been pressed into the wreckage and separating the woman's remains from the squashed trailer would take a significant amount of time. The task would also expose the companions to several dangers, not the least of which being a collapse that would kill anyone in the wrong place at the wrong time.

"At least the lizards won't get her," Kendra said.

Oscar wasn't so sure.

The scavenging efforts yielded fruit, but not much. Roscoe handed over the Benelli, and she was able to pry the revolver from Shelly's crushed hand. One ammunition case was retrieved, but it had busted open, and only four boxes of shotgun shells—twenty #4 turkey and twenty slugs, and a cracked open box of bullets for the .38 were all that was recovered. Kendra had her service pistol and two spare magazines clipped to her utility belt, her badge gleaming in the midday sun.

"Shotgun," Oscar said as he headed for the patrol car.

The screech of tearing metal and breaking glass froze the group in place.

A mutant appeared from behind the overturned trailer across the street, this one much bigger than the one Roscoe had dispatched. Its legs churned as it plowed through the devastation and launched itself onto the roof of Kendra's patrol car.

Metal flexed and snapped, glass shattered, and tires popped as the car sagged on its suspension. The monster threw back its long head, mouth falling open, retracting gums revealing razor-sharp teeth. Green stripes ran up and down the beast, and as it roared the lines glowed with an inner power.

The lizard rose on its hindlegs, its tail snaking to the ground for balance. It jumped onto the hood of the car, its weight crushing the suspension and pressing the cruiser to the ground.

"Son of a bitch," Kendra said as she drew her Glock and marched toward the beast like the Terminator.

The creature cackled, and to Oscar, it sounded like laughter. A thick red forked tongue lashed out, but it came up several feet short of its prey.

Kendra spread her legs and planted her feet as she brought up the gun. She locked it in a two-handed grip and aimed at the beast's head.

The lizard was unmoved by the show of force, and with a speed that startled Oscar and made him take a step back, the mutant lunged at Kendra, pushing off the vehicle and almost flipping the destroyed car over.

The cop didn't flinch. Kendra pulled the trigger methodically, peppering the lizard's face with 9 MM full metal jacket rounds that tore through flesh, splintered bone, and cleaved muscle. Nine shots thumped into the mutant before it crashed to the ground before Kendra, its tail still striking out wildly as the beast's brain issued its final orders.

With a womp of air and a billowing cloud of dust and gun smoke, the monster collapsed to the ground ten feet from Kendra.

"Oorah," she said as she blew on the tip of her gun's barrel, twirled the weapon by the trigger guard, and holstered the weapon like an old-school outlaw.

The dead creature deflated like a dying balloon, and the beast's final breath pushed a nasty cloud of stink over the scene.

Giving the dead beast a wide berth, Oscar walked out to the street which was littered with the devastation of Twilight Dunes. Overturned cars and crushed trailers dotted a field of branches, pieces of fence, and the detritus of lives torn open.

The creak of a car door being pulled open broke the quiet. Kendra had pried open her patrol car and brought forth a pump action shotgun which sat in a holster next to her dash computer, which was dead.

"I'm not going to even try and start it," Kendra said.

"Why would you?" Roscoe asked. "Unless you've got four spare wheels. Unfortunately, mine's in no better shape." She pointed at her car which was on its side.

A sense of helplessness flowed through Oscar.

"You've come too far, honey," came Monica's voice from the void. "You can't give up now."

Oscar sighed. "Grab anything worth carrying and grab it fast," he said.

"You have a plan?" Kendra asked.

Oscar said nothing but instead pointed up the street at a red pickup that still sat upright in its driveway.

29

The group eased around the dead lizard Kendra had killed. As they passed the monster's corpse it sagged further, and a nasty cloud of blood mist spewed from the beast's nostrils and mouth. Everyone ducked except Kendra, who casually lifted her Glock and put a shot into the side of the deflating carcass.

"Don't worry, it's dead," Kendra said.

"Then why are you wasting ammo?" Roscoe asked.

Kendra harrumphed and continued down the street, heading for the red pickup.

The sun was going full blast, the morning mist had burned away, and the tangy-sweet scent of mesquite and devil grass carried through the remains of Twilight Dunes.

Oscar rolled his shoulders and cracked his back as he held back a tempest of grief. The park was an apocalyptic wasteland. Trailers not tipped over or crushed had been knocked around, some dragged from their support blocks by their couplers, others having been pushed aside by flying vehicles or falling trees. Here and there mangled corpses lay strewn in open doors and hung through destroyed windows, but it was the body parts that turned Oscar's stomach.

As he made his way down the street he saw a severed hand, part of a leg, and what he thought was a crushed eyeball. He went into Army mode and stared forward into a tunnel so narrow there was nothing to see except the next step. The ringing in his head rose and his vision grew blurry. This had been his home. It hadn't been much, but it had been his home. Now it was gone and everything in the Dunes would end up in the Fill.

Kendra screamed.

Oscar dropped to a knee, put the Benelli stock to his shoulder, and eased his finger onto the trigger. There was a slug in the chamber, which gave him more accuracy for close-in work.

Kendra stood with her gun at her side, staring at the ground.

Ziggy was an orange tabby named after the iconic comic strip character. A prominent member of the Pride, Oscar had fed Ziggy many times, and the feline had spent more than one night in his screen porch on a chair. If Oscar had a cat friend, Ziggy would have been it.

The beast's entrails spilled from a huge gash that ran from the dead cat's neck to a stump, the tail mostly gone. Ziggy's glassy eyes gazed at the sky, his jaws open, whiskers askew, lips pulled back, teeth bared in a final show of aggression.

Oscar felt the red-hot heat of anger then. It surprised him. He'd been numb after all the death. Seeing those closest to him die in horrible ways. Hell, he'd almost bitten the donut himself a couple of times, and he had started to accept that his well of anger had run dry. But then there it was again like an old friend. A reason to live. A purpose to hold onto. Something to drive him forward and give him a reason to go on.

He ground his teeth, bit his lip, and took his finger off the trigger.

"Come on, Oscar," Roscoe said. "There's nothing you can do for him now."

Mr. Erickson's car was gone, and there was no sign of him or his poodle Henry. The old man's fancy doublewide looked basically intact, and a quick inspection revealed no blood, so with the car gone, there was hope that Mr. E and his best friend had gotten out of Dodge in time.

Oscar noticed that many cars were missing. "Looks like some folks got away."

Nobody responded.

With Kendra and Tank on point, the party threaded through the destruction and traversed Mr. E's yard to the end of the street.

Teddy Preston's place was so rusted and old that its original color was no longer discernable, but his 2015 Ford F150 pickup shined with the attention of an overindulgent father. Chrome glistened, the deep black metallic paint sparkled, and every piece of dark rubber shone as if newly coated with rejuvenation oil.

The yard was torn up, and Teddy's camper door swung in the breeze.

Kendra said, "Oscar, with me. Tank and Roscoe wait here and watch our backs." The deputy sheriff raised her Glock in a doublehanded grip as she made her way toward the camper.

Oscar pursed his lips, smiled at Roscoe, and said, "O.K., then."

A great braying and shrieking and wailing rose above the wind, but Kendra didn't slow. When she reached the open trailer door, she pinned it back and stepped inside as she ranged her weapon around.

Oscar put the stock of the M2 to his shoulder as he followed.

Kendra moved through the small camper as Oscar's eyes adjusted to the light. The camper was a pigsty. The small kitchen sink was overflowing with dishes and glasses, and a cloud of flies hovered above the mini-landfill. Empty beer cans, liquor bottles, forlorn pizza boxes, and piles of dirty clothes filled every vertical surface. Flies dive-bombed his head and Oscar swiped them away, the bright sunlight barely making it through the grime-coated windows.

"Clear!" yelled Kendra.

Oscar relaxed and hung the Benelli from his shoulder.

There was no sign of Teddy. No blood or body parts, and there were no indications that there'd been a struggle, though it was hard to tell with all the trash strewn about.

"Everything O.K.?" Roscoe yelled from outside.

"All good," Oscar answered.

"Any sign of his keys?" Kendra said.

Oscar sucked on his lips and started searching.

"How can a person live like this?" Kendra said. She was using salad tongs to pick through Teddy's dirty clothes. "And the truck. What's the deal with that?"

"Outward verses inner perceptions," Oscar said.

"I suppose, but still…"

When the pair didn't find the keys, Oscar moved to the small bedroom and adjoining bathroom while Kendra went through the kitchen area.

Flies attacked Oscar as he moved stacks of papers, looking under loose clothing and in dresser drawers. A thick cloud of gnats hung over a mound on the bed, and for a heartbeat, Oscar thought he'd found Teddy, but it was only a bundle of dirty sheets and blankets.

"Got them!" shouted Kendra.

Her announcement was answered by a long roar, which was followed by faint chirping and an elongated hiss.

Oscar emerged to find Kendra holding a set of keys with a white rabbit's foot hanging from the ring.

Kendra held up the good luck charm. "Now if he'd had this…" She let the thought go unfinished and a scowl slid over her features.

Oscar understood. Given everything that had gone down it was easy to see any situation in a negative light. "He might have caught a ride with someone," Oscar postulated, but as soon as the words left his mouth, he knew they were bullshit.

"And leave his truck?" She chuckled.

Outside, Kendra used the key fob to unlock the pickup and the companions piled in. It was tight, but even Tank managed to squeeze into the cab, and nobody had to sit in the load bed, which was coated in black plastic and looked to have never been used.

The truck started right up, and Oscar backed out onto the road. It was slow going because the street was littered with vehicles, debris, and the occasional body part.

When they came to Ms. Perriweather's trailer, Oscar brought the pickup to a halt. Several members of the Pride kept watch out front of the old lady's doublewide. The trailer was one of the few undisturbed campers in the park as if some halo of protection encompassed the place.

Oscar put the truck in park and opened the door.

"What are you doing?" Roscoe asked.

"If she's in there we'll bring her with us," Oscar said.

"Hurry," Kendra said.

Oscar was only gone a couple of minutes because the old woman made it very clear that she wasn't leaving her cats. "She said unless I can round up the entire Pride, she wasn't going anywhere."

"Didn't she hear the Army's warning?" Kendra asked.

Oscar nodded. "She said she'll stay indoors. She's got several cats inside with her already, and she's not going to stop until they're all with her. She asked me to help."

"Ouch," Roscoe said.

"Yeah." He started the pickup and put it in gear.

The truck had only rolled a few feet before a scream pierced the day. "Oscar! That you? Oscar. Help. Please help!"

Oscar glanced at the rearview mirror and saw Stacey dragging her son Joey through the devastation.

Roscoe said, "Your girlfriend."

"Not," Oscar said. "But we can't leave the kid."

"Or her," Kendra said.

Oscar said nothing.

Stacey was dirty and reeked of alcohol. Her eyes were beet red, her hair a rat's nest, and there were yellow stains all over her white tank top.

Joey was in pajamas and the boy had dried spaghetti sauce all over his face.

"Hit the back," Roscoe said to Stacey as she opened her door and jumped down to the road. "You take my seat. O.K., Joey?"

The boy nodded as he peeled himself from his mother and let Roscoe boost him into the cab.

Something moved in a pile of rubbish on the side of the road and Tank leaped past the kid. The canine growled and surged forward, ignoring the pleas of Oscar and the others.

"Shit," Oscar said as he slipped from the cab with the Benelli.

Tank was nosing through debris, and the face of a corpse peered up through the garbage.

Oscar didn't recognize the person, and he tugged on Tank's collar and dragged him away.

A mutant lizard the size of a massive gator trundled out of the wreckage of a trailer and Oscar and Tank froze.

As the monster worked its way between two ruined trailers it didn't see Oscar and Tank.

Oscar didn't move, and Tank needed no instruction.

The creature's thick bowed legs cycled forward, narrow head swinging side to side, tongue lashing out, the large protrusions along the monster's back swaying as the creature moved. Green bioluminescent stripes gyrated, and the mutant's tail swung lazily and indiscriminately pounded what was left of Twilight Dunes.

Oscar held his breath.

Stacey had disappeared within the pickup's bed, and the truck's cab looked empty.

The boom and tinkle of breaking glass echoed over the Dunes as a rock shattered the front window of a camper.

Oscar searched for the source of the rock and saw Tommy hiding in a hedgerow.

The monster paused, its head turning toward the sound, before investigating.

Oscar let the breath he'd been holding escape his lips.

When the beast was gone, Tommy emerged from hiding.

"Thanks, kid," Oscar said. "Where's your mom?"

"She never came home last night."

Oscar bit his lip.

The kid hiked his shoulders and looked at the ground.

"Here," said Kendra. She handed her pump action shotgun to the boy. "Do you know how to work that?"

"He sure does," Oscar said. "But..." He looked at Roscoe, who nodded.

"Take this one," she said as she handed over Oscar's revolver. "Easy to handle."

Tommy didn't protest and he and Roscoe traded weapons.

Oscar took the driver's seat, and Kendra leaned across the cab and wiped sweat from his brow with a rag. "Are you O.K.?" She handed him a bottle of water.

"She might be a keeper," came Monica's voice across the void.

Oscar felt a stirring he hadn't felt in a long time as the heat of attraction consumed him. His face grew hot as he said, "I'm O.K." But it was a lie.

Once the cab was packed and Roscoe and Stacey had taken up positions in the load bed, Oscar dropped the truck in gear and said, "Everybody hold on now." He looked around at the destroyed trailer park one last time as he headed for the exit.

30

"Joey, do you want to play a game?" Kendra asked, the sound of rocks hitting the wheel wells and the pop of rubber crunching pebbles like background static.

The boy nodded eagerly.

"It's called underwater."

Joey frowned and said, "I can't swim."

Kendra did her best fake laugh. "Don't worry. You don't need to swim. This game is pretend. Two people close their eyes and the first person to open them loses. Like breathing underwater."

"What will I win?"

"What do you want?"

The boy looked back through the pickup's long rear cab window at his mother where she sat huddled against the side of the load bed like a war criminal on her way to the gallows. "Can you help my mom if I win?"

A piece of Oscar's heart gave way then, and acid crept up his throat into his mouth. What would his child have been had Monica not miscarried? Was fate and her body warning her even then? Sorrow threatened to suck him into despair, memories of a child he never had weighing down his already heavy baggage.

Kendra coughed gently as she restrained her emotions, and said, "Yes. If you win, I can do that."

"What do you want?" the boy said eagerly.

"If I win you have to read an entire book and complete twenty math dittos."

Joey's face soured as his gaze strayed to his mother again. "Deal." He held out his pinky finger.

Kendra wrapped her finger around the boy's and the pair closed their eyes.

Oscar stared ahead, but even his narrow tunnel vision couldn't block out the devastation. Without conversation or discussion, he and Kendra had fallen into complete parental sync. Tommy had already seen the horrors of what the creatures could do, and he was older, so there was no way to keep him from the nightmare that was now Twilight Dunes. Joey, however, was trying to save his mom, and in doing so might save himself.

Tank sat between Tommy and Joey, and all three youngsters had their heads down and their tails between their legs. The cab smelled like a wet dog and self-doubt.

Oscar brought the truck to a stop before the remains of the portcullis that marked the entrance to Twilight Dunes and led through the border of vegetation. The Twilight Dunes sign was broken and lay face down in the sand, and the main structure of old wood and discarded metal covered in kudzu vine had collapsed on one side.

The remains of the entryway scraped the Ford as Oscar squeezed the pickup through. He said, "If Teddy was here, I'd have a bunch of tiny metal pellets in my butt."

As the truck churned free of the cut that led out of the shallow arroyo, Oscar saw a dark line of clouds marching across the western horizon. To the north, a black haze hung over the Fill, and the desert was a chaotic jumble of dust clouds and shadows, stray beams of sunlight streaking through the growing cloud cover.

There were two opposing storms coming.

Oscar made a right onto West End Avenue and headed south toward Main Street, the primary thoroughfare that led to the interstate which was the fastest way out of Scorched Mesa and the restricted zone.

Dust billowed over the road, and Oscar's view was intermittently blocked by thick clouds of grit. He slowed, tension massaging his groin, the knot in his neck pounding on his last nerve. The same nerve Roscoe had been working on.

"Oh, shit," Oscar said.

There was a Chevy Malibu dumped in the culvert that ran alongside the road. It was Mr. Erickson's ride.

Oscar put the pickup in park, opened his door, and said, "Tank!"

The canine scampered over Tommy and Oscar's laps and jumped down to the road. "Kendra, with me. Tommy, keep an eye on Joey. Both of you get down and don't peek your heads up. No matter what. Understand?"

Both boys nodded emphatically.

Oscar and Kendra counted to three, then slipped out of the pickup's cab. "Keep a bead on us, Roscoe."

Roscoe held her rifle at the ready, her elbows braced on the truck cab's roof.

He tossed his head toward Stacey. "And make sure she doesn't do something stu—overzealous."

Tank prowled across the road like a cat, chest pressed low, nose sniffing the ground, tail out straight, a low growl seeping from between bared teeth. The dog approached the abandoned car like a police officer, taking a wide angle so that he could see the front of the vehicle. Tank disappeared from view, and his growling was replaced by whimpering.

The ground trembled.

Waves of heat rolled over the sand, the desert awash in gloom. The stubby shadows of sand dunes and the spidery fingers of the vegetation were all that moved, and of the mutants, there was no sign.

The hood of Mr. E's car was crushed, and the front passenger side tire was flat, but other than that the vehicle looked fine. The driver's side door stood open, and what was left of Mr. E was sprawled on the side of the road.

Oscar knew it was Mr. E because of the tweed jacket still clinging to the corpse and the lizard skin boot that adorned the remaining foot, but that was all that was left of the man he'd known. Mr. E had been decapitated, and one of his legs and both his arms were gone, the stumps like bloody spaghetti as they leaked muscle, gristle, bone, and blood. A mutant had gnawed on the man, but decided dragging the carcass back to its den was too much work in the mid-day heat, so the beast had left the old man's remains to rot. He guessed it made sense. There was no shortage of food.

"Are those pawprints?" asked Kendra.

Oscar examined the tracks, and either a very small coyote had run away from the scene of the crime, or Mr. E's poodle, Henry, had left his master for dead. "Looks like the little guy got away," he said.

Only silence, the bitching wind, and the scouring sand responded.

An unnerving screech surfed Oscar's spine and closed out on his lower back.

A mutant appeared like magic from behind a sand dune, its camouflage skin shifting, the green bioluminescent stripes fading as the beast raced across the desert leaving a trail of dust, its legs moving so fast they were a blur.

Oscar and Kendra took cover behind the Malibu, the deputy sheriff using the hood to brace her arms, and Oscar using the roof.

Dust and grit hid the creature as it came on, and though Oscar was aware of the party's limited amount of ammunition and the distance, he squeezed the trigger twice, breathing between shots as the Benelli spit turkey shot.

Oscar couldn't tell if his shots hit home, but it didn't matter. The beast was out of range, and he'd taken the shots hoping they might scare the creature. No such luck.

The massive lizard came on, thirty feet of rippling muscle shuffling across the desert, two glowing eyes staring out from the gathering dust storm. Green streaks knifed through the grit and sand, and when the creature had closed half the distance to Oscar it let loose with a screech that made the maggots churning in his stomach attack with a newfound fury.

Roscoe's M4 carbine had much better range and accuracy, and she squeezed off shots as the beast charged.

When the gigantic lizard was thirty yards out, Oscar's skin crawling with tension, sweat dripping down his forehead and back, his fingertips stinging with pain, he fired his remaining three shots. The Benelli thundered, and the snap of the empty shotgun shells bouncing off the Malibu's roof was a welcome sound. When the gun clicked empty, Oscar ducked behind the car and let Kendra go to work.

Tank barked incessantly, slime dripping from his jaws.

It was Kendra's turn and the deputy sheriff held her Glock in a doublehanded grip and pulled the trigger as fast as she could, 9 MM rounds thumping into the creature's face, mouth, and eyes. Kendra's gun clicked empty. She dropped the magazine, pulled a fresh one from her belt, slammed it home, chambered a round, and then continued to pepper the monster with face shots.

Roscoe hadn't backed down either. She still fired methodically, the crack of her rifle and the plunk of bullets piercing the creature's armor rising above the tumult.

The mutant staggered as it ran, then faceplanted, its narrow head pushing sand like a snowplow. A death wail marked the beast's final moments as it collapsed to the hardpan and deflated like so many popped balloons. Sand showered the Malibu as the creature's momentum propelled its spasming body forward, and it crashed into the car and the pickup.

Oscar, Kendra, and Tank were tossed like trash, and Oscar landed inches away from a tall cactus that would have permanently altered his love life—not that he had one.

Kendra landed beside him, her gun still in her hand.

Tank pulled 'a cat' and somehow managed to land on his feet, the bandage on his side once again stained crimson.

Stacey was thrown from the load bed as the pickup rocked on its springs. She danced in the air, trying to right herself, but she hit the ground hard. Her head smacked a rock with a sickening crack, her arms flailing as she screamed.

The wail went through Oscar like bad chicken, but at least she was alive. But no sooner had that thought floated through his adrenaline-soaked brain, when the dead beast's tail spasmed and whipped in a sharp arc, destroying the thicket of bushes.

Stacey's scream was choked off as the tail hammered her, and the sound of breaking bones and tearing muscles echoed over the devastation.

Oscar screamed, the rage taking control, all the loss and heartbreak and frustration coming back at him like a storm tide. He aimed the Benelli at the dead creature and pulled the trigger, but the gun was empty.

"Don't let the boy see his mother," Monica said from the void.

Oscar's eyes ranged to the pickup's cab. Tommy and Joey couldn't be seen. They'd listened. His stomach was on fire, and the thought of telling Joey his mother was dead burned a hole through him. But at least the kid hadn't watched his mother die. With Joey's face printed on the inside of his eyeballs, and Monica urging him on, Oscar knew what needed to be done.

"Help me," Oscar said.

The partners put Stacey's broken body in the backseat of the Malibu and did the same with Mr. E's remains, Tank eyeballing the duo the entire time. Oscar didn't want the beasts to get to them, and until it wasn't possible, he'd respect the dead because he could soon join their ranks.

"Come on, Oscar," Kendra said. "We're running out of time."

There were no planes in the skies to the east, but that would change soon.

Oscar locked up the Malibu as Tank and Kendra headed back to the pickup. A deep sense of loss washed through him, that feeling of shame after having survived yet again when others had died. Wind pushed sand over sand, and Oscar shielded his eyes with his hands.

When he arrived, the interior of the pickup's cab was quiet, the tinkle of sand and the wind forcing its way through the window's weatherstripping the only sounds.

The pickup shifted as Roscoe climbed back into the load bed and gave a thumbs up.

Joey looked back. "Where's my mom?"

Kendra put her arm around the boy but said nothing.

The kid stared at the floor, a tear leaking down his cheek as his face went red.

Oscar started the truck and put it in gear. As he headed for Main Street, he tried not to look back, but he couldn't help himself.

Storm clouds rolled across the western horizon, the desert a chaotic mix of smoke, dust, and desperation.

31

Oscar and crew were cruising south on West End Avenue when the distant roar of an army of planes and copters coming to life carried on the easterly breeze. Dark clouds marched across the western horizon, the two opposing forces like armies arrayed on an ancient battlefield.

"Oscar!" came Roscoe's voice from the back of the pickup. She was pointing northeast across the desert at a surging knot of sand that was rolling across the desert. Sagebrush flew, trees toppled, and a wave of earth cascaded toward the road.

Main Street was still two miles off, and the next cross street, Willow Brook Way, was nothing more than a dirt path that ran between two large ranches. Oscar pressed the F-150's pedal to the floor. The eight-cylinder engine roared, the rear tires chirped, and the front end lifted slightly as the rear wheels tore at the hardpan road.

The truck wasn't loaded down, nor was it empty, and it only took a few seconds for Oscar and company to be barreling down the uneven road at 80 mph, the arc of the desert tidal wave angling to cut them off.

"We're not gonna make it!" Kendra yelled.

Oscar didn't know if they were going to make it or not, but as the truck gained speed, he had his doubts. The truck swayed gently in the breeze, and he felt himself slowly losing control of the vehicle. Teddy had gotten an extended lift on the truck, which meant every turn was magnified, every wind gust a potential nor'easter, and every rock and pebble had the potential to break the windshield and cause a crash.

But it was go all out now or it wouldn't matter. As the fist of sand grew, Oscar considered slamming on the brakes and pulling the old 'let them pass trick'. But he could see the creature had adjusted its course with the increased speed of the truck. It sensed its prey with a surreal extrasensory perception that he couldn't escape.

Oscar glanced at Joey, Tank, and Tommy... He had to escape, or at least try and help the boys escape. He owed that to them... and himself.

"And Kendra," came Monica's voice. "Pay attention to the road."

He gripped the wheel so tight his knuckles hurt, and sweat dripped into his eyes, the stinging pain helping him focus on the tunnel ahead that was narrowing by the second. Oscar searched his memory, his thoughts streaming back to the tunnels, to the giant millipedes. Could a Ford F-150 take one out? Head-to-head? Both going full tilt, both intent on one thing, killing the other?

Oscar eased his foot off the gas and the truck slowed. He watched the knot of sand as it cut over the desert, throwing vegetation, and he thought that he saw the slightest adjustment in the beast's course. The mutant was on him like a heat-seeking missile.

What does one do when outmatched and outmanned and all is lost? You go on offense.

With new resolve and the skeleton of a plan forming, Oscar put the gas pedal to the floor, and the truck swayed as its oversized tires bit the road.

He drove the Ford as fast as he could while still taking safety into account, given the lift and oversized tires. He eased off the gas, his glance constantly shifting from the road to the mound of undulating earth that was closing fast.

When Oscar judged three hundred yards separated the truck from the beast, he eased off the gas more. If the truck was moving too fast upon impact, he'd lose control of the vehicle.

"Everyone hold onto something!" Oscar yelled. "Tommy, hold onto Tank."

The canine had been silent throughout the chase, his teeth bared, eyes locked on the approaching wave of sand.

"Come here, Joey," Kendra said. The cop enveloped the kid like a mother placing its young under its wing.

Joey put his arms around Kendra and squeezed his eyes closed.

Roscoe was lying flat in the load bed, her feet pressing one side, her hands the other as she braced herself for impact.

Two hundred yards.

Sagebrush, sand, and devil grass heaved before the fist of earth, and cable-like antennas poked from the wave.

Oscar slowed a little more, the truck coasting at fifty miles per hour.

At one hundred yards the monster adjusted its course, the creature rising from the desert like a leviathan from the sea. It was massive, stretching at least thirty feet in length, its elongated, cylindrical body consisting of slithering and shifting segments, each adorned with two pairs of legs.

Fifty yards.

The monster's vibrant coloration shone through the flowing sand, the beast's exoskeleton a stunning array of red, orange, pink, and brown. The colors formed an intricate puzzle, and as the creature moved, the design shifted, concealing the beast against the desert. Two shining eyes emerged from the undulating mass of dirt and sand and dead vegetation.

Oscar made his move. With a battle cry he hadn't ordered his brain to issue, he stomped on the accelerator and twisted the wheel left.

Tires caught and screamed, the truck listed sharply, and everyone in the cab was tossed around as the truck bumped down off the road, launched across a shallow culvert, and smashed into the side of the surging knot of sand.

The creature was unable to adjust, and the pickup drove through the sand and a loud *crack* reverberated over the desert.

Oscar's seatbelt bit into his chest as the companions were driven forward, and the side window shattered and sprayed tiny squares of glass across the cab.

Roscoe slammed into the head of the load bed but somehow didn't get tossed from the truck.

Tank howled and Tommy clung to the dog like he was his mother.

Kendra still enveloped Joey in her protective cocoon.

The giant millipede bucked and heaved as it skidded to a stop, and an avalanche of earth flowed over the truck.

"Shiiiitttttt," shouted Oscar.

The momentum of the monster and the onrush of sand and dead plants hit the pickup and it flipped onto its side and skidded over the hardpan. An acrid chemical smell filled Oscar's nostrils as the pickup screeched to a halt against a tangle of vegetation. Sand filtered into the cab through the broken window, the creature shrieked, and the ground trembled and shifted as the mutant fought to free itself.

"Everyone O.K.?" Oscar shouted.

A chorus of yes and O.K.

The truck balanced on the driver's side. Oscar's door was blocked, and Tommy, Tank, Joey, and Kendra were stacked loosely atop him, a roiling mass of flesh and tension worming and shifting for position. A foot connected with Oscar's head, and he screamed, "Everyone stop moving!"

Roscoe appeared above, her head and shoulders silhouetted in the broken passenger side window, her hand extended into the cab.

Kendra braced herself against the dashboard, boosted Joey up, and Roscoe pulled the boy free.

The reek of gasoline filled the cab, and the ants of tension marched up Oscar's spine and went to work on his neck.

Tommy was halfway through the window when the truck shook and slewed through the sand as the creature poked the vehicle. The kid either saw his last chance, or Roscoe had tugged on the boy, because Tommy launched from the cab, leaving only Tank, Kendra, and Oscar.

Gunshots rang out, and Roscoe screamed instructions, but Oscar couldn't understand what she was saying.

Kendra did, because the cop clawed at the side of the cab as she pulled herself through the window into the gray mist proceeding the storm.

The pickup lurched hard and flipped over onto its roof.

Oscar hit the windshield and it finally gave up the ghost. He was sprayed with glass shards as he reached for the Benelli, which had been reloaded with slugs. With the pickup upside-down and the windshield smashed, he saw his way out. The truck whined and popped as it slid, the tapping and tinkle of legs scuttling over metal filling the cab.

Tank darted out through the broken windshield.

The canine's escape sparked Oscar's adrenaline-addled brain, and he forced his way through the broken windshield. He rolled and pressed to his feet like a surfer getting up on a longboard as he struggled to move away from the floundering mutant.

A gentle mist massaged Oscar's face, and then Kendra was there, taking him by the arm and leading him away, the Benelli clutched in his hands.

The creature was half buried, but the collision had injured the beast. Two severed legs writhed on the hardpan, blood seeping into the sand. With a squeal, the monster reared up, a single antenna swaying, the other a wriggling stump, its beady black eyes aglow, its many segments shifting.

Roscoe's rifle barked.

The creature wailed and churned the ground with its many legs.

Kendra and Oscar broke into a run, Tommy and Joey fleeing across the desert before them. His heart hammered in his chest, and he was starting to believe he might get away when the howls of Tank rose above the tumult.

The canine stood his ground before the creature, his jaws agape, his vicious snarl ranging over the desert.

With astonishing speed, the monster dove beneath the sand, and a huge wave of earth plowed toward the dog.

"No!" Roscoe screamed, but there was nothing she could do.

The sand wave crested, Tank raging, but then a second, much less intense barking carried over the fight.

Oscar searched for the source of the noise, and he laughed when he found it. He couldn't help himself.

Henry, Mr. E's poodle, stood with his feet planted, his cubic zirconia diamond collar glinting in the gloom. The canine barked with all the force of a pit bull, and it was enough.

The surging fist of sand slowed and changed direction slightly.

Tank bolted forward, and attempted to climb up the shifting dune, but soon gave up and retreated.

Roscoe and the dogs fell in alongside the rest of the party as they fled from the mutant.

"What the hell were you thinking, Tank?" Oscar said.

Tank whined but didn't stop running.

The truck was on fire, and the creature appeared and disappeared in the clouds of smoke and grit that covered the desert.

"Keep going," Roscoe yelled as she slowed.

Oscar's mouth fell open, an objection on his tongue, but he thought better of it. Roscoe was a crack shot, and if she thought she could take the beast down who the hell was he to tell her otherwise?

Roscoe stopped running, spun around, and got down on one knee. She aimed the M4 and fired, and she didn't stop until the weapon clicked empty.

The creature's exoskeleton cracked and popped as the shots tore into it, and the monster gave one last surge of effort as its dying brain fought for survival. But the beast wasn't a worm, and it couldn't live without its primitive brain which Roscoe had just turned into oatmeal.

A wail of pain and failure carried over the desert, and the hill of sand that engulfed the giant millipede fell flat, and the only sign the beast was still there was its remaining antenna, which stuck from the sand and swayed in the wind.

Henry barked his approval, and Tank turned and licked the smaller dog on the snout.

"Looks like you've got two dogs now," said Monica, her voice a port in a storm.

Oscar looked down at the dogs. Tank wasn't his, but he would see him at the Fill every day, or would he? Suddenly Oscar understood that he'd never work at the Fill again. Where he would work, he didn't know, but it wouldn't be at the landfill.

Kendra sidled up to Oscar and took his hand. "You alright?"

"She likes you," Monica said. "And I like her."

Oscar said, "I'll be happy when we're out of the restricted area."

The grumble of the approaching air armada spurred Oscar and his friends into motion once more.

32

Back up on the road, the wrecked pickup in their rearview, Oscar and company ran the final leg to Main Street, where they hoped to catch a ride. The sky to the east was thick with approaching helicopters, followed by planes that were dropping tiny bioweapons that thudded to the ground before breaking open and releasing their poison.

Oscar and his friends couldn't run any faster, but even if they could, the companions wouldn't make it to Main Street before they were overcome. He saw no other vehicles or people. No signs of life other than the birds and beasts fleeing west.

The scant collection of buildings along the road appeared to be sealed up tight, and Oscar doubted anyone hiding within would risk their lives to lower their drawbridge. But he had kids with him, and that might sway some people.

Kendra chugged up beside him, their eyes met, and she looked at the ground. "We need to find shelter. Anything."

Oscar nodded and focused on his tunnel.

"Give her more than that, Oscar." Monica sounded irritated.

"There will never be another," he muttered. The memory of the night Monica died came rushing back, her final plea etched into his brain.

"Never is a very long word. Try. For me. I'm not saying tomorrow, or the next day, but someday. Please. I know I'm the greatest, but…"

"Where are you?" Kendra asked as she jogged beside him.

"I really like her," said Oscar's dead wife.

He said nothing.

The cluster of buildings at West End and Main was still a ways off, so Oscar picked a structure close to the road and veered east, heading for a small metal building that looked like a warehouse for a construction company or something similar. A row of vans was parked on the side of the building, and the place's metal security shutters were down. There were no other cars in the parking lot.

When the party reached the building's main entrance, Tank and Henry barked and Roscoe said, "I agree. What's the plan?"

"We break in," Oscar said as he gripped the door handle and pulled.

The door didn't move. "Blow it!" Oscar screamed.

"Stand back," said Roscoe as she pointed her rifle at the door's hardware.

"What the hell is that?" said Kendra. She now had Tommy as well as Joey in her protective cocoon.

A line of dust trailed down Main Street from the east behind a racing vehicle, the armada of planes right behind it.

Hope surged through him, and for the first time in a long time, the pain in his stomach eased. "Let's get to it," Oscar yelled. "Double-time it!"

Tank and Henry led the way as the companions went back to the road and set off at a run again.

The advance line of helicopters thundered overhead, kicking up dust and grit and limiting visibility to a hundred yards.

Mutant Gila monsters fled before the approaching air strike, the monsters sensing something was wrong and understanding there was no time to dig in. Tongues licked the desert wind, and sand pelted Oscar's face as he threw himself forward in an awkward gait, his muscles shrieking, his knees threatening to come unhinged. He looked back and took inventory: Kendra herded Tommy and Joey before her, and Roscoe took up the rear.

Oscar didn't think the fleeing monsters were going to make it, but as the desert camouflage-colored military transport rounded the corner off Main onto West End it became clear that he and his friends just might.

The wind eased—the calm before the storm, and the transport skidded to a stop and a team of soldiers wearing body armor streamed from the vehicle. Cracks and pops echoed over the desert as the soldiers laid cover fire for Oscar and his team, and shame washed through him when he saw Colonel Jefferies step from the transport onto the hardpan. Oscar had wished the man dead a few times and opined about how he only cared about other greenies, but here he was saving Oscar's civilian ass.

"We saw you guys running," the Colonel said as he helped Oscar and the others aboard.

The military transport had eight huge wheels and three millipede-like parts that moved separately but were connected, and the vehicle was packed with people.

Oscar had never been so happy to see the greenies. He'd been so quick to condemn his old tribe, but suddenly once again he owed them a great debt.

He remembered little of the ride out of the restricted zone. The growl of the engine, the pop, and snap of rubber kicking pebbles and stones, the colonel prattling in his ear, the cloud of planes right on their tail.

Tank and Henry were entwined and curled up in a ball on a seat, and Oscar decided he wasn't going to break the pair up. Trash-master was dead, and who would care if Tank never went back to the Fill? Hell, he was never going back, and it was possible nobody ever would.

Joey and Tommy were more difficult.

Kendra clung to Joey like he was her son, and all indications were pointing in that direction. The boy's mother was dead, maybe for the better, and Kendra was a Deputy Sheriff with a bright future and the ability to support the youngster, no matter where she ended up. There would be paperwork and interviews, but Oscar was certain that in the end Joey and Kendra wouldn't be separated.

Theoretically, Tommy's mother was alive, so Oscar resolved to cross that bridge when he came to it.

Kendra felt him watching her, and she detached from the boys and squeezed in beside him. She asked, "Where are you going? When this is over, I mean?" The unspoken sub-context was that she wouldn't be returning to Scorched Mesa.

"I figure they'll put us up somewhere for a bit until things can be figured out," Oscar said.

"Yeah," she said.

There are moments in life when you "lean in" as the young folks say. Oscar wasn't sure what the phrase meant, but he was pretty sure it meant take a chance. Of regrets, he had a few, but still…

"If you blow this you will regret it for the rest of your days," came Monica's distant voice.

"Maybe we should stick together for a bit?" Oscar offered.

"Good. Now more…" Monica said.

"We need to take care of Joey and make sure Tommy finds his mom. Then there's the dogs."

"Sounds complicated," she said, a thin smile spreading across her dirt-smeared face. "You sure you can handle it?"

"I think I'm ready for complicated," he said.

She took his hand. "But do you want it?"

Time and tragedy had marked Kendra without extinguishing the fire in her eyes. Oscar put his arms around her and hugged her as tightly as he could.

"Now that's what I'm talking about," came Monica's voice through the void, but it sounded distant and weak. "Peace out," she said.

Oscar screamed into the void, mentally calling for his wife, but Monica was gone.

Back at the Collection Center, Oscar and his friends were dumped off with all the others. Roscoe was greeted by her husband, who had raced home when he'd heard what was happening. She'd almost bit the donut multiple times, but she was laughing, her carelines gone. Their eyes met, and Oscar nodded. The partners would always be friends, but things had already changed.

What hadn't? His entire life had been swept away, and he'd lost several good friends, and a few he didn't particularly like, but still… As he looked at Tommy and Joey, he no longer felt the guilt of failure, and for the first time since Monica died, he believed he'd done something good, maybe even made the world a better place. That realization made him ask the hard question: can you take the next step? He believed with Kendra's help… and Tank's… he could.

There would be memorials, masses, and fundraisers, but Oscar didn't plan to go to any of them. Kendra's question clouded his head, and she, the boys, and the dogs were all he cared about.

Then the cleansing rain came, and still Monica hadn't spoken to him. Dark clouds reached across the desert, one the size and shape of a large arrow, its tip pointed east toward the Cactus Ridge Proving Ground. That arrow was for others to follow.

CODA

Memorandum

Office of the President of the United States
To: All Government Agencies and Relevant Departments
Subject: Scorched Mesa Closure
Date: June 8th, 2026
Classification: Top Secret

Dear Esteemed Colleagues,

I trust this memo finds you well. I write to address a matter of utmost national importance that demands immediate attention and discretion. In light of recent classified events, I have made the difficult decision to temporarily close Scorched Mesa, the expansive desert region surrounding the Cactus Ridge Proving Ground.

The closure of Scorched Mesa is imperative to safeguard our national security and protect the citizens of our great nation. While the details surrounding the event remain classified, rest assured that this action is taken with the utmost consideration for the well-being and prosperity of our citizens.

Effective immediately, access to Scorched Mesa is restricted to authorized personnel only. The closure will be enforced by a joint task force comprised of military, intelligence, and law enforcement agencies. The Cactus Ridge Base is off limits to all but the Army, and a comprehensive report of what's left there will be made available when possible. Any violations of these orders will be treated with the utmost severity under the law.

I understand the potential impact of this decision on local communities, businesses, and individuals with interests in the area. Rest assured, compensatory measures will be implemented to mitigate economic repercussions. Additionally, a comprehensive communication plan will be rolled out to address public concerns without compromising classified information.

I appreciate your unwavering commitment to the security of our nation and trust that you will cooperate fully with the designated authorities during this critical period. The decision to close Scorched Mesa is not taken lightly, but it is a necessary step in ensuring the continued safety and prosperity of our beloved nation.

Sincerely,
Mrs. Carol Ann Castro
President of the United States

OTHER SEVERED PRESS NOVELS BY EDWARD J. MCFADDEN III:

CRICS, Terror Lake, TRAGIC, Predators & Prey, Wolves of the Sea, Fortune's Cypher, Crimson Falls (#1 Amazon Bestseller Tag), Hell Creek, Barracuda Swarm, The Cryptid Club, Dinosaur Red, Drop Off (#1 Amazon Bestseller Tag), Jurassic Ark, Keepers of the Flame, Throwback, Sea Tremors, Primeval Valley, Shadow of the Abyss (#1 Amazon Bestseller Tag), Awake, and The Breach (#1 Amazon Bestseller Tag, Amazon #1 Hot New Audio Release Tag). His other novels include: Terror Peak (#1 Amazon Bestseller Tag), the Ellis Parker Adventure Thriller series: The Modern Pharoh, The Doomsday Deception, and The Sigils of Solomon, the Theo Ramage Thriller series: Quick Sands, Sandbagged, and Too Much Grit, and Dogs Get Ten Lives, The Black Death of Babylon, and HOAXERS. Ed lives on Long Island with his wife Dawn, their daughter Samantha, and their cats Snoop and Skittles.

CHECK OUT OTHER GREAT
KAIJU NOVELS

KAIJU SPAWN
by David Robbins
& Eric S Brown

Wally didn't believe it was really the end of the world until he saw the Kaiju with his own eyes. The great beasts rose from the Earth's oceans, laying waste to civilization. Now Wally must fight his way across the Kaiju ravaged wasteland of modern day America in search of his daughter. He is the only hope she has left . . . and the clock is ticking.

From authors David Robbins (Endworld) and Eric S Brown (Kaiju Apocalypse), Kaiju Spawn is an action packed, horror tale of desperate determination and the battle to overcome impossible odds.

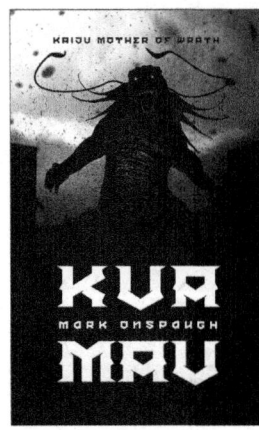

KUA MAU
by Mark Onspaugh

The Spider Islands. A mysterious ship has completed a treacherous journey to this hidden island chain. Their mission: to capture the legendary monster, Kua'Mau. Thinking they are successful, they sail back to the United States, where the terrifying creature will be displayed at a new luxury casino in Las Vegas. But the crew has made a horrible mistake - they did not trap Kua'Mau, they took her offspring. Now hot on their heels comes a living nightmare, a two hundred foot, one hundred ton tentacled horror, Kua'Mau, Kaiju Mother of Wrath, who will stop at nothing to safeguard her young. As she tears across California heading towards Vegas, she leaves a monumental body-count in her wake, and not even the U. S. military or private black ops can stop this city-crushing, havoc-wreaking monstrous mother of all Kaiju as she seeks her revenge.

CHECK OUT OTHER GREAT KAIJU NOVELS

ATOMIC REX
by Matthew Dennion

The war is over, humanity has lost, and the Kaiju rule the earth.

Three years have passed since the US government attempted to use giant mechs to fight off an incursion of kaiju. The eight most powerful kaiju have carved up North America into their respective territories and their mutant offspring also roam the continent. The remnants of humanity are gathered in a remote settlement with Steel Samurai, the last of the remaining mechs, as their only protection. The mech is piloted by Captain Chris Myers who realizes that humanity will not survive if they stay at the settlement. In order to preserve the human race, he leaves the settlement unprotected as he engages on a desperate plan to draw the eight kaiju into each other's territories. His hope is that the kaiju will destroy each other. Chris will encounter horrors including the amorphous Amebos, Tortiraus the Giant turtle , and the nuclear powered mutant dinosaur Atomic Rex!

KAIJU DEADFALL
by JE Gurley

Death from space. The first meteor landed in the Pacific Ocean near San Francisco, causing an earthquake and a tsunami. The second wiped out a small Indiana city. The third struck the deserts of Nevada. When gigantic monsters- Ishom, Girra, and Nusku- emerge from the impact craters, the world faces a threat unlike any it had ever known - Kaiju . NASA catastrophist Gate Rutherford and Special Ops Captain Aiden Walker must find a way to stop the creatures before they destroy every major city in America..

CHECK OUT OTHER GREAT KAIJU NOVELS

MURDER WORLD | KAIJU DAWN
by Jason Cordova
& Eric S Brown

Captain Vincente Huerta and the crew of the Fancy have been hired to retrieve a valuable item from a downed research vessel at the edge of the enemy's space.
It was going to be an easy payday.
But what Captain Huerta and the men, women and alien under his command didn't know was that they were being sent to the most dangerous planet in the galaxy.
Something large, ancient and most assuredly evil resides on the planet of Gorgon IV. Something so terrifying that man could barely fathom it with his puny mind. Captain Huerta must use every trick in the book, and possibly write an entirely new one, if he wants to escape Murder World.

KAIJU ARMAGEDDON
by Eric S. Brown

The attacks began without warning. Civilian and Military vessels alike simply vanished upon the waves. Crypto-zoologist Jerry Bryson found himself swept up into the chaos as the world discovered that the legendary beasts known as Kaiju are very real. Armies of the great beasts arose from the oceans and burrowed their way free of the Earth to declare war upon mankind. Now Dr. Bryson may be the human race's last hope in stopping the Kaiju from bringing civilization to its knees.
This is not some far distant future. This is not some alien world. This is the Earth, here and now, as we know it today, faced with the greatest threat its ever known. The Kaiju Armageddon has begun.

Printed in Great Britain
by Amazon

62609053R00111